THE JEWEL OF SEVEN STARS

THE JEWEL OF SEVEN STARS

BY

BRAM STOKER

AUTHOR OF "THE MYSTERY OF THE SEA," "DRACULA"
"THE SNAKE'S PASS," "THE WATTER'S MOU'," ETC.

Amereon House
MATTITUCK

TO THE READER

It is our pleasure to keep available uncommon
titles and to this end, at the time of publication,
we have used the best available sources. To aid
catalogers and collectors, this title is printed in
an edition limited to 300 copies. ——— **Enjoy!**

To order contact
AMEREON HOUSE, the publishing division of
Amereon Ltd.
Postal Box 1200
Mattituck, New York 11952

Manufactured in the United States

CONTENTS

THE JEWEL OF SEVEN STARS

CHAPTER I

IT all seemed so real that I could hardly imagine that
it had ever occurred before; and yet each episode
came, not as a fresh step in the logic of things,
but as something expected. It is in such wise that
memory plays its pranks for good or ill; for pleasure
or pain; for weal or woe. It is thus that life is bitter-
sweet, and that which has been done becomes eternal.

Again, the light skiff, ceasing to shoot through the
lazy water as when the oars flashed and dripped,
glided out of the fierce July sunlight into the cool
shade of the great drooping willow branches — I
standing up in the swaying boat, she sitting still and
with deft fingers guarding herself from stray twigs
or the freedom of the resilience of moving boughs.
Again, the water looked golden-brown under the
canopy of translucent green; and the grassy bank
was of emerald hue. Again, we sat in the cool shade,
with the myriad noises of nature both without and
within our bower merging into that drowsy hum in
whose sufficing environment the great world with its
disturbing trouble, and its more disturbing joys, can

be effectually forgotten. Again, in that blissful solitude the young girl lost the convention of her prim, narrow upbringing, and told me in a natural, dreamy way of the loneliness of her new life. With an undertone of sadness she made me feel how in that spacious home each one of the household was isolated by the personal magnificence of her father and herself ; that there confidence had no altar, and sympathy no shrine ; and that there even her father's face was as distant as the old country life seemed now. Once more, the wisdom of my manhood and the experience of my years laid themselves at the girl's feet. It was seemingly their own doing ; for the individual "I" had no say in the matter, but only juSt obeyed imperative orders. And once again the flying seconds multiplied themselves endlessly. For it is in the arcana of dreams that existences merge and renew themselves, change and yet keep the same—like the soul of . a musician in a fugue. And so memory swooned, again and again, in sleep.

It seems that there is never to be any perfect rest. Even in Eden the snake rears its head among the laden boughs of the Tree of Knowledge. The silence of the dreamless night is broken by the roar of the avalanche ; the hissing of sudden floods ; the clanging of the engine bell marking its sweep through a sleeping American town ; the clanking of distant paddles over the sea. . . . Whatever it is, it is breaking the charm of my Eden. The canopy of greenery above us, starred with diamond-points of light, seems to quiver in the ceaseless beat of paddles ; and the restless bell seems as though it would never cease. . . .

All at once the gates of Sleep were thrown wide open, and my waking ears took in the cause of the disturbing sounds. Waking existence is prosaic enough—there was somebody knocking and ringing at someone's street door.

I was pretty well accustomed in my Jermyn Street chambers to passing sounds; usually I did not concern myself, sleeping or waking, with the doings, however noisy, of my neighbours. But this noise was too continuous, too insistent, too imperative to be ignored. There was some active intelligence behind that ceaseless sound; and some stress or need behind the intelligence. I was not altogether selfish, and at the thought of someone's need I was, without premeditation, out of bed. Instinctively I looked at my watch. It was just three o'clock; there was a faint edging of grey round the green blind which darkened my room. It was evident that the knocking and ringing were at the door of our own house; and it was evident, too, that there was no one awake to answer the call. I slipped on my dressing-gown and slippers, and went down to the hall door. When I opened it there stood a dapper groom, with one hand pressed unflinchingly on the electric bell whilst with the other he raised a ceaseless clangour with the knocker. The instant he saw me the noise ceased; one hand went up instinctively to the brim of his hat, and the other produced a letter from his pocket. A neat brougham was opposite the door, the horses were breathing heavily as though they had come fast. A policeman, with his night lantern still alight at his belt, stood by attracted to the spot by the noise.

"Beg pardon, sir, I'm sorry for disturbing you, but my orders was imperative; I was not to lose a moment, but to knock and ring till someone came. May I ask you, sir, if Mr. Malcolm Ross lives here?"

"I am Mr. Malcolm Ross."

"Then this letter is for you, sir, and the bro'am is for you too, sir!"

I took, with a strange curiosity, the letter which he handed to me. As a barrister I had had, of course, odd experiences now and then, including sudden demands upon my time; but never anything like this. I stepped back into the hall, closing the door to, but leaving it ajar; then I switched on the electric light. The letter was directed in a strange hand, a woman's. It began at once without "dear sir" or any such address:

"You said you would like to help me if I needed it; and I believe you meant what you said. The time has come sooner than I expected. I am in dreadful trouble, and do not know where to turn, or to whom to apply. An attempt has, I fear, been made to murder my Father; though, thank God, he still lives. But he is quite unconscious. The doctors and police have been sent for; but there is no one here whom I can depend on. Come at once, if you are able to; and forgive me if you can. I suppose I shall realise later what I have done in asking such a favour; but at present I cannot think. Come! Come at once!

"MARGARET TRELAWNY."

Pain and exultation struggled in my mind as I read; but the mastering thought was that she was in trouble and had called on me—me! My dreaming of her, then, was not altogether without a cause. I called out to the groom:

"Wait! I shall be with you in a minute!" Then I flew upstairs.

A very few minutes sufficed to wash and dress; and we were soon driving through the streets as fast as the horses could go. It was market morning, and when we got out on Piccadilly there was an endless stream of carts coming from the west; but for the rest the roadway was clear, and we went quickly. I had told the groom to come into the brougham with me so that he could tell me what had happened as we went along. He sat awkwardly, with his hat on his knees as he spoke.

"Miss Trelawny, sir, sent a man to tell us to get out a carriage at once; and when we was ready she come herself and gave me the letter and told Morgan —the coachman, sir—to fly. She said as I was to lose not a second, but to keep knocking till someone come."

"Yes, I know, I know—you told me! What I want to know is, why she sent for me. What happened in the house?"

"I don't quite know myself, sir; except that master was found in his room senseless, with the sheets all bloody, and a wound on his head. He couldn't be waked nohow. 'Twas Miss Trelawny herself as found him."

"How did she come to find him at such an hour? It was late in the night, I suppose?"

"I don't know, sir; I didn't hear nothing at all of the details."

As he could tell me no more, I stopped the carriage for a moment to let him get out on the box; then I turned the matter over in my mind as I sat alone. There were many things which I could have asked the servant; and for a few moments after he had gone I was angry with myself for not having used my

opportunity. On second thought, however, I was
glad the temptation was gone. I felt that it would be
more delicate to learn what I wanted to know of Miss
Trelawny's surroundings from herself, rather than
from her servants.

We bowled swiftly along Knightsbridge, the small
noise of our well-appointed vehicle sounding hollowly
in the morning air. We turned up the Kensington
Palace Road and presently stopped opposite a great
house on the left-hand side, nearer, so far as I could
judge, the Notting Hill than the Kensington end of
the avenue. It was a truly fine house, not only with
regard to size but to architecture. Even in the dim
grey light of the morning, which tends to diminish the
size of things, it looked big.

Miss Trelawny met me in the hall. She was not in
any way shy. She seemed to rule all around her with
a sort of high-bred dominance, all the more remarkable as she was greatly agitated and as pale as snow.
In the great hall were several servants, the men standing together near the hall door, and the women cling-
ing together in the further corners and doorways.
A police superintendent had been talking to Miss
Trelawny ; two men in uniform and one plain-clothes
man stood near him. As she took my hand impulsively there was a look of relief in her eyes, and she
gave a gentle sigh of relief. Her salutation was
simple.

"I knew you would come!"

The clasp of the hand can mean a great deal, even
when it is not intended to mean anything especially.
Miss Trelawny's hand somehow became lost in my
own. It was not that it was a small hand; it was
fine and flexible, with long delicate fingers—a rare

and beautiful hand; it was the unconscious self-surrender. And though at the moment I could not dwell on the cause of the thrill which swept me, it came back to me later.

She turned and said to the police superintendent:

"This is Mr. Malcolm Ross." The police officer saluted as he answered:

"I know Mr. Malcolm Ross, miss. Perhaps he will remember I had the honour of working with him in the Brixton Coining case." I had not at first glance noticed who it was, my whole attention having been taken with Miss Trelawny.

"Of course, Superintendent Dolan, I remember very well!" I said as we shook hands. I could not but note that the acquaintanceship seemed a relief to Miss Trelawny. There was a certain vague uneasiness in her manner which took my attention; instinctively I felt that it would be less embarrassing for her to speak with me alone. So I said to the Superintendent:

"Perhaps it will be better if Miss Trelawny will see me alone for a few minutes. You, of course, have already heard all she knows; and I shall understand better how things are if I may ask some questions. I will then talk the matter over with you if I may."

"I shall be glad to be of what service I can, sir," he answered heartily.

Following Miss Trelawny, I moved over to a dainty room which opened from the hall and looked out on the garden at the back of the house. When we had entered and I had closed the door she said:

"I will thank you later for your goodness in coming to me in my trouble; but at present you can best help me when you know the facts."

"Go on," I said. "Tell me all you know and spare

no detail, however trivial it may at the present time seem to be." She went on at once:

"I was awakened by some sound; I do not know what. I only know that it came through my sleep; for all at once I found myself awake, with my heart beating wildly, listening anxiously for some sound from my Father's room. My room is next Father's, and I can often hear him moving about before I fall asleep. He works late at night, sometimes very late indeed; so that when I wake early, as I do occasionally, or in the grey of the dawn, I hear him still moving. I tried once to remonstrate with him about staying up so late, as it cannot be good for him; but I never ventured to repeat the experiment. You know how stern and cold he can be—at least you may remember what I told you about him; and when he is polite in this mood he is dreadful. When he is angry I can bear it much better; but when he is slow and deliberate, and the side of his mouth lifts up to show the sharp teeth, I think I feel—well, I don't know how! Last night I got up softly and stole to the door, for I really feared to disturb him. There was not any noise of moving, and no kind of cry at all; but there was a queer kind of dragging sound, and a slow, heavy breathing. Oh! it was dreadful, waiting there in the dark and the silence, and fearing—fearing I did not know what!

"At last I took my courage à deux mains, and turning the handle of the door as softly as I could, I opened the door a tiny bit. It was quite dark within; I could just see the outline of the windows. But in the darkness the sound of breathing, becoming more distinct, was appalling. As I listened, this continued; but there was no other sound. I pushed the door open all at once. I was afraid to open it slowly; I felt as if there might be some dreadful thing behind it ready to pounce out on me! Then I switched on the electric light, and stepped into the room. I looked first at the bed. The sheets were all crumpled up, so that I knew Father had been in bed; but there was a great dark red patch in the centre of the bed, and spreading to the edge of it, that made my heart stand still. As I was gazing at it the sound of the breathing came across the room, and my eyes followed to it. There was Father on his right side with the other arm under him, just as if his dead body had been thrown there all in a heap. The track of blood went across the room up to the bed, and there was a pool all around him which looked terribly red and glittering as I bent over to examine him. The place where he lay was right in front of the big safe. He was in his pyjamas. The left sleeve was torn, showing his bare arm, and stretched out toward the safe. It looked—oh! so terrible, patched all with blood, and with the flesh torn or cut all around a gold chain bangle on his wrist. I did not know he wore such a thing, and it seemed to give me a new shock of surprise."

She paused a moment; and as I wished to relieve her by a moment's divergence of thought, I said:

"Oh, that need not surprise you. You will see the most unlikely men wearing bangles. I have seen a judge condemn a man to death, and the wrist of the hand he held up had a gold bangle." She did not seem to heed much the words or the idea; the pause, however, relieved her somewhat, and she went on in a steadier voice:

"I did not lose a moment in summoning aid, for I feared he might bleed to death. I rang the bell, and then went out and called for help as loudly as I could. In what must have been a very short time—though it seemed an incredibly long one to me—some of the servants came running up; and then others, till the room seemed full of staring eyes, and dishevelled hair, and night clothes of all sorts.

"We lifted Father on a sofa ; and the housekeeper, Mrs. Grant, who seemed to have her wits about her more than any of us, began to look where the flow of blood came from. In a few seconds it became apparent that it came from the arm which was bare. There was a deep wound—not clean-cut as with a knife, but like a jagged rent or tear—close to the wrist, which seemed to have cut into the vein. Mrs. Grant tied a handkerchief round the cut, and screwed it up tight with a silver paper-cutter ; and the flow of blood seemed to be checked at once. By this time I had come to my senses—or such of them as remained ; and I sent off one man for the doctor and another for the police. When they had gone, I felt that, except for the servants, I was all alone in the house, and that I knew nothing—of my Father or anything else ; and a great longing came to me to have someone with me who could help me. Then I thought of you and your kind offer in the boat under the willow-tree ; and, without waiting to think, I told the men to get a carriage ready at once, and I scribbled a note and sent it on to you."

She paused. I did not like to say just then anything of how I felt. I looked at her ; I think she understood, for her eyes were raised to mine for a moment and then fell, leaving her cheeks as red as peony roses. With a manifest effort she went on with her story :

" The Doctor was with us in an incredibly short time. The groom had met him letting himself into his house with his latchkey, and he came here running. He made a proper tourniquet for poor Father's arm, and then went home to get some appliances. I dare say he will be back almost immediately. Then a policeman came, and sent a message to the station ; and very soon the Superintendent was here.. Then you came."

There was a long pause, and I ventured to take her hand for an instant. Without a word more we opened the door, and joined the Superintendent in the hall. He hurried up to us, saying as he came :

" I have been examining everything myself, and have sent off a message to Scotland Yard. You see, Mr. Ross, there seemed so much that was odd about the case that I thought we had better have the best man of the Criminal Investigation Department that we could get. So I sent a note asking to have Sergeant Daw sent at once. You remember him, sir, in that American poisoning case at Hoxton."

" Oh yes," I said, " I remember him well ; in that and other cases, for I have benefited several times by his skill and acumen. He has a mind that works as truly as any that I know. When I have been for the defence, and believed my man was innocent, I was glad to have him against us ! "

" That is high praise, sir ! " said the Superintendent gratified : " I am glad you approve of my choice ; that I did well in sending for him."

I answered heartily :

" Could not be better. I do not doubt that between

you we shall get at the facts—and what lies behind
them !"

We ascended to Mr. Trelawny's room, where we
found everything exactly as his daughter had described.

There came a ring at the house bell, and a minute
later a man was shown into the room. A young man
with aquiline features, keen grey eyes, and a forehead
that stood out square and broad as that of a thinker.
In his hand he had a black bag which he at once
opened. Miss Trelawny introduced us : "Doctor
Winchester, Mr. Ross, Superintendent Dolan." We
bowed mutually, and he, without a moment's delay,
began his work. We all waited, and eagerly watched
him as he proceeded to dress the wound. As he went
on he turned now and again to call the Superintendent's attention to some point about the wound, the
latter proceeding to enter the fact at once in his note-
book.

"See ! several parallel cuts or scratches beginning
on the left side of the wrist and in some places
endangering the radial artery.

"These small wounds here, deep and jagged,
seem as if made with a blunt instrument. This in
particular would seem as if made with some kind of
sharp wedge; the flesh round it seems torn as if with
lateral pressure."

Turning to Miss Trelawny he said presently :

"Do you think we might remove this bangle ? It
is not absolutely necessary, as it will fall lower on the
wrist where it can hang loosely ; but it might add
to the patient's comfort later on." The poor girl
flushed deeply as she answered in a low voice :

"I do not know. I—I have only recently come to
live with my Father ; and I know so little of his life

or his ideas that I fear I can hardly judge in such a matter. The Doctor, after a keen glance at her, said in a very kindly way:

"Forgive me! I did not know. But in any case you need not be distressed. It is not required at present to move it. Were it so I should do so at once on my own responsibility. If it be necessary later on, we can easily remove it with a file. Your Father doubtless has some object in keeping it as it is. See! there is a tiny key attached to it. . . ." As he was speaking he stopped and bent lower, taking from my hand the candle which I held and lowering it till its light fell on the bangle. Then motioning me to hold the candle in the same position, he took from his pocket a magnifying-glass which he adjusted. When he had made a careful examination he stood up and handed the magnifying-glass to Dolan, saying as he did so:

"You had better examine it yourself. That is no ordinary bangle. The gold is wrought over triple steel links; see where it is worn away. It is manifestly not meant to be removed lightly; and it would need more than an ordinary file to do it."

The Superintendent bent his great body; but not getting close enough that way knelt down by the sofa as the Doctor had done. He examined the bangle minutely, turning it slowly round so that no particle of it escaped observation. Then he stood up and handed the magnifying-glass to me. "When you have examined it yourself," he said, "let the lady look at it if she will," and he commenced to write at length in his note-book.

I made a simple alteration in his suggestion. I held out the glass toward Miss Trelawny, saying:

"Had you not better examine it first?" She drew back, slightly raising her hand in disclaimer, as she said impulsively:

"Oh no! Father would doubtless have shown it to me had he wished me to see it. I would not like to without his consent." Then she added, doubtless fearing lest her delicacy of view should give offence to the rest of us:

"Of course it is right that you should see it. You have to examine and consider everything; and indeed —indeed I am grateful to you. . . ."

She turned away; I could see that she was crying quietly. It was evident to me that even in the midst of her trouble and anxiety there was a chagrin that she knew so little of her father; and that her ignorance had to be shown at such a time and amongst so many strangers. That they were all men did not make the shame more easy to bear, though there was a certain relief in it. Trying to interpret her feelings I could not but think that she must have been glad that no woman's eyes—of understanding greater than man's—were upon her in that hour.

When I stood up from my examination, which verified to me that of the Doctor, the latter resumed his place beside the couch and went on with his ministrations. Superintendent Dolan said to me in a whisper:

"I think we are fortunate in our doctor!" I nodded, and was about to add something in praise of his acumen, when there came a low tapping at the door.

CHAPTER II

STRANGE INSTRUCTIONS

SUPERINTENDENT DOLAN went quietly to the door;
by a sort of natural understanding he had taken
possession of affairs in the room. The rest of us
waited. He opened the door a little way; and then
with a gesture of manifest relief threw it wide, and
a young man stepped in. A young man clean-shaven,
tall and slight; with an eagle face and bright, quick
eyes that seemed to take in everything around him
at a glance. As he came in, the Superintendent held
out his hand; the two men shook hands warmly.

"I came at once, sir, the moment I got your
message. I am glad I still have your confidence."

"That you'll always have," said the Superintendent
heartily. "I have not forgotten our old Bow Street
days, and I never shall!" Then, without a word of
preliminary, he began to tell everything he knew up
to the moment of the newcomer's entry. Sergeant
Daw asked a few questions—a very few—when it
was necessary for his understanding of circumstances
or the relative positions of persons; but as a rule
Dolan, who knew his work thoroughly, forestalled
every query, and explained all necessary matters as
he went on. Sergeant Daw threw occasionally swift
glances round him; now at one of us; now at the

room or some part of it; now at the wounded man lying senseless on the sofa.

When the Superintendent had finished, the Sergeant turned to me and said:

"Perhaps you remember me, sir. I was with you in that Hoxton case."

"I remember you very well," I said as I held out my hand. The Superintendent spoke again:

"You understand, Sergeant Daw, that you are put in full charge of this case."

"Under you I hope, sir," he interrupted. The other shook his head and smiled as he said:

"It seems to me that this is a case that will take all a man's time and his brains. I have other work to do; but I shall be more than interested, and if I can help in any possible way I shall be glad to do so!"

"All right, sir," said the other, accepting his responsibility with a sort of modified salute; straightway he began his investigation.

First he came over to the Doctor and, having learned his name and address, asked him to write a full report which he could use, and which he could refer to headquarters if necessary. Doctor Winchester bowed gravely as he promised. Then the Sergeant approached me and said *sotto voce:*

"I like the look of your doctor. I think we can work together!" Turning to Miss Trelawny he asked:

"Please let me know what you can of your Father; his ways of life, his history—in fact of anything of whatsoever kind which interests him, or in which he may be concerned." I was about to interrupt to tell him what she had already said of her ignorance in all matters of her father and his ways, but her warning hand was raised to me pointedly and she spoke herself.

"Alas! I know little or nothing. Superintendent Dolan and Mr. Ross know already all I can say."

"Well, ma'am, we must be content to do what we can," said the officer genially. "I'll begin by making a minute examination. You say that you were outside the door when you heard the noise?"

"I was in my room when I heard the queer sound —indeed it must have been the early part of whatever it was which woke me. I came out of my room at once. Father's door was shut, and I could see the whole landing and the upper slopes of the staircase. No one could have left by the door unknown to me, if that is what you mean!"

"That is just what I do mean, miss. If every one who knows anything will tell me as well as that, we shall soon get to the bottom of this."

He then went over to the bed, looked at it carefully, and asked:

"Has the bed been touched?"

"Not to my knowledge," said Miss Trelawny, "but I shall ask Mrs. Grant—the housekeeper," she added as she rang the bell. Mrs. Grant answered it in person. "Come in," said Miss Trelawny. "These gentlemen want to know, Mrs. Grant, if the bed has been touched."

"Not by me, ma'am."

"Then," said Miss Trelawny, turning to Sergeant Daw, "it cannot have been touched by any one. Either Mrs. Grant or I myself was here all the time, and I do not think any of the servants who came when I gave the alarm were near the bed at all. You see, Father lay here just under the great safe, and every one crowded round him. We sent them all away in a very short time." Daw, with a motion of his hand, asked us all to stay at the other side of the room whilst with a magnifying-glass he examined the bed, taking care as he moved each fold of the bed-clothes to replace it in exact position. Then he examined with his magnifying-glass the floor beside it, taking especial pains where the blood had trickled over the side of the bed, which was of heavy red wood handsomely carved. Inch by inch, down on his knees, carefully avoiding any touch with the stains on the floor, he followed the blood-marks over to the spot, close under the great safe, where the body had lain. All around and about this spot he went for a radius of some yards; but seemingly did not meet with anything to arrest special attention. Then he examined the front of the safe; round the lock, and along the bottom and top of the double doors, more especially at the places of their touching in front.

Next he went to the windows, which were fastened down with the hasps.

"Were the shutters closed?" he asked Miss Trelawny in a casual way as though he expected the negative answer, which came.

All this time Doctor Winchester was attending to his patient; now dressing the wounds in the wrist or making minute examination all over the head and throat, and over the heart. More than once he put his nose to the mouth of the senseless man and sniffed. Each time he did so he finished up by unconsciously looking round the room, as though in search of something.

Then we heard the deep strong voice of the Detective:

"So far as I can see, the object was to bring that key to the lock of the safe. There seems to be some secret in the mechanism that I am unable to guess at, though I served a year in Chubb's before I joined the police. It is a combination lock of seven letters ; but there seems to be a way of locking even the combination. It is one of Chatwood's ; I shall call at their place and find out something about it." Then turning to the Doctor, as though his own work were for the present done, he said :

"Have you anything you can tell me at once, Doctor, which will not interfere with your full report? If there is any doubt I can wait, but the sooner I know something definite the better." Doctor Winchester answered at once :

"For my own part I see no reason in waiting. I shall make a full report of course. But in the meantime I shall tell you all I know—which is after all not very much, and all I think—which is less definite. There is no wound on the head which could account for the state of stupor in which the patient continues. I must, therefore, take it that either he has been drugged or is under some hypnotic influence. So far as I can judge, he has not been drugged—at least by means of any drug of whose qualities I am aware. Of course, there is ordinarily in this room so much of mummy smell that it is difficult to be certain about anything having a delicate aroma. I dare say that you have noticed the peculiar Egyptian scents, bitumen, nard, aromatic gums and spices, and so forth. It is quite possible that somewhere in this room, amongst the curios and hidden by stronger scents, is some substance or liquid which may have the effect we see. It is possible that the patient has taken some drug, and that he may in some sleeping phase have injured himself. I do not think this is likely; and circumstances, other than those which I have myself been investigating, may prove that this surmise is not correct. But in the meantime it is possible; and must, till it be disproved, be kept within our purview." Here Sergeant Daw interrupted:

"That may be, but if so, we should be able to find the instrument with which the wrist was injured. There would be marks of blood somewhere."

"Exactly so!" said the Doctor, fixing his glasses as though preparing for an argument. "But if it be that the patient has used some strange drug, it may be one that does not take effect at once. As we are as yet ignorant of its potentialities—if, indeed, the whole surmise is correct at all—we must be prepared at all points."

Here Miss Trelawny joined in the conversation:

"That would be quite right, so far as the action of the drug was concerned; but according to the second part of your surmise the wound may have been self-inflicted, and this *after* the drug had taken effect."

"True!" said the Detective and the Doctor simultaneously. She went on.

"As however, Doctor, your guess does not exhaust the possibilities, we must bear in mind that some other variant of the same root-idea may be correct. I take it, therefore, that our first search, to be made on this assumption, must be for the weapon with which the injury was done to my Father's wrist."

"Perhaps he put the weapon in the safe before he became quite unconscious," said I, giving voice foolishly to a half-formed thought.

"That could not be," said the Doctor quickly. "At

least I think it could hardly be," he added cautiously, with a brief bow to me. "You see, the left hand is covered with blood ; but there is no blood mark whatever on the safe."

"Quite right ! " I said, and there was a long pause. The first to break the silence was the Doctor.

"We shall want a nurse here as soon as possible ; and I know the very one to suit. I shall go at once to get her if I can. I must ask that till I return some of you will remain constantly with the patient. It may be necessary to remove him to another room later on ; but in the meantime he is best left here. Miss Trelawny, may I take it that either you or Mrs. Grant will remain here—not merely in the room, but close to the patient and watchful of him—till I return ? "

She bowed in reply, and took a seat beside the sofa. The Doctor gave her some directions as to what she should do in case her father should become conscious before his return.

The next to move was Superintendent Dolan, who came close to Sergeant Daw as he said :

"I had better return now to the station—unless, of course, you should wish me to remain for a while."

He answered, "Is Johnny Wright still in your division ? "

"Yes ! Would you like him to be with you ? " The other nodded reply. "Then I will send him on to you as soon as can be arranged. He shall then stay with you as long as you wish. I will tell him that he is to take his instructions entirely from you."

The Sergeant accompanied him to the door, saying as he went :

"Thank you, sir ; you are always thoughtful for men who are working with you. It is a pleasure

to me to be with you again. I shall go back to
Scotland Yard and report to my chief. Then I shall
call at Chatwood's; and I shall return here as soon
as possible. I suppose I may take it, miss, that I
may put up here for a day or two, if required. It
may be some help, or possibly some comfort to you,
if I am about, until we unravel this mystery."

"I shall be very grateful to you." He looked keenly
at her for a few seconds before he spoke again.

"Before I go have I permission to look about your
Father's table and desk? There might be something
which would give us a clue—or a lead at all events."
Her answer was so unequivocal as almost to surprise
him.

"You have the fullest possible permission to do
anything which may help us in this dreadful trouble
—to discover what it is that is wrong with my Father,
or which may shield him in the future!"

He began at once a systematic search of the dress-
ing-table, and after that of the writing-table in the
room. In one of the drawers he found a letter sealed;
this he brought at once across the room and handed
to Miss Trelawny.

"A letter—directed to me—and in my Father's
hand!" she said as she eagerly opened it. I watched
her face as she began to read; but seeing at once
that Sergeant Daw kept his keen eyes on her face,
unflinchingly watching every flitting expression, I
kept my eyes henceforth fixed on his. When Miss
Trelawny had read her letter through, I had in my
mind a conviction, which, however, I kept locked in
my own heart. Amongst the suspicions in the mind
of the Detective was one, rather perhaps potential
than definite, of Miss Trelawny herself.

For several minutes Miss Trelawny held the letter in her hand with her eyes downcast, thinking. Then she read it carefully again; this time the varying expressions were intensified, and I thought I could easily follow them. When she had finished the second reading, she paused again. Then, though with some reluctance, she handed the letter to the Detective. He read it eagerly but with unchanging face; read it a second time, and then handed it back with a bow. She paused a little again, and then handed it to me. As she did so she raised her eyes to mine for a single moment appealingly; a swift blush spread over her pale cheeks and forehead.

With mingled feelings I took it, but, all said, I was glad. She did not show any perturbation in giving the letter to the Detective — she might not have shown any to anyone else. But to me . . . I feared to follow the thought further; but read on, conscious that the eyes of both Miss Trelawny and the Detective were fixed on me.

"MY DEAR DAUGHTER,—I want you to take this letter as an instruction—absolute and imperative, and admitting of no deviation whatever—in case anything untoward or unexpected by you or by others should happen to me. If I should be suddenly and mysteriously stricken down—either by sickness, accident or attack—you must follow these directions implicitly. If I am not already in my bedroom when you are made cognisant of my state, I am to be brought there as quickly as possible. Even should I be dead, my body is to be brought there. Thenceforth, until I am either conscious and able to give instructions on my own account, or buried, I am never to be left alone—

not for a single instant. From nightfall to sunrise at least two persons must remain in the room. It will be well that a trained nurse be in the room from time to time, and will note any symptoms, either permanent or changing, which may strike her. My solicitors, Marvin & Jewkes, of 27B Lincoln's Inn, have full instructions in case of my death; and Mr. Marvin has himself undertaken to see personally my wishes carried out. I should advise you, my dear Daughter, seeing that you have no relative to apply to, to get some friend whom you can trust to either remain within the house where instant communication can be made, or to come nightly to aid in the watching, or to be within call. Such friend may be either male or female; but, whichever it may be, there should be added one other watcher or attendant at hand of the opposite sex. Understand, that it is of the very essence of my wish that there should be, awake and exercising themselves to my purposes, both masculine and feminine intelligences. Once more, my dear Margaret, let me impress on you the need for observation and just reasoning to conclusions, howsoever strange. If I am taken ill or injured, this will be no ordinary occasion; and I wish to warn you, so that your guarding may be complete.

"Nothing in my room—I speak of the curios—must be removed or displaced in any way, or for any cause whatever. I have a special reason and a special purpose in the placing of each; so that any moving of them would thwart my plans.

"Should you want money or counsel in anything, Mr. Marvin will carry out your wishes; to the which he has my full instructions.

"ABEL TRELAWNY."

I read the letter a second time before speaking, for I feared to betray myself. The choice of a friend might be a momentous occasion for me. I had already ground for hope, in that she had asked me to help her in the first throe of her trouble; but love makes its own doubtings, and I feared. My thoughts seemed to whirl with lightning rapidity, and in a few seconds a whole process of reasoning became formulated. I must not volunteer to be the friend that the father advised his daughter to have to aid in her vigil; and yet that one glance had a lesson which I must not ignore. Also, did not she, when she wanted help, send to me—to me a stranger, except for one meeting at a dance and one brief afternoon of companionship on the river? Would it not humiliate her to make her ask me twice? Humiliate her! No! that pain I could at all events save her; it is not humiliation to refuse. So, as I handed her back the letter, I said:

"I know you will forgive me, Miss Trelawny, if I presume too much; but if you will permit me to aid in the watching I shall be proud. Though the occasion is a sad one, I shall be so far happy to be allowed the privilege."

Despite her manifest and painful effort at self-control, the red tide swept her face and neck. Even her eyes seemed suffused, and in stern contrast with her pale cheeks when the tide had rolled back. She answered in a low voice:

"I shall be very grateful for your help!" Then in an afterthought she added:

"But you must not let me be selfish in my need! I know you have many duties to engage you; and though I shall value your help highly—most highly— it would not be fair to monopolise your time."

"As to that," I answered at once, "my time is yours. I can for to-day easily arrange my work so that I can come here in the afternoon and stay till morning. After that, if the occasion still demands it, I can so arrange my work that I shall have more time still at my disposal."

She was much moved. I could see the tears gather in her eyes, and she turned away her head. The Detective spoke:

"I am glad you will be here, Mr. Ross. I shall be in the house myself, as Miss Trelawny will allow me, if my people in Scotland Yard will permit." That letter seems to put a different complexion on every-thing; though the mystery remains greater than ever. If you can wait here an hour or two I shall go to headquarters, and then to the safe makers. After that I shall return; and you can go away easier in your mind, for I shall be here."

When he had gone, we two, Miss Trelawny and I, remained in silence. At last she raised her eyes and looked at me for a moment; after that I. would not have exchanged places with a king. For a while she busied herself round the extemporised bedside of her father. Then, asking me to be sure not to take my eyes off him till she returned, she hurried out.

In a few minutes she came back with Mrs. Grant and two maids and a couple of men, who bore the entire frame and furniture of a light iron bed. This they proceeded to put together and to make. When the work was completed, and the servants had with-drawn, she said to me:

"It will be well to be all ready when the Doctor returns. He will surely want to have Father put to bed; and a proper bed will be better for him than the sofa." She then got a chair close beside her father, and sat down watching him.

I went about the room, taking accurate note of all I saw. And truly there were enough things in the room to evoke the curiosity of any man—even though the attendant circumstances were less strange. The whole place, excepting those articles of furniture necessary to a well-furnished bedroom, was filled with magnificent curios, chiefly Egyptian. As the room was of immense size there was opportunity for the placing of a large number of them, even if, as with these, they were of huge proportions.

Whilst I was still investigating the room there came the sound of wheels on the gravel outside the house. There was a ring at the hall door, and a few minutes later, after a preliminary tap at the door and an answering "Come in!" Doctor Winchester entered, followed by a young woman in the dark dress of a nurse.

"I have been fortunate!" he said as he came in. "I found her at once and free. Miss Trelawny, this is Nurse Kennedy!"

CHAPTER III

I WAS struck by the way the two young women looked at each other. I suppose I have been so much in the habit of weighing up in my own mind the personality of witnesses and of forming judgment by their unconscious action and mode of bearing themselves, that the habit extends to my life outside as well as within the court-house. At this moment of my life anything that interested Miss Trelawny interested me; and as she had been struck by the newcomer I instinctively weighed her up also. By comparison of the two I seemed somehow to gain a new knowledge of Miss Trelawny. Certainly, the two women made a good contrast. Miss Trelawny was of fine figure; dark, straight-featured. She had marvellous eyes; great, wide-open, and as black and soft as velvet, with a mysterious depth. To look in them was like gazing at a black mirror such as Doctor Dee used in his wizard rites. I heard an old gentleman at the picnic, a great oriental traveller, describe the effect of her eyes "as looking at night at the great distant lamps of a mosque through the open door." The eyebrows were typical. Finely arched and rich in long curling hair, they seemed like the proper architectural environment of the deep, splendid eyes.

Her hair was black also, but was as fine as silk. Generally black hair is a type of animal strength and seems as if some strong expression of the forces of a strong nature; but in this case there could be no such thought. There were refinement and high breeding; and though there was no suggestion of weakness, any sense of power there was, was rather spiritual than animal. The whole harmony of her being seemed complete. Carriage, figure, hair, eyes; the mobile, full mouth, whose scarlet lips and white teeth seemed to light up the lower part of the face—as the eyes did the upper; the wide sweep of the jaw from chin to ear; the long, fine fingers; the hand which seemed to move from the wrist as though it had a sentience of its own. All these perfections went to make up a personality that dominated either by its grace, its sweetness, its beauty, or its charm.

Nurse Kennedy, on the other hand, was rather under than over a woman's average height. She was firm and thickset, with full limbs and broad, strong, capable hands. Her colour was in the general effect that of an autumn leaf. The yellow-brown hair was thick and long, and the golden-brown eyes sparkled from the freckled, sunburnt skin. Her rosy cheeks gave a general idea of rich brown. The red lips and white teeth did not alter the colour scheme, but only emphasized it. She had a snub nose—there was no possible doubt about it; but like such noses in general it showed a nature generous, untiring, and full of good-nature. Her broad white forehead, which even the freckles had spared, was full of forceful thought and reason.

Doctor Winchester had on their journey from the hospital, coached her in the necessary particulars, and without a word she took charge of the patient and set to work. Having examined the new-made bed and shaken the pillows, she spoke to the Doctor, who gave instructions; presently we all four, stepping together, lifted the unconscious man from the sofa.

Early in the afternoon, when Sergeant Daw had returned, I called at my rooms in Jermyn Street, and sent out such clothes, books and papers as I should be likely to want within a few days. Then I went on to keep my legal engagements.

The Court sat late that day as an important case was ending; it was striking six as I drove in at the gate of the Kensington Palace Road. I found myself installed in a large room close to the sick chamber.

That night we were not yet regularly organised for watching, so that the early part of the evening showed an unevenly balanced guard. Nurse Kennedy, who had been on duty all day, was lying down, as she had arranged to come on again by twelve o'clock. Doctor Winchester, who was dining in the house, remained in the room until dinner was announced; and went back at once when it was over. During dinner Mrs. Grant remained in the room, and with her Sergeant Daw, who wished to complete a minute examination which he had undertaken of everything in the room and near it. At nine o'clock Miss Trelawny and I went in to relieve the Doctor. She had lain down for a few hours in the afternoon so as to be refreshed for her work at night. She told me that she had determined that for this night at least she would sit up and watch. I did not try to dissuade her, for I knew that her mind was made up. Then and there I made up my mind that I would watch with her—unless, of course, I should see that she really did not wish it. I said nothing of my intentions for the present. We came in on tiptoe, so silently that the Doctor, who was bending over the bed, did not hear us, and seemed a little startled when suddenly looking up he saw our eyes upon him. I felt that the mystery of the whole thing was getting on his nerves, as it had already got on the nerves of some others of us. He was, I fancied, a little annoyed with himself for having been so startled, and at once began to talk in a hurried manner as though to get over our idea of his embarrassment :

" I am really and absolutely at my wits'-end to find any fit cause for this stupor. I have made again as accurate an examination as I know how, and I am satisfied that there is no injury to the brain, that is, no external injury. Indeed, all his vital organs seem unimpaired. I have given him, as you know, food several times and it has manifestly done him good. His breathing is strong and regular, and his pulse is slower and stronger than it was this morning. I cannot find evidence of any known drug, and his unconsciousness does not resemble any of the many cases of hypnotic sleep which I saw in the Charcot Hospital in Paris. And as to these wounds "—he laid his finger gently on the bandaged wrist which lay outside the coverlet as he spoke, " I do not know what to make of them. They might have been made by a carding-machine ; but that supposition is untenable. It is within the bounds of possibility that they might have been made by a wild animal if it had taken care to sharpen its claws. That too is, I take it, impossible. By the way, have you any strange pets here in the house ;

anything of an exceptional kind, such as a tiger-cat
or anything out of the common?" Miss Trelawny
smiled a sad smile which made my heart ache, as she
made answer:

"Oh no! Father does not like animals about the
house, unless they are dead and mummied." This was
said with a touch of bitterness—or jealousy, I could
hardly tell which. "Even my poor kitten was only
allowed in the house on sufferance; and though he
is the dearest and best-conducted cat in the world,
he is now on a sort of parole, and is not allowed into
this room."

As she was speaking a faint rattling of the door
handle was heard. Instantly Miss Trelawny's face
brightened. She sprang up and went over to the
door, saying as she went:

"There he is! That is my Silvio. He stands on
his hind legs and rattles the door handle when he
wants to come into a room." She opened the door,
speaking to the cat as though he were a baby: "Did
him want his movver? Come then; but he must
stay with her!" She lifted the cat, and came back
with him in her arms. He was certainly a magnificent
animal. A chinchilla grey Persian with long silky
hair; a really lordly animal with a haughty bearing,
despite his gentleness; and with great paws which
spread out as he placed them on the ground. Whilst
she was fondling him, he suddenly gave a wriggle like
an eel and slipped out of her arms. He ran across
the room and stood opposite a low table on which
stood the mummy of an animal, and began to mew
and snarl. Miss Trelawny was after him in an instant
and lifted him in her arms, kicking and struggling and
wriggling to get away; but not biting or scratching,

for evidently he loved his beautiful mistress. He ceased to make a noise the moment he was in her arms; in a whisper she admonished him:

"O you naughty Silvio! You have broken your parole that mother gave for you. Now, say goodnight to the gentlemen, and come away to mother's room!" As she was speaking she held out the cat's paw to me to shake. As I did so I could not but admire its size and beauty. "Why," said I, "his paw seems like a little boxing-glove full of claws." She smiled:

"So. it ought to. Don't you notice that my Silvio has seven toes, see!" she opened the paw; and surely enough there were seven separate claws, each of them sheathed in a delicate, fine, shell-like case. As I gently stroked the foot the claws emerged and one of them accidentally—there was no anger now and the cat was purring—stuck into my hand. Instinctively I said as I drew back:

"Why, his claws are like razors!"

Doctor Winchester had come close to us and was bending over looking at the cat's claws; as I spoke he said in a quick, sharp way:

"Eh!" I could hear the quick intake of his breath. Whilst I was stroking the now quiescent cat, the Doctor went to the table and tore off a piece of blotting-paper from the writing-pad and came back. He laid the paper on his palm and, with a simple "pardon me!" to Miss Trelawny, placed the cat's paw on it and pressed it down with his other hand. The haughty cat seemed to resent somewhat the familiarity, and tried to draw its foot away. This was plainly what the Doctor wanted, for in the act the cat opened the sheaths of its claws and made several reefs in the soft paper. Then Miss Trelawny took her pet away. She returned in a couple of minutes ; as she came in she said :

" It is most odd about that mummy ! When Silvio came into the room first—indeed I took him in as a kitten to show to Father—he went on just the same way. He jumped up on the table, and tried to scratch and bite the mummy. That was what made Father so angry, and brought the decree of banishment on poor Silvio. Only his parole, given through me, kept him in the house."

Whilst she had been gone, Doctor Winchester had taken the bandage from her father's wrist. The wound was now quite clear, as the separate cuts showed out in fierce red lines. The Doctor folded the blotting-paper across the line of punctures made by the cat's claws, and held it down close to the wound. As he did so, he looked up triumphantly and beckoned us over to him.

The cuts in the paper corresponded with the wounds in the wrist ! No explanation was needed, as he said :

" It would have been better if master Silvio had not broken his parole ! "

We were all silent for a little while. Suddenly Miss Trelawny said :

" But Silvio was not in here last night ! "

" Are you sure ? Could you prove that if necessary ? " She hesitated before replying :

" I am certain of it ; but I fear it would be difficult to prove. Silvio sleeps in a basket in my room. I certainly put him to bed last night ; I remember distinctly laying his little blanket over him, and tucking him in. This morning I took him out of the basket myself. I certainly never noticed him in here ; though, of course, that would not mean much, for I was too concerned about poor father, and too much occupied with him, to notice even Silvio."

The Doctor shook his head as he said with a certain sadness :

" Well, at any rate it is no use trying to prove anything now. Any cat in the world would have cleaned blood-marks—did any exist—from his paws in a hundredth part of the time that has elapsed."

Again we were all silent ; and again the silence was broken by Miss Trelawny :

" But now that I think of it, it could not have been poor Silvio that injured Father. My door was shut when I first heard the sound ; and Father's was shut when I listened at it. When I went in, the injury had been done ; so that it must have been before Silvio could possibly have got in." This reasoning commended itself, especially to me as a barrister, for it was proof to satisfy a jury. It gave me a distinct pleasure to have Silvio acquitted of the crime— possibly because he was Miss Trelawny's cat and was loved by her. Happy cat ! Silvio's mistress was manifestly pleased as I said :

" Verdict, ' not guilty ! ' " Doctor Winchester after a pause observed :

" My apologies to master Silvio on this occasion ; but I am still puzzled to know why he is so keen against that mummy. Is he the same toward the other mummies in the house ? There are, I suppose, a lot of them. I saw three in the hall as I came in."

" There are lots of them," she answered. " I sometimes don't know whether I am in a private house or the British Museum. But Silvio never concerns himself about any of them except that particular one. I suppose it must be because it is of an animal, not a man or a woman."

"Perhaps it is of a cat!" said the Doctor as he started up and went across the room to look at the mummy more closely. "Yes," he went on, "it is the mummy of a cat; and a very fine one, too. If it hadn't been a special favourite of some very special person it would never have received so much honour. See! A painted case and obsidian eyes— just like a human mummy. It is an extraordinary thing, that knowledge of kind to kind. Here is a dead cat—that is all; it is perhaps four or five thousand years old—and another cat of another breed, in what is practically another world, is ready to fly at it, just as it would if it were not dead. I should like to experiment a bit about that cat if you don't mind, Miss Trelawny." She hesitated before replying:

"Of course, do anything you may think necessary or wise; but I hope it will not be anything to hurt or worry my poor Silvio." The Doctor smiled as he answered:

"Oh, Silvio would be all right : it is the other one that my sympathies would be reserved for."

"How do you mean ?"

"Master Silvio will do the attacking ; the other one will do the suffering."

"Suffering ?" There was a note of pain in her voice. The Doctor smiled more broadly:

"Oh, please make your mind easy as to that. The other won't suffer as we understand it ; except perhaps in his structure and outfit."

"What on earth do you mean ?"

"Simply this, my dear young lady, that the antagonist will be a mummy cat like this one. There are, I take it, plenty of them to be had in Museum Street. I shall get one and place it here instead of that one—you won't think that a temporary exchange will violate your Father's instructions, I hope. We shall then find out, to begin with, whether Silvio objects to all mummy cats, or only to this one in particular."

"I don't know," she said doubtfully. "Father's instructions seem very uncompromising." Then after a pause she went on: "But of course under the circumstances anything that is to be ultimately for his good must be done. I suppose there can't be anything very particular about the mummy of a cat."

Doctor Winchester said nothing. He sat rigid, with so grave a look on his face that his extra gravity passed on to me; and in its enlightening perturbation I began to realise more than I had yet done the strangeness of the case in which I was now so deeply concerned. When once this thought had begun there was no end to it. Indeed it grew, and blossomed, and reproduced itself in a thousand different ways. The room and all in it gave grounds for strange thoughts. There were so many ancient relics that unconsciously one was taken back to strange lands and strange times. There were so many mummies or mummy objects, round which there seem to cling for ever the penetrating odours of bitumen, and spices and gums—"Nard and Circassia's balmy smells"—that one was unable to forget the past. Of course, there was but little light in the room, and that carefully shaded; so that there was no glare anywhere. None of that direct light which can manifest itself as a power or an entity,

and so make for companionship. The room was
a large one, and lofty in proportion to its size. In
its vastness was place for a multitude of things not
often found in a bedchamber. In far corners of
the room were shadows of uncanny shape. More
than once as I thought, the multitudinous presence
of the dead and the past took such hold on me
that I caught myself looking round fearfully as
though some strange personality or influence was
present. Even the manifest presence of Doctor
Winchester and Miss Trelawny could not altogether
comfort or satisfy me at such moments. It was with
a distinct sense of relief that I saw a new personality
in the room in the shape of Nurse Kennedy. There
was no doubt that that business-like, self-reliant,
capable young woman added an element of security
to such wild imaginings as my own. She had a
quality of common sense that seemed to pervade
everything around her, as though it were some kind
of emanation. Up to that moment I had been
building fancies around the sick man ; so that finally
all about him, including myself, had become involved
in them, or enmeshed, or saturated, or . . . But now
that she had come, he relapsed into his proper perspective as a patient ; the room was a sick-room, and
the shadows lost their fearsome quality. The only
thing which it could not altogether abrogate was the
strange Egyptian smell. You may put a mummy
in a glass case and hermetically seal it so that no
corroding air can get within ; but all the same it will
exhale its odour. One might think that four or five
thousand years would exhaust the olfactory qualities
of anything ; but experience teaches us that these
smells remain, and that their secrets are unknown

to us. To-day they are as much mysteries as they
were when the embalmers put the body in the bath
of natron. . . .

All at once I sat up. I had become lost in an
absorbing reverie. The Egyptian smell had seemed
to get on my nerves—on my memory—on my very
will.

At that moment I had a thought which was like an
inspiration. If I was influenced in such a manner by
the smell, might it not be that the sick man, who lived
half his life or more in the atmosphere, had gradually
and by slow but sure process taken into his system
something which had permeated him to such degree
that it had a new power derived from quantity—or
strength—or . . .

I was becoming lost again in a reverie. This would
not do. I must take such precaution that I could
remain awake, or free from such entrancing thought.
I had had but half a night's sleep last night; and this
night I must remain awake. Without stating my
intention, for I feared that I might add to the trouble
and uneasiness of Miss Trelawny, I went downstairs
and out of the house. I soon found a chemist's shop,
and came away with a respirator. When I got back,
it was ten o'clock; the Doctor was going for the
night. The Nurse came with him to the door of the
sick-room, taking her last instructions. Miss Trelawny sat ll beside the bed. Sergeant Daw, who
had entered as the Doctor went out, was some
little distance off.

When Nurse Kennedy joined us, we arranged that
she should sit up till two o'clock, when Miss Trelawny
would relieve her. Thus, in accordance with Mr.
Trelawny's instructions, there would always be a man

and a woman in the room ; and each one of us would overlap, so that at no time would a new set of watchers come on duty without some one to tell of what—if anything—had occurred. I lay down on a sofa in my own room, having arranged that one of the servants should call me a little before twelve. In a few moments I was asleep.

When I was waked, it took me several seconds to get back my thoughts so as to recognise my own identity and surroundings. The short sleep had, however, done me good, and I could look on things around me in a more practical light than I had been able to do earlier in the evening. I bathed my face, and thus refreshed went into the sick-room. I moved very softly. The Nurse was sitting by the bed, quiet and alert ; the Detective sat in an arm-chair across the room in deep shadow. He did not move when I crossed, until I got close to him, when he said in a dull whisper :

"It is all right ; I have not been asleep !" An unnecessary thing to say, I thought—it always is, unless it be untrue in spirit. When I told him that his watch was over ; that he might go to bed till I should call him at six o'clock, he seemed relieved and went with alacrity. At the door he turned and, coming back to me, said in a whisper :

"I sleep lightly and I shall have my pistols with me. I won't feel so heavy-headed when I get out of this mummy smell."

He too, then, had shared my experience of drowsiness !

I asked the Nurse if she wanted anything. I noticed that she had a vinaigrette in her lap. Doubtless she, too, had felt some of the influence which had so affected me. She said that she had all she required, but that if she should want anything she would at once let me know. I wished to keep her from noticing my respirator, so I went to the chair in the shadow where her back was toward me. Here I quietly put it on, and made myself comfortable.

For what seemed a long time, I sat and thought and thought. It was a wild medley of thoughts, as might have been expected from the experiences of the previous day and night. Again I found myself thinking of the Egyptian smell; and I remember that I felt a delicious satisfaction that I did not experience it as I had done. The respirator was doing its work.

It must have been that the passing of this disturbing thought made for repose of mind, which is the corollary of bodily rest, for, though I really cannot remember being asleep or waking from it, I saw a vision—I dreamed a dream, I scarcely know which.

I was still in the room, seated in the chair. I had on my respirator and knew that I breathed freely. The Nurse sat in her chair with her back toward me. She sat quite still. The sick man lay as still as the dead. It was rather like the picture of a scene than the reality; all were still and silent; and the stillness and silence were continuous. Outside, in the distance I could hear the sounds of a city, the occasional roll of wheels, the shout of a reveller, the far-away echo of whistles and the rumbling of trains. The light was very, very low; the reflection of it under the green-shaded lamp was a dim relief to the darkness, rather than light. The green silk fringe of the lamp had merely the colour of an emerald seen in the moonlight. The room, for all its darkness, was full of shadows. It seemed in my whirling thoughts as though all the real things had become shadows— shadows which moved, for they passed the dim out- line of the high windows. Shadows which had sentience. I even thought there was sound, a faint sound as of the mew of a cat—the rustle of drapery and a metallic clink as of metal faintly touching metal. I sat as one entranced. At last I felt, as in nightmare, that this was sleep, and that in the passing of its portals all my will had gone.

All at once my senses were full awake. A shriek rang in my ears. The room was filled suddenly with a blaze of light. There was the sound of pistol shots— one, two; and a haze of white smoke in the room. When my waking eyes regained their power, I could have shrieked with horror myself at what I saw before me.

CHAPTER IV

THE SECOND ATTEMPT

THE sight which met my eyes had the horror of a
dream within a dream, with the certainty of reality
added. The room was as I had seen it last; except
that the shadowy look had gone in the glare of the
many lights, and every article in it stood stark and
solidly real.

By the empty bed sat Nurse Kennedy, as my eyes
had last seen her, sitting bolt upright in the arm-chair
beside the bed. She had placed a pillow behind her,
so that her back might be erect; but her neck was
fixed as that of one in a cataleptic trance. She was,
to all intents and purposes, turned into stone. There
was no special expression on her face—no fear, no
horror; nothing such as might be expected of one in
such a condition. Her open eyes showed neither
wonder nor interest. She was simply a negative existence, warm, breathing, placid; but absolutely unconscious of the world around her. The bedclothes were
disarranged, as though the patient had been drawn
from under them without throwing them back. The
corner of the upper sheet hung upon the floor; close
by it lay one of the bandages with which the Doctor
had dressed the wounded wrist. Another and another
lay further along the floor, as though forming a clue

to where the sick man now lay. This was almost exactly where he had been found on the previous night, under the great safe. Again, the left arm lay toward the safe. But there had been a new outrage, an attempt had been made to sever the arm close to the bangle which held the tiny key. A heavy "kukri" knife — one of the leaf - shaped knives which the Gurkhas and others of the hill tribes of India use with such effect—had been taken from its place on the wall, and with it the attempt had been made. It was manifest that just at the moment of striking, the blow had been arrested, for only the point of the knife and not the edge of the blade had struck the flesh. As it was, the outer side of the arm had been cut to the bone and the blood was pouring out. In addition, the former wound in front of the arm had been cut or torn about terribly, one of the cuts seemed to jet out blood as if with each pulsation of the heart. By the side of her father knelt Miss Trelawny, her white nightdress stained with the blood in which she knelt. In the middle of the room Sergeant Daw, in his shirt and trousers and stocking feet, was putting fresh cartridges into his revolver in a dazed mechanical kind of way. His eyes were red and heavy, and he seemed only half awake, and less than half conscious of what was going on around him. Several servants, bearing lights of various kinds, were clustered round the doorway.

As I rose from my chair and came forward, Miss Trelawny raised her eyes toward me. When she saw me she shrieked and started to her feet, pointing towards me. Never shall I forget the strange picture she made, with her white drapery all smeared with blood which, as she rose from the pool, ran in streaks toward her bare feet. I believe that I had only been asleep; that whatever influence had worked on Mr. Trelawny and Nurse Kennedy—and in less degree on Sergeant Daw—h ⌐ not touched me. The respirator had been of some service, though it had not kept off the tragedy whose dire evidences were before me. I can understand now—I could understand even then— the fright, added to that which had gone before, which my appearance must have evoked. I had still on the respirator, which covered mouth and nose; my hair had been tossed in my sleep. Coming suddenly forward, thus enwrapped and dishevelled, in that horrified crowd, I must have had, in the strange mixture of lights, an extraordinary and terrifying appearance. It was well that I recognised all this in time to avert another catastrophe; for the half-dazed, mechanically-acting Detective put in the cartridges and had raised his revolver to shoot at me when I succeeded in wrenching off the respirator and shouting to him to hold his hand. In this also he acted mechanically; the red, half-awake eyes had not in them even then the intention of conscious action. The danger, however, was averted. The relief of the situation, strangely enough, came in a simple fashion. Mrs. Grant, seeing that her young mistress had on only her nightdress, had gone to fetch a dressing-gown, which she now threw over her. This simple act brought us all back to the region of fact. With a long breath, one and all seemed to devote themselves to the most pressing matter before us, that of staunching the flow of blood from the arm of the wounded man. Even as the thought of action came, I rejoiced; for the bleeding was very proof that Mr. Trelawny still lived.

Last night's lesson was not thrown away. More

than one of those present knew now what to do in such an emergency, and within a few seconds willing hands were at work on a tourniquet. A man was at once despatched for the doctor, and several of the servants disappeared to make themselves respectable. We lifted Mr. Trelawny on to the sofa where he had lain yesterday; and, having done what we could for him, turned our attention to the Nurse. In all the turmoil she had not stirred; she sat there as before, erect and rigid, breathing softly and naturally and with a placid smile. As it was manifestly of no use to attempt anything with her till the doctor had come, we began to think of the general situation.

Mrs. Grant had by this time taken her mistress away and changed her clothes; for she was back presently in a dressing-gown and slippers, and with the traces of blood removed from her hands. She was now much calmer, though she trembled sadly; and her face was ghastly white. When she had looked at her father's wrist, I holding the tourniquet, she turned her eyes round the room, resting them now and again on each one of us present in turn, but seeming to find no comfort. It was so apparent to me that she did not know where to begin or whom to trust that, to reassure her, I said:

"I am all right now; I was only asleep." Her voice had a gulp in it as she said in a low voice:

"Asleep! You! and my Father in danger! I thought you were on the watch!" I felt the sting of justice in the reproach; but I really wanted to help her, so I answered:

"Only asleep. It is bad enough, I know; but there is something more than an 'only' round us here. Had it not been that I took a definite precaution I

might have been like the Nurse there." She turned
her eyes swiftly on the weird figure, sitting grimly
upright like a painted statue; and then her face
softened. With the action of habitual courtesy she
said :

"Forgive me! I did not mean to be rude. But
I am in such distress and fear that I hardly know
what I am saying. Oh, it is dreadful! I fear for
fresh trouble and horror and mystery every moment."
This cut me to the very heart, and out of the heart's
fulness I spoke :

"Don't give me a thought! I don't deserve it. I
was on guard, and yet I slept. All that I can say
is that I didn't mean to, and I tried to avoid it; but
it was over me before I knew it. Anyhow, it is done
now; and can't be undone. Probably some day we
may understand it all; but now let us try to get at
some idea of what has happened. Tell me what you
remember!" The effort to recollect seemed to stimu-
late her; she became calmer as she spoke :

"I was asleep, and woke suddenly with the same
horrible feeling on me that Father was in great and
immediate danger. I jumped up and ran, just as I
was, into his room. It was nearly pitch dark, but
as I opened the door there was light enough to see
Father's nightdress as he lay on the floor under the
safe, just as on that first awful night. Then I think
I must have gone mad for a moment." She stopped
and shuddered. My eyes lit on Sergeant Daw, still
fiddling in an aimless way with the revolver. Mindful
of my work with the tourniquet, I said calmly :

"Now tell us, Sergeant Daw, what did you fire
at?" The policeman seemed to pull himself together
with the habit of obedience. Looking around at the

servants remaining in the room, he said with that air of importance which, I take it, is the regulation attitude of an official of the law before strangers :

"Don't you think, sir, that we can allow the servants to go away ? We can then better go into the matter." I nodded approval; the servants took the hint and withdrew, though unwillingly, the last one closing the door behind him. Then the Detective went on :

"I think I had better tell you my impressions, sir, rather than recount my actions. That is, so far as I remember them." There was a mortified deference now in his manner, which probably arose from his consciousness of the awkward position in which he found himself. "I went to sleep half-dressed—as I am now, with a revolver under my pillow. It was the last thing I remember thinking of. I do not know how long I slept. I had turned off the electric light, and it was quite dark. I thought I heard a scream ; but I can't be sure, for I felt thick-headed as a man does when he is called too soon after an extra long stretch of work. Not that such was the case this time. Anyhow my thoughts flew to the pistol. I took it out, and ran on to the landing. Then I heard a sort of scream, or rather a call for help, and ran into this room. The room was dark, for the lamp beside the Nurse was out, and the only light was that from the landing, coming through the open door. Miss Trelawny was kneeling on the floor beside her father, and was screaming. I thought I saw something move between me and the window; so, without thinking, and being half dazed and only half awake, I shot at it. It moved a little more to the right between the windows, and I shot again. Then you

came up out of the big chair with all that muffling
on your face. It seemed to me, being as I say half
dazed and only half awake—I know, sir, you will take
this into account—as if it had been you, being in the
same direction as the thing I had fired at. And so
I was about to fire again when you pulled off the
wrap." Here I asked him—I was cross-examining
now and felt at home:

"You say you thought I was the thing you fired
at. What thing?" The man scratched his head,
but made no reply.

"Come, sir," I said, "what thing; what was it
like?" The answer came in a low voice:

"I don't know, sir. I thought there was something; but what it was, or what it was like, I haven't
the faintest notion. I suppose it was because I had
been thinking of the pistol before I went to sleep, and
because when I came in here I was half dazed and
only half awake—which I hope you will in future, sir,
always remember." He clung to that formula of
excuse as though it were his sheet-anchor. I did not
want to antagonise the man; on the contrary I
wanted to have him with us. Besides, I had on me
at that time myself the shadow of my own default;
so I said as kindly as I knew how:

"Quite right! Sergeant. Your impulse was correct; though of course in the half-somnolent condition
in which you were, and perhaps partly affected by
the same influence—whatever it may be—which made
me sleep and which has put the Nurse in that cataleptic trance, it could not be expected that you would
pause to weigh matters. But now, whilst the matter
is fresh, let me see exactly where you stood and where
I sat. We shall be able to trace the course of your

bullets." The prospect of action and the exercise of his habitual skill seemed to brace him at once; he seemed a different man as he set about his work. I asked Mrs. Grant to hold the tourniquet, and went and stood where he had stood and looked where, in the darkness, he had pointed. I could not but notice the mechanical exactness of his mind, as when he showed me where he had stood, or drew, as a matter of course, the revolver from his pistol pocket, and pointed with it. The chair from which I had risen still stood in its place. Then I asked him to point with his hand only, as I wished to move in the track of his shot.

Just behind my chair, and a little back of it, stood a high buhl cabinet. The glass door was shattered. I asked:

"Was this the direction of your first shot or your second?" The answer came promptly:

"The second; the first was over there!"

He turned a little to the left, more toward the wall where the great safe stood, and pointed. I followed the direction of his hand and came to the low table whereon rested, amongst other curios, the mummy of the cat which had raised Silvio's ire. I got a candle and easily found the mark of the bullet. It had broken a little glass vase and a tazza of black basalt, exquisitely engraved with hieroglyphics, the graven lines being filled with some faint green cement and the whole thing being polished to an equal surface. The bullet, flattened against the wall, lay on the table.

I then went to the broken cabinet. It was evidently a receptacle for valuable curios; for in it were some great scarabs of gold, agate, green jasper, amethyst, lapis lazuli, opal, granite, and blue-green china. None

of these things happily were touched. The bullet
had gone through the back of the cabinet; but no
other damage, save the shattering of the glass, had
been done. I could not but notice the strange arrangement of the curios on the shelf of the cabinet. All
the scarabs, rings, amulets, &c. were arranged in an
uneven oval round an exquisitely-carved golden minia-
ture figure of a hawk-headed God crowned with a disk
and plumes. I did not wait to look further at present, for my attention was demanded by more pressing
things; but I determined to make a more minute
examination when I should have time. It was evident
that some of the strange Egyptian smell clung to
these old curios; through the broken glass came an
added whiff of spice and gum and bitumen, almost
stronger than those I had already noticed as coming
from others in the room.

All this had really taken but a few minutes. I was
surprised when my eye met, through the chinks between the dark window blinds and the window cases,
the brighter light of the coming dawn. When I went
back to the sofa and took the tourniquet from Mrs.
Grant, she went over and pulled up the blinds.

It would be hard to imagine anything more ghastly
than the appearance of the room with the faint grey
light of early morning coming in upon it. As the
windows faced north, any light that came was a fixed
grey light without any of the rosy possibility of dawn
which comes in the eastern quarter of the heavens.
The electric lights seemed dull and yet glaring; and
every shadow was of a hard intensity. There was
nothing of morning freshness; nothing of the softness
of night. All was hard and cold, and inexpressibly
dreary. The face of the senseless man on the sofa

seemed of a ghastly yellow; and the Nurse's face had taken a suggestion of green from the shade of the lamp near her. Only Miss Trelawny's face looked white; and it was of a pallor which made my heart ache. It looked as if nothing on God's earth could ever again bring back to it the colour of life and happiness.

It was a relief to us all when Doctor Winchester came in, breathless with running. He only asked one question:

"Can anyone tell me anything of how this wound was gotten?" On seeing the headshake which went round us under his glance, he said no more, but applied himself to his surgical work. For an instant he looked up at the Nurse sitting so still; but then bent himself to his task, a grave frown contracting his brows. It was not till the arteries were tied and the wounds completely dressed that he spoke again, except, of course, when he had asked for anything to be handed to him or to be done for him. When Mr. Trelawny's wounds had been thoroughly cared for, he said to Miss Trelawny:

"What about Nurse Kennedy?" She answered at once:

"I really do not know. I found her when I came into the room at half-past two o'clock, sitting exactly as she does now. We have not moved her, or changed her position. She has not wakened since. Even Sergeant Daw's pistol-shots did not disturb her."

"Pistol-shots? Have you then discovered any cause for this new outrage?" The rest were silent, so I answered:

"We have discovered nothing. I was in the room watching with the Nurse. Earlier in the evening I fancied that the mummy smells were making me drowsy, so I went out and got a respirator. I had it on when I came on duty; but it did not keep me from going to sleep. I awoke to see the room full of people; that is, Miss Trelawny and Sergeant Daw and the servants. The Nurse was sitting in her chair just as I had seen her. Sergeant Daw, being only half awake and still stupefied by the same scent or influence which had affected us, fancied that he saw something moving through the shadowy darkness of the room, and fired twice. When I rose out of my chair, with my face swathed in the respirator, he took me for the cause of the trouble. Naturally enough, he was about to fire again, when I was fortunately in time to manifest my identity. Mr. Trelawny was lying beside the safe, just as he was found last night; and was bleeding profusely from the new wound in his wrist. We lifted him on the sofa, and made a tourniquet. That is, literally and absolutely, all that any of us know as yet. We have not touched the knife, which you see lies close by the pool of blood. Look!" I said, going over and lifting it, "The point is red with the blood which has dried."

Doctor Winchester stood quite still a few minutes before speaking:

"Then the doings of this night are quite as mysterious as those of last night?"

"Quite!" I answered. He said nothing in reply, but turning to Miss Trelawny said:

"We had better take Nurse Kennedy into another room. I suppose there is nothing to prevent it?"

"Nothing! Please, Mrs. Grant, see that Nurse Kennedy's room is ready; and ask two of the men to come and carry her in." Mrs. Grant went out immediately; and in a few minutes came back saying:

"The room is quite ready; and the men are here." By her direction two footmen came into the room and, lifting up the rigid body of Nurse Kennedy under the supervision of the Doctor, carried her out of the room. Miss Trelawny remained with me in the sick chamber, and Mrs. Grant went with the Doctor into the Nurse's room.

When we were alone Miss Trelawny came over to me, and taking both my hands in hers, said:

"I hope you won't remember what I said. I did not mean it, and I was distraught." I did not make reply; but I held her hands and kissed them. There are different ways of kissing a lady's hands. This way was intended as homage and respect; and it was accepted as such in the high-bred, dignified way which marked Miss Trelawny's bearing and every movement. I went over to the sofa and looked down at the senseless man. The dawn had come much nearer in the last few minutes, and there was something of the clearness of day in the light. As I looked at the stern, cold, set face, now as white as a marble monument in the pale grey light, I could not but feel that there was some deep mystery beyond all that had happened within the last twenty-six hours. Those beetling brows screened some massive purpose; that high, broad forehead held some finished train of reasoning, which the broad chin and massive jaw would help to carry into effect. As I looked and wondered, there began to steal over me again that phase of wandering thought which had last night heralded the approach of sleep. I resisted it, and held myself sternly to the present. This was easier to do when Miss Trelawny came close to me, and, leaning her forehead against my shoulder, began to cry silently. Then all the manhood in me woke, and to present purpose. It was of little use trying to speak; words were inadequate to thought. But we understood each other; she did not draw away when I put my arm protectingly over her shoulder as I used to do with my little sister long ago when in her childish trouble she would come to her big brother to be comforted. That very act or attitude of protection made me more resolute in my purpose, and seemed to clear my brain of idle, dreamy wandering in thought. With an instinct of greater protection, however, I took away my arm as I heard the Doctor's footstep outside the door.

When Doctor Winchester came in he looked intently at the patient before speaking. His brows were set, and his mouth was a thin, hard line. Presently he said:

"There is much in common between the sleep of your Father and Nurse Kennedy. Whatever influence has brought it about has probably worked the same way in both cases. In Kennedy's case the coma is less marked. I cannot but feel, however, that with her we may be able to do more and more quickly than with this patient, as our hands are not tied. I have placed her in a draught; and already she shows some signs, though very faint ones, of ordinary unconsciousness. The rigidity of her limbs is less, and her skin seems more sensitive—or perhaps I should say less insensitive—to pain."

"How is it, then," I asked, "that Mr. Trelawny is still in this state of insensibility; and yet, so far as we know, his body has not had such rigidity at all?"

"That I cannot answer. The problem is one which we may solve in a few hours; or it may need a few days. But it will be a useful lesson in diagnosis to us all; and perhaps to many and many others after us, who knows!" he added, with the genuine fire of an enthusiast.

As the morning wore on, he flitted perpetually between the two rooms, watching anxiously over both patients. He made Mrs. Grant remain with the Nurse, but either Miss Trelawny or I, generally both of us, remained with the wounded man. We each managed, however, to get bathed and dressed; the Doctor and Mrs. Grant remained with Mr. Trelawny whilst we had breakfast.

Sergeant Daw went off to report at Scotland Yard the progress of the night; and then to the local station to arrange for the coming of his comrade, Wright, as fixed with Superintendent Dolan. When he returned I could not but think that he had been hauled over the coals for shooting in a sick-room; or perhaps for shooting at all without certain and proper cause. His remark to me enlightened me in the matter:

"A good character is worth something, sir, in spite of what some of them say. See! I've still got leave to carry my revolver."

That day was a long and anxious one. Toward nightfall Nurse Kennedy so far improved that the rigidity of her limbs entirely disappeared. She still breathed quietly and regularly; but the fixed expression of her face, though it was a calm enough expression, gave place to fallen eyelids and the negative look of sleep. Doctor Winchester had, towards evening, brought two more nurses, one of whom was to remain with Nurse Kennedy and the other to share in the watching with Miss Trelawny, who had insisted on remaining up herself. She had, in order to prepare for the duty, slept for several hours in the afternoon. We had all taken counsel together, and had arranged thus for the watching in Mr. Trelawny's room. Mrs. Grant was to remain beside the patient till twelve, when Miss Trelawny would relieve her. The new nurse was to sit in Miss Trelawny's room, and to visit the sick chamber each quarter of an hour. The Doctor would remain till twelve; when I was to relieve him. One or other of the detectives was to remain within hail of the room all night; and to pay periodical visits to see that all was well. Thus, the watchers would be watched; and the possibility of such events as last night, when the watchers were both overcome, would be avoided.

When the sun set, a strange and grave anxiety fell on all of us; and in our separate ways we prepared for the vigil. Doctor Winchester had evidently been thinking of my respirator, for he told me he would go out and get one. Indeed, he took to the idea so kindly that I persuaded Miss Trelawny also to have one which she could put on when her time for watching came.

And so the night drew on.

CHAPTER V

MORE STRANGE INSTRUCTIONS

WHEN I came from my room at half-past eleven o'clock I found all well in the sick-room. The new nurse, prim, neat, and watchful, sat in the chair by the bedside where Nurse Kennedy had sat last night. A little way off, between the bed and the safe, sat Dr. Winchester alert and wakeful, but looking strange and almost comic with the respirator over mouth and nose. As I stood in the doorway looking at them I heard a slight sound; turning round I saw the new detective, who nodded, held up the finger of silence and withdrew quietly. Hitherto no one of the watchers was overcome by sleep.

I took a chair outside the door. As yet there was no need for me to risk coming again under the subtle influence of last night. Naturally my thoughts went revolving round the main incidents of the last day and night, and I found myself arriving at strange conclusions, doubts, conjectures; but I did not lose myself, as on last night, in trains of thought. The sense of the present was ever with me, and I really felt as should a sentry on guard. Thinking is not a slow process; and when it is earnest the time can pass quickly. It seemed a very short time indeed till the door, usually left ajar, was pulled

open and Dr. Winchester emerged, taking off his
respirator as he came. His act, when he had it
off, was demonstrative of his keenness. He turned
up the outside of the wrap and smelled it carefully.

"I am going now," he said. "I shall come early
in the morning; unless, of course, I am sent for
before. But all seems well to-night."

The next to appear was Sergeant Daw, who went
quietly into the room and took the seat vacated by
the Doctor. I still remained outside; but every few
minutes looked into the room. This was rather a
form than a matter of utility, for the room was so
dark that coming even from the dimly-lighted corridor it was hard to distinguish anything.

A little before twelve o'clock Miss Trelawny came
from her room. Before coming to her father's she
went into that occupied by Nurse Kennedy. After
a couple of minutes she came out, looking, I thought,
a trifle more cheerful. She had her respirator in her
hand, but before putting it on, asked me if anything
special had occurred since she had gone to lie down.
I answered in a whisper—there was no loud talking
in the house to-night—that all was safe, was well.
She then put on her respirator, and I mine; and we
entered the room. The Detective and the Nurse rose
up, and we took their places. Sergeant Daw was the
last to go out; he closed the door behind him as we
had arranged.

For a while I sat quiet, my heart beating. The
place was grimly dark. The only light was a faint
one from the top of the lamp which threw a white
circle on the high ceiling, except the emerald sheen
of the shade as the light took its under edges. Even
the light only seemed to emphasize the blackness of

the shadows. These presently began to seem, as on last night, to have a sentience of their own. I did not myself feel in the least sleepy ; and each time I went softly over to look at the patient, which I did about every ten minutes, I could see that Miss Trelawny was keenly alert. Every quarter of an hour one or other of the policemen looked in through the partly opened door. Each time both Miss Trelawny and I said through our mufflers, "all right," and the door was closed again.

As the time wore on, the silence and the darkness seemed to increase. The circle of light on the ceiling was still there, but it seemed less brilliant than at first. The green edging of the lamp-shade became like Maori greenstone rather than emerald. The sounds of the night without the house, and the starlight spreading pale lines along the edges of the window-cases, made the pall of black within more solemn and more mysterious.

We heard the clock in the corridor chiming the quarters with its silver bell till two o'clock ; and then a strange feeling came over me. I could see from Miss Trelawny's movement as she looked round, that she also had some new sensation. The new detective had just looked in ; we two were alone with the unconscious patient for another quarter of an hour.

My heart began to beat wildly. There was a sense of fear over me. Not for myself ; my fear was impersonal. It seemed as though some new person had entered the room, and that a strong intelligence was awake close to me. Something brushed against my leg. I put my hand down hastily and touched the furry coat of Silvio. With a very faint far-away

sound of a snarl he turned and scratched at me.   I
felt blood on my hand.   I rose gently and came over
to the bedside.   Miss Trelawny, too, had stood up
and was looking behind her, as though there was
something close to her.   Her eyes were wild, and
her breast rose and fell as though she were fighting
for air.   When I touched her she did not seem to
feel me ; she worked her hands in front of her, as
though she was fending off something.

There was not an instant to lose.   I seized her in
my arms and rushed over to the door, threw it open,
and strode into the passage, calling loudly :

" Help ! Help ! "

In an instant the two Detectives, Mrs. Grant, and
the Nurse appeared on the scene.   Close on their
heels came several of the servants, both men and
women.   Immediately Mrs. Grant came near enough,
I placed Miss Trelawny in her arms, and rushed back
into the room, turning up the electric light as soon as
I could lay my hand on it.   Sergeant Daw and the
Nurse followed me.

We were just in time.   Close under the great safe,
where on the two successive nights he had been found,
lay Mr. Trelawny with his left arm, bare save for the
bandages, stretched out.   Close by his side was a leaf-
shaped Egyptian knife which had lain amongst the
curios on the shelf of the broken cabinet.   Its point
was stuck in the parquet floor, whence had been
removed the blood-stained rug.

But there was no sign of disturbance anywhere ;
nor any sign of any one or anything unusual.   The
Policemen and I searched the room accurately, whilst
the Nurse and two of the servants lifted the wounded
man back to bed ; but no sign or clue could we get.

Very soon Miss Trelawny returned to the room. She was pale but collected. When she came close to me she said in a low voice:

"I felt myself fainting. I did not know why; but I was afraid!"

The only other shock I had was when Miss Trelawny cried out to me, as I placed my hand on the bed to lean over and look carefully at her father:

"You are wounded. Look! look! your hand is bloody. There is blood on the sheets!" I had, in the excitement, quite forgotten Silvio's scratch. As I looked at it, the recollection came back to me; but before I could say a word Miss Trelawny had caught hold of my hand and lifted it up. When she saw the parallel lines of the cuts she cried out again:

"It is the same wound as Father's!" Then she laid my hand down gently but quickly, and said to me and to Sergeant Daw:

"Come to my room! Silvio is there in his basket." We followed her, and found Silvio sitting in his basket awake. He was licking his paws. The Detective said:

"He is there sure enough; but why licking his paws?"

Margaret—Miss Trelawny—gave a moan as she bent over and took one of the forepaws in her hand; but the cat seemed to resent it and snarled. At that Mrs. Grant came into the room. When she saw that we were looking at the cat she said:

"The Nurse tells me that Silvio was asleep on Nurse Kennedy's bed ever since you went to your Father's room until a while ago. He came there just after you had gone to master's room. Nurse says that Nurse Kennedy is moaning and muttering in her sleep as though she had a nightmare. I think we should send for Dr. Winchester."

"Do so at once, please!" said Miss Trelawny; and we went back to the room.

For a while Miss Trelawny stood looking at her father, with her brows wrinkled. Then, turning to me, as though her mind were made up, she said:

"Don't you think we should have a consultation on Father? Of course I have every confidence in Doctor Winchester; he seems an immensely clever young man. But he *is* a young man; and there must be men who have devoted themselves to this branch of science. Such a man would have more knowledge and more experience; and his knowledge and experience might help to throw light on poor Father's case. As it is, Doctor Winchester seems to be quite in the dark. Oh! I don't know what to do. It is all so terrible!" Here she broke down a little and cried; and I tried to comfort her.

Doctor Winchester arrived quickly. His first thought was for his patient; but when he found him without further harm, he visited Nurse Kennedy. When he saw her, a hopeful look came into his eyes. Taking a towel, he dipped a corner of it in cold water and flicked her on the face. The skin coloured, and she stirred slightly. He said quietly to the new nurse —Sister Doris he called her:

"She is all right. She will wake in a few hours at latest. She may be dizzy and distraught at first, or perhaps hysterical. If so, you know how to treat her."

"Yes, sir!" answered Sister Doris demurely; and we went back to Mr. Trelawny's room. As soon as we had entered, Mrs. Grant and the Nurse went out so that only Doctor Winchester, Miss Trelawny, and myself remained in the room. When the door had been closed Doctor Winchester asked me as to what had occurred. I told him fully, giving exactly every detail so far as I could remember. Throughout my narrative, which did not take long, however, he kept asking me questions as to who had been present and the order in which each one had come into the room. He asked other things, but nothing of any importance; these were all that took my attention, or remained in my memory. When our conversation was finished, he said, in a very decided way indeed, to Miss Trelawny:

"I think, Miss Trelawny, that we had better have a consultation on this case." She answered at once, seemingly a little to his surprise:

"I am glad you have mentioned it. I quite agree. Who would you suggest?"

"Have you any choice yourself?" he asked. "Any one to whom your Father is known? Has he ever consulted any one?"

"Not to my knowledge. But I hope you will choose whoever you think would be best. My dear Father should have all the help that can be had; and I shall be deeply obliged by your choosing. Who is the best man in London—anywhere else—in such a case?"

"There are several good men; but they are scattered all over the world. Somehow, the brain specialist is born, not made; though a lot of hard work goes to the completing of him and fitting him for his work. He comes from no country. The most daring investigator up to the present is Chiuni, the Japanese; but he is rather a surgical experimentalist than a practitioner. Then there is Zammerfest of Upsala, and

Fenelon of the University of Paris, and Morfessi of
Naples.   These, of course, are in addition to our own
men, Morrison of Aberdeen and Richardson of Birmingham.   But before them all I would put Frere of
King's College.   Of all that I have named he best unites
theory and practice.   He has no hobbies—that have
been discovered at all events; and his experience is
immense.   It is the regret of all of us who admire
him that the nerve so firm and the hand so dexterous
must yield to time.   For my own part I would rather
have Frere than any one living."

"Then," said Miss Trelawny decisively, "let us
have Doctor Frere—by the way, is he 'Doctor' or
'Mister'? — as early as we can get him in the
morning!"

A weight seemed removed from him, and he spoke
with greater ease and geniality than he had yet shown:

"He is Sir James Frere.   I shall go to him myself
as early as it is possible to see him, and shall ask him
to come here at once."   Then turning to me he said:

"You had better let me dress your hand."

"It is nothing," I said.

"Nevertheless it should be seen to.   A scratch from
any animal might turn out dangerous; there is nothing
like being safe."   I submitted; forthwith he began to
dress my hand.   He examined with a magnifying-glass
the several parallel wounds, and compared them with
the slip of blotting-paper, marked with Silvio's claws,
which he took from his pocket-book.   He put back
the paper, simply remarking:

"It's a pity that Silvio slips in—and out—just
when he shouldn't."

The morning wore slowly on.   By ten o'clock
Nurse Kennedy had so far recovered that she was

able to sit up and talk intelligibly. But she was still hazy in her thoughts ; and could not remember anything that had happened on the previous night, after her taking her place by the sick-bed. As yet she seemed neither to know nor care what had happened.

It was nearly eleven o'clock when Doctor Winchester returned with Sir James Frere. Somehow I felt my heart sink when from the landing I saw them in the hall below ; I knew that Miss Trelawny was to have the pain of telling yet another stranger of her ignorance of her father's life.

Sir James Frere was a man who commanded attention followed by respect. He knew so thoroughly what he wanted himself, that he placed at once on one side all wishes and ideas of less definite persons. The mere flash of his piercing eyes, or the set of his resolute mouth, or the lowering of his great eyebrows, seemed to compel immediate and willing obedience to his wishes. Somehow, when we had all been introduced and he was well amongst us, all sense of mystery seemed to melt away. It was with a hopeful spirit that I saw him pass into the sick-room with Doctor Winchester.

They remained in the room a long time ; once they sent for the Nurse, the new one, sister Doris, but she did not remain long. Again they both went into Nurse Kennedy's room. He sent out the nurse attendant on her. Doctor Winchester told me afterward that Nurse Kennedy, though she was ignorant of later matters, gave full and satisfactory answers to all Doctor Frere's questions relating to her patient up to the time she became unconscious. Then they went to the study, where they remained so long, and their voices raised in heated discussion seemed in such determined opposition, that I began to feel uneasy. As for Miss Trelawny, she was almost in a state of collapse from nervousness before they joined us. Poor girl! she had had a sadly anxious time of it, and her nervous strength had almost broken down.

They came out at last, Sir James first, his grave face looking as unenlightening as that of the sphinx. Doctor Winchester followed him closely; his face was pale, but with that kind of pallor which looked like a reaction. It gave me the idea that it had been red not long before. Sir James asked that Miss Trelawny would come into the study. He suggested that I should come also. When we had entered, Sir James turned to me and said :

"I understand from Doctor Winchester that you are a friend of Miss Trelawny, and that you have already considerable knowledge of this case. Perhaps it will be well that you should be with us. I know you already as a keen lawyer, Mr. Ross, though I never had the pleasure of meeting you. As Doctor Winchester tells me that there are some strange matters outside this case which seem to puzzle him— and others—and in which he thinks you may yet be specially interested, it might be as well that you should know every phase of the case. For myself I do not take much account of mysteries — except those of science ; and as there seems to be some idea of an attempt at assassination or robbery, all I can say is that if assassins were at work they ought to take some elementary lessons in anatomy before their next job, for they seem thoroughly ignorant. If robbery were their purpose, they seem to have worked with marvellous inefficiency. That, however, is not my business."

Here he took a big pinch of snuff, and turning to Miss

Trelawny, went on : " Now as to the patient. Leaving out the cause of his illness, all we can say at present is that he appears to be suffering from a marked attack of catalepsy. At present nothing can be done, except to sustain his strength. The treatment of my friend Doctor Winchester is mainly such as I approve of ; and I am confident that should any slight change arise he will be able to deal with it satisfactorily. It is an interesting case—most interesting ; and should any new or abnormal development arise I shall be happy to come at any time. There is just one thing to which I wish to call your attention ; and I put it to you, Miss Trelawny, directly, since it is your responsibility. Doctor Winchester informs me that you are not yourself free in the matter, but are bound by an instruction given by your Father in case just such a condition of things should arise. I would strongly advise that the patient be removed to another room ; or, as an alternative, that those mummies and all such things should be removed from his chamber. Why, it's enough to put any man into an abnormal condition, to have such an assemblage of horrors round him, and to breathe the atmosphere which they exhale. You have evidence already of how such mephitic odour may act. That nurse—Kennedy, I think you said, Doctor—isn't yet out of her state of catalepsy ; and you, Mr. Ross, have, I am told, experienced something of the same effects. I know this "— here his eyebrows came down more than ever, and his mouth hardened—" if I were in charge here I should insist on the patient having a different atmosphere ; or I would throw up the case. Doctor Winchester already knows that I can only be again consulted on this condition being fulfilled. But I

trust that you will see your way, as a good daughter to
my mind should, to looking to your Father's health
and sanity rather than to any whim of his—whether
supported or not by a foregoing fear, or by any
number of 'penny dreadful' mysteries. The day has
hardly come yet, I am glad to say, when the British
Museum and St. Thomas's Hospital have exchanged
their normal functions. Good-day, Miss Trelawny.
I earnestly hope that I may soon see your Father
restored. Remember, that should you fulfil the
elementary condition which I have laid down, I am at
your service day or night. Good-morning, Mr. Ross.
I hope you will be able to report to me soon, Doctor
Winchester."

When he had gone we stood silent, till the rumble
of his carriage wheels died away. The first to speak
was Doctor Winchester:

"I think it well to say that to my mind, speaking
purely as a physician, he is quite right. I feel as if
I could have assaulted him when he made it a condition of not giving up the case; but all the same he
is right as to treatment. He does not understand
that there is something odd about this special case;
and he will not realise the knot that we are all tied up
in by Mr. Trelawny's instructions. Of course—" He
was interrupted by Miss Trelawny:

"Doctor Winchester, do you, too, wish to give up
the case; or are you willing to continue it under the
conditions you know?"

"Give it up! Less now than ever. Miss Trelawny,
I shall never give it up, so long as life is left to him or
any of us!" She said nothing, but held out her hand,
which he took warmly.

"Now," said she, "if Sir James Frere is a type of

the cult of Specialists, I want no more of them. To start with, he does not seem to know any more than you do about my Father's condition; and if he were a hundredth part as much interested in it as you are, he would not stand on such punctilio. Of course, I am only too anxious about my poor Father; and if I can see· a way to meet either of Sir James Frere's conditions, I shall do so. I shall ask Mr. Marvin to come here to-day, and advise me as to the limit of Father's wishes. If he thinks I am free to act in any way on my own responsibility, I shall not hesitate to do so." Then Doctor Winchester took his leave.

Miss Trelawny sat down and wrote a letter to Mr. Marvin, telling him of the state of affairs, and asking him to come and see her and to bring with him any papers which might throw any light on the subject. She sent the letter off with a carriage to bring back the solicitor; we waited with what patience we could for his coming.

It is not a very long journey for oneself from Kensington Palace Gardens to Lincoln's Inn Fields; but it seemed endlessly long when waiting for someone else to take it. All things, however, are amenable to Time; it was less than an hour all told when Mr. Marvin was with us.

He recognised Miss Trelawny's impatience, and when he had learned sufficient of her father's illness, he said to her:

"Whenever you are ready I can go with you into particulars regarding your Father's wishes."

"Whenever you like," she said, with an evident ignorance of his meaning. "Why not now?" He looked at me, as to a fellow man of business, and stammered out:

" We are not alone."

" I have brought Mr. Ross here on purpose," she answered. " He knows so much at present, that I want him to know more." The solicitor was a little disconcerted, a thing which those knowing him only in courts would hardly have believed. He answered, however, with some hesitation :

" But, my dear young lady—Your Father's wishes !— Confidence between father and child——"

Here she interrupted him ; there was a tinge of red in her pale cheeks as she did so :

" Do you really think that applies to the present circumstances, Mr. Marvin ? My Father never told me anything of his affairs ; and I can now, in this sad extremity, only learn his wishes through a gentleman who is a stranger to me and of whom I never even heard till I got my Father's letter, written to be shown to me only in extremity. Mr. Ross is a new friend ; but he has all my confidence, and I should like him to be present. Unless, of course," she added, "such a thing is forbidden by my Father. Oh ! forgive me, Mr. Marvin, if I seem rude ; but I have been in such dreadful trouble and anxiety lately, that I have hardly command of myself." She covered her eyes with her hand for a few seconds ; we two men looked at each other and waited, trying to appear unmoved. She went on more firmly ; she had recovered herself :

" Please ! please do not think I am ungrateful to you for your kindness in coming here and so quickly. I really am grateful ; and I have every confidence in your judgment. If you wish, or think it best, we can be alone." I stood up ; but Mr. Marvin made a dissentient gesture. He was evidently pleased with

her attitude; there was geniality in his voice and
manner as he spoke:

"Not at all! Not at all! There is no restriction
on your Father's part; and on my own I am quite
willing. Indeed, all told, it may be better. From
what you have said of Mr. Trelawny's illness, and the
other—incidental—matters, it will be well in case of
any—grave—eventuality, that it was understood from
the first, that circumstances were ruled by your
Father's own imperative instructions. For, please,
understand me, his instructions are imperative—most
imperative. They are so unyielding that he has given
me a Power of Attorney, under which I have undertaken to act, authorising me to see his written wishes
carried out. Please believe once for all, that he
intended fully everything mentioned in that letter to
you! Whilst he is alive he is to remain in his own
room; and none of his property is to be removed
from it under any circumstances whatever. He has
even given an inventory of the articles which are not
to be displaced."

Miss Trelawny was silent. She looked somewhat
distressed; so, thinking that I understood the immediate cause, I asked:

"May we see the list? Miss Trelawny's face at
once brightened; but it fell again as the lawyer
answered promptly—he was evidently prepared for
the question:

"Not unless I am compelled to take action on the
Power of Attorney. I have brought that instrument
with me. You will recognise, Mr. Ross "—he said this
with a sort of business conviction which I had noticed
in his professional work, as he handed me the deed—
"how strongly it is worded, and how the grantor

made his wishes apparent in such a way as to leave
no loophole. It is his own wording, except for
certain legal formalities; and I assure you I have
seldom seen a more iron-clad document. Even I
myself have no power to make the slightest relaxation
of the instructions, without committing a distinct
breach of faith. And that, I need not tell you, is
impossible." He evidently added the last words in
order to prevent an appeal to his personal consideration. He did not like the seeming harshness of his
words, however, for he added:

"I do hope, Miss Trelawny, that you understand
that I am willing—frankly and unequivocally willing—
to do anything I can, within the limits of my power,
to relieve your distress. But your Father had, in all
his doings, some purpose of his own which he did
not disclose to me. So far as I can see, there is not
a word of his instructions that he had not thought
over fully. Whatever idea he had in his mind was the
idea of a lifetime; he had studied it in every possible
phase, and was prepared to guard it at every point.

"Now I fear I have distressed you, and I am truly
sorry for it; for I see you have much—too much—to
bear already. But I have no alternative. If you
want to consult me at any time about anything, I
promise you I will come without a moment's delay,
at any hour of the day or night. There is my private
address," he scribbled in his pocket-book as he spoke,
"and under it the address of my club, where I am
generally to be found in the evening." He tore out
the paper and handed it to her. She thanked him. He
shook hands with her and with me and withdrew.

As soon as the hall door was shut on him, Mrs.
Grant tapped at the door and came in. There was

such a look of distress in her face that Miss Trelawny
stood up, deadly white, and asked her :

"What is it, Mrs. Grant? What is it? Any new
trouble?"

"I grieve to say, miss, that the servants, all but two,
have given notice and want to leave the house to-day.
They have talked the matter over among themselves;
the butler has spoken for the rest. He says as how
they are willing to forego their wages, and even to pay
their legal obligations instead of notice; but that go
to-day they must."

"What reason do they give?"

"None, miss. They say as how they're sorry, but
that they've nothing to say. I asked Jane, the upper
housemaid, miss, who is not with the rest but stops
on; and she tells me confidential that they've got
some notion in their silly heads that the house is
haunted!"

We ought to have laughed, but we didn't. I could
not look in Miss Trelawny's face and laugh. The
pain and horror there showed no sudden paroxysm
of fear; there was a fixed idea of which this was a
confirmation. For myself, it seemed as if my brain
had found a voice. But the voice was not complete; there was some other thought, darker and
deeper, which lay behind it, whose voice had not
sounded as yet.

CHAPTER VI

SUSPICIONS

THE first to get full self-command was Miss Trelawny. There was a haughty dignity in her bearing as she said :

"Very well, Mrs. Grant; let them go! Pay them up to to-day, and a month's wages. They have hitherto been very good servants; and the occasion of their leaving is not an ordinary one. We must not expect much faithfulness from any one who is beset with fears. Those who remain are to have in future double wages; and please send these to me presently when I send word." Mrs. Grant bristled with smothered indignation; all the housekeeper in her was outraged by such generous treatment of servants who had combined to give notice :

"They don't deserve it, miss; them to go on so, after the way they have been treated here. Never in my life have I seen servants so well treated or anyone so good to them and gracious to them as you have been. They might be in the household of a King for treatment. And now, just as there is trouble, to go and act like this. It's abominable, that's what it is!"

Miss Trelawny was very gentle with her, and smothered her ruffled dignity; so that presently

she went away with, in her manner, a lesser measure of hostility to the undeserving. In quite a
different frame of mind she returned presently to
ask if her mistress would like her to engage a full
staff of other servants, or at any rate try to do so.
"For you know, ma'am," she went on, "when once
a scare has been established in the servants' hall,
it's wellnigh impossible to get rid of it. Servants
may come; but they go away just as quick. There's
no holding them. They simply won't stay; or even
if they work out their month's notice, they lead you
that life that you wish every hour of the day that you
hadn't kept them. The women are bad enough, the
huzzies; but the men are worse!" There was neither
anxiety nor indignation in Miss Trelawny's voice or
manner as she said:

"I think, Mrs. Grant, we had better try to do with
those we have. Whilst my dear Father is ill we shall
not be having any company, so that there will be only
three now in the house to attend to. If those servants
who are willing to stay are not enough, I should only
get sufficient to help them to do the work. It will
not, I should think, be difficult to get a few maids;
perhaps some that you know already. And please
bear in mind, that those whom you get, and who are
suitable and will stay, are henceforth to have the same
wages as those who are remaining. Of course, Mrs.
Grant, you well understand that though I do not
group you in any way with the servants, the rule of
double salary applies to you too." As she spoke she
extended her long, fine-shaped hand, which the other
took and then, raising it to her lips, kissed it impres-
sively with the freedom of an elder woman to a
younger. I could not but admire the generosity of

her treatment of her servants. In my mind I en-
dorsed Mrs. Grant's *sotto voce* remark as she left the
room:

"No wonder the house is like a King's house, when
the mistress is a Princess!"

"A Princess!" That was it. The idea seemed to
satisfy my mind, and to bring back in a wave of light
the first moment when she swept across my vision at
the ball in Belgrave Square. A queenly figure! tall
and slim, bending, swaying, undulating as the lily or
the lotos. Clad in a flowing gown of some filmy black
material shot with gold. For ornament in her hair
she wore an old Egyptian jewel, a tiny crystal disk,
set between rising plumes carved in lapis lazuli. On
her wrist was a broad bangle or bracelet of antique
work, in the shape of a pair of spreading wings
wrought in gold, with the feathers made of coloured
gems. For all her gracious bearing toward me,
when our hostess introduced me, I was then afraid
of her. It was only when later, at the picnic on
the river, I had come to realise her sweet and
gentle nature, that my awe changed to something
else.

For a while she sat, making some notes or memo-
randa. Then putting them away, she sent for the
faithful servants. I thought that she had better
have this interview alone, and so left her. When I
came back there were traces of tears in her eyes.

The next phase in which I had a part was even
more disturbing, and infinitely more painful. Late
in the afternoon Sergeant Daw came into the study
where I was sitting. After closing the door carefully
and looking all round the room to make certain that
we were alone, he came close to me.

"What is it?" I asked him. "I see you wish to speak to me privately."

"Quite so, sir! May I speak in absolute confidence?"

"Of course you may. In anything that is for the good of Miss Trelawny—and of course of Mr. Trelawny—you may be perfectly frank. I take it that we both want to serve them to the best of our powers." He hesitated before replying:

"Of course you know that I have my duty to do; and I think you know me well enough to know that I will do it. I am a policeman—a detective; and it is my duty to find out the facts of any case I am ·put on, without fear or favour to anyone. I would rather speak to you alone, in confidence if I may, without reference to any duty of anyone to anyone, except mine to Scotland Yard."

"Of course! of course!" I answered mechanically, my heart sinking, I did not know why. "Be quite frank with me. I assure you of my confidence."

"Thank you, sir. I take it that what I say is not to pass beyond you—not to anyone. Not to Miss Trelawny herself, or even to Mr. Trelawny when he becomes well again."

"Certainly, if you make it a condition!" I said a little more stiffly. The man recognised the change in my voice or manner, and said apologetically:

"Excuse me, sir, but I am going outside my duty in speaking to you at all on the subject. I know you, however, of old; and I feel that I can trust you. Not your word, sir, that is all right; but your discretion!"

I bowed. "Go on!" I said. He began at once:

"I have gone over this case, sir, till my brain begins

to reel; but I can't find any ordinary solution of it. At the time of each attempt no one has seemingly come into the house; and certainly no one has got out. What does it strike you is the inference?"

"That the somebody—or the something—was in the house already," I answered, smiling in spite of myself.

"That's just what I think," he said, with a manifest sigh of relief. "Very well! Who can be that some-one?"

"'Someone, or something,' was what I said," I answered.

"Let us make it 'someone,' Mr. Ross! That cat, though he might have scratched or bit, never pulled the old gentleman out of bed, and tried to get the bangle with the key off his arm. Such things are all very well in books where your amateur detectives, who know everything before it's done, can fit them into theories; but in Scotland Yard, where the men aren't all idiots either, we generally find that when crime is done, or attempted, it's people, not things, that are at the bottom of it."

"Then make it 'people' by all means, Sergeant."

"We were speaking of 'someone,' sir."

"Quite right. *Someone*, be it!"

"Did it ever strike you, sir, that on each of the three separate occasions where outrage was effected, or attempted, there was one person who was the first to be present and to give the alarm?"

"Let me see! Miss Trelawny, I believe, gave the alarm on the first occasion. I was present myself, if fast asleep, on the second; and so was Nurse Kennedy. When I woke there were several people in the room; you were one of them. I understand

that on that occasion also Miss Trelawny was before
you. At the last attempt I was in the room when
Miss Trelawny fainted. I carried her out and went
back. In returning, I was first ; and I think you were
close behind me."

Sergeant Daw thought for a moment before
replying :

"She was present, or first, in the room on all the
occasions ; there was only damage done in the first
and second !"

The inference was one which I, as a lawyer, could
not mistake. I thought the best thing to do was to
meet it half-way. I have always found that the
best way to encounter an inference is to cause it
to be turned into a statement.

"You mean," I said, "that as on the only occasions
when actual harm was done, Miss Trelawny's being
the first to discover it is a proof that she did it ; or
was in some way connected with the attempt, as well
as the discovery ?"

"I didn't venture to put it as clear as that ; but
that is where the doubt which I had leads." Sergeant
Daw was a man of courage ; he evidently did not
shrink from any conclusion of his reasoning on
facts.

We were both silent for a while. Fears began
crowding in on my own mind. Not doubts of Miss
Trelawny, or of any act of hers ; but fears lest such
acts should be misunderstood. There was evidently
a mystery somewhere ; and if no solution to it could
be found, the doubt would be cast on someone. In
such cases the guesses of the majority are bound to
follow the line of least resistance ; and if it could be
proved that any personal gain to anyone would

follow Mr. Trelawny's death, should such ensue, it
might prove a difficult task for anyone to prove
innocence in the face of suspicious facts. I found
myself instinctively taking that deferential course
which, until the plan of battle of the prosecution is
unfolded, is so safe an attitude for the defence. It
would never do for me, at this stage, to combat any
theories which a detective might form. I could best
help Miss Trelawny by listening and understanding.
When the time should come for the dissipation and
obliteration of the theories, I should be quite willing
to use all my militant ardour, and all the weapons at
my command.

"You will of course do your duty, I know," I said,
"and without fear. What course do you intend to
take ? "

"I don't know as yet, sir. You see, up to now it
isn't with me even a suspicion. If any one else told
me that that sweet young lady had a hand in such a
matter, I would think him a fool ; but I am bound
to follow my own conclusions. I know well that
just as unlikely persons have been proved guilty,
when a whole court—all except the prosecution who
knew the facts, and the judge who had taught his
mind to wait—would have sworn to innocence. I
wouldn't, for all the world, wrong such a young lady ;
more especial when she has such a cruel weight to
bear. And you will be sure that I won't say a word
that'll prompt anyone else to make such a charge.
That's why I speak to you in confidence, man to
man. You are skilled in proofs ; that is your profession. Mine only gets so far as suspicions, and
what we call our own proofs—which are nothing
but *ex parte* evidence after all. You know Miss

Trelawny better than I do; and though I watch
round the sick-room, and go where I like about
the house and in and out of it, I haven't the same
opportunities as you have of knowing the lady and
what her life is, or her means are; or of anything
else which might give me a clue to her actions. If
I were to try to find out from her, it would at once
arouse her suspicions. Then, if she were guilty, all
possibility of ultimate proof would go; for she would
easily find a way to baffle discovery. But if she be
innocent, as I hope she is, it would be doing a cruel
wrong to accuse her. I have thought the matter over
according to my lights before I spoke to you; and if
I have taken a liberty, sir, I am truly sorry."

"No liberty in the world, Daw," I said warmly, for
the man's courage and honesty and consideration
compelled respect. "I am glad you have spoken to
me so frankly. We both want to find out the truth;
and there is so much about this case that is strange—
so strange as to go beyond all experiences—that to
aim at truth is our only chance of making anything
clear in the long-run—no matter what our views are,
or what object we wish to achieve ultimately!" The
Sergeant looked pleased as he went on:

"I thought, therefore, that if you had it once in
your mind that somebody else held to such a possibility, you would by degrees get proof; or at any
rate such ideas as would convince yourself, either for
or against it. Then we would come to some conclusion; or at any rate we should so exhaust all other
possibilities that the most likely one would remain as
the nearest thing to proof, or strong suspicion, that
we could get. After that we should have to——"

Just at this moment the door opened and Miss

Trelawny entered the room. The moment she saw us she drew back quickly, saying :

"Oh, I beg pardon! I did not know you were here, and engaged." By the time I had stood up, she was about to go back.

"Do come in," I said ; "Sergeant Daw and I were only talking matters over."

Whilst she was hesitating, Mrs. Grant appeared, saying as she entered the room : " Doctor Winchester is come, miss, and is asking for you."

I obeyed Miss Trelawny's look ; together we left the room.

When the Doctor had made his examination, he told us that there was seemingly no change. He added that nevertheless he would like to stay in the house that night if he might. Miss Trelawny looked glad, and sent word to Mrs. Grant to get a room ready for him. Later in the day, when he and I happened to be alone together, he said suddenly :

" I have arranged to stay here to-night because I want to have a talk with you. And as I wish it to be quite private, I thought the least suspicious way would be to have a cigar together late in the evening when Miss Trelawny is watching her father." We still kept to our arrangement that either the sick man's daughter or I should be on watch all night. We were to share the duty at the early hours of the morning. I was anxious about this, for I knew from our conversation that the Detective would watch in secret himself, and would be particularly alert about that time.

The day passed uneventfully. Miss Trelawny slept in the afternoon ; and after dinner went to relieve the Nurse. Mrs. Grant remained with her, Sergeant Daw being on duty in the corridor. Doctor Winchester and I took our coffee in the library. When we had lit our cigars he said quietly :

" Now that we are alone I want to have a confidential talk. We are ' tiled,' of course ; for the present at all events ? "

" Quite so ! " I said, my heart sinking as I thought of my conversation with Sergeant Daw in the morning, and of the disturbing and harrowing fears which it had left in my mind. He went on :

" This case is enough to try the sanity of all of us concerned in it. The more I think of it, the madder I seem to get ; and the two lines, each continually strengthened, seem to pull harder in opposite directions."

" What two lines ? " He looked at me keenly for a moment before replying. Doctor Winchester's look at such moments was apt to be disconcerting. It would have been so to me had I had a personal part, other than my interest in Miss Trelawny, in the matter. As it was, however, I stood it unruffled. I was now an attorney in the case ; an *amicus curiæ* in one sense, in another retained for the defence. The mere thought that in this clever man's mind were two lines, equally strong and opposite, was in itself so consoling as to neutralise my anxiety as to a new attack. As he began to speak, the Doctor's face wore an inscrutable smile ; this, however, gave place to a stern gravity as he proceeded :

" Two lines : Fact and—Fancy ! In the first there is this whole thing : attacks ; attempts at robbery and murder ; stupefyings ; organised catalepsy which points to either criminal hypnotism and thought suggestion, or some simple form of poisoning unclassified yet in our toxicology. In the other there is some influence at work which is not classified in any book that I know—outside the pages of romance. I never felt in my life so strongly the truth of Hamlet's words :

> 'There are more things in Heaven and earth . . .
> Than are dreamt of in your philosophy.'

"Let us take the 'Fact' side first. Here we have a man in his home ; amidst his own household ; plenty of servants of different classes in the house, which forbids the possibility of an organised attempt made from the servants' hall. He is wealthy, learned, clever. From his physiognomy there is no doubting that he is a man of iron will and determined purpose. His daughter—his only child, I take it, a young girl bright and clever—is sleeping in the very next room to his. There is seemingly no possible reason for expecting any attack or disturbance of any kind ; and no reasonable opportunity for any outsider to effect it. And yet we have an attack made ; a brutal and remorseless attack, made in the middle of the night. Discovery is made quickly ; made with that rapidity which in criminal cases generally is found to be not accidental, but of premeditated intent. The attacker, or attackers, are manifestly disturbed before the completion of their work, whatever their ultimate intent may have been. And yet there is no possible sign of their escape ; no clue, no disturbance of anything ; no open door or window ; no sound. Nothing whatever to show who had done the deed, or even that a deed has been done ; except the victim, and his surroundings incidental to the deed !

"The next night a similar attempt is made, though
the house is full of wakeful people ; and though there
are on watch in the room and around it a detective
officer, a trained nurse, an earnest friend, and the
man's own daughter.   The nurse is thrown into a
catalepsy, and the watching friend—though protected
by a respirator—into a deep sleep.   Even the detective is so far overcome with some phase of stupor
that he fires off his pistol in the sick-room, and can't
even tell what he thought he was firing at.   That
respirator of yours is the only thing that seems to
have a bearing on the 'fact' side of the affair.   That
you did not lose your head as the others did—the
effect in such case being in proportion to the amount
of time each remained in the room—points to the
probability that the stupefying medium was not
hypnotic, whatever else it may have been.   But
again, there is a fact which is contradictory.   Miss
Trelawny, who was in the room more than any of
you—for she was in and out all the time and did her
share of permanent watching also—did not seem
to be affected at all.   This would show that the
influence, whatever it is, does not affect generally—
unless, of course, it was that she was in some way
inured to it.   If it should turn out that it be some
strange exhalation from some of those Egyptian
curios, that might account for it ; only, we are then
face to face with the fact that Mr. Trelawny, who
was most of all in the room—who, in fact, lived
more than half his life in it—was affected worst of
all.   What kind of influence could it be which would
account for all these different and contradictory
effects ?   No ! the more I think of this form of the
dilemma, the more I am bewildered !   Why, even if

it were that the attack, the physical attack, on Mr. Trelawny had been made by some one residing in the house and not within the sphere of suspicion, the oddness of the stupefyings would still remain a mystery. It is not easy to put anyone into a catalepsy. Indeed, so far as is known yet in science, there is no way to achieve such an object at will. The crux of the whole matter is Miss Trelawny, who seems to be subject to none of the influences, or possibly of the variants of the same influence at work. Through all she goes unscathed, except for that one slight semi-faint. It is most strange!"

I listened with a sinking heart; for, though his manner was not illuminative of distrust, his argument was disturbing. Although it was not so direct as the suspicion of the Detective, it seemed to single out Miss Trelawny as different from all others concerned; and in a mystery to be alone is to be suspected, ultimately if not immediately. I thought it better not to say anything. In such a case silence is indeed golden; and if I said nothing now I might have less to defend, or explain, or take back later. I was, therefore, secretly glad that his form of putting his argument did not require any answer from me—for the present, at all events. Doctor Winchester did not seem to expect any answer—a fact which, when I recognised it, gave me pleasure, I hardly knew why. He paused for a while, sitting with his chin in his hand, his eyes staring at vacancy, whilst his brows were fixed. His cigar was held limp between his fingers; he had apparently forgotten it. In an even voice, as though commencing exactly where he had left off, he resumed his argument:

"The other horn of the dilemma is a different affair

altogether ; and if we once enter on it we must leave everything in the shape of science and experience behind us. I confess that it has its fascinations for me ; though at every new thought I find myself romancing in a way that makes me pull up suddenly and look facts resolutely in the face. I sometimes wonder whether the influence or emanation from the sick-room at times affects me as it did the others—the Detective, for instance. Of course it may be that if it is anything chemical, any drug, for example, in vaporeal form, its effects may be cumulative. But then, what could there be that could produce such an effect ? The room is, I know, full of mummy smell ; and no wonder, with so many relics from the tomb, let alone the actual mummy of that animal which Silvio attacked. By the way, I am going to test him to-morrow ; I have been on the trace of a mummy cat, and am to get possession of it in the morning. When I bring it here we shall find out if it be a fact that racial instinct can survive a few thousand years in the grave. However, to get back to the subject in hand. These very mummy smells arise from the presence of substances, and combinations of substances, which the Egyptian priests, who were the learned men and scientists of their time, found by the experience of centuries to be strong enough to arrest the natural forces of decay. There must be powerful agencies at work to effect such a purpose ; and it is possible that we may have here some rare substance or combination whose qualities and powers are not understood in this later and more prosaic age. I wonder if Mr. Trelawny has any knowledge, or even suspicion, of such a kind ? I only know this for certain, that a worse atmosphere for a sick chamber could not possibly be imagined; and I admire the courage of Sir James Frere in refusing to have anything to do with a case under such conditions. These instructions of Mr. Trelawny to his daughter, and from what you have told me, the care with which he has protected his wishes through his solicitor, show that he suspected something, at any rate. Indeed, it would almost seem as if he expected something to happen. . . . I wonder if it would be possible to learn anything about that! Surely his papers would show or suggest something. . . . It is a difficult matter to tackle; but it might have to be done. His present condition cannot go on for ever; and if anything should happen there would have to be an inquest. In such case full examination would have to be made into everything. . . . As it stands, the police evidence would show a murderous attack more than once repeated. As no clue is apparent, it would be necessary to seek one in a motive."

He was silent. The last words seemed to come in a lower and lower tone as he went on. It had the effect of hopelessness. It came to me as a conviction that now was my time to find out if he had any definite suspicion; and as if in obedience to some command, I asked:

"Do you suspect anyone?" He seemed in a way startled rather than surprised as he turned his eyes on me:

"Suspect anyone? Any thing, you mean. I certainly suspect that there is some influence; but at present my suspicion is held within such limit. Later on, if there be any sufficiently definite conclusion to my reasoning, or my thinking—for there are not proper data for reasoning—I may suspect; at present, however——"

He stopped suddenly and looked at the door. There was a faint sound as the handle turned. My own heart seemed to stand still. There was over me some grim, vague apprehension. The interruption in the ·morning, when I was talking with the Detective, came back upon me with a rush.

The door opened, and Miss Trelawny entered the room.

When she saw us, she started back; and a deep flush swept her face. For a few seconds she paused; at such a time a few succeeding seconds seem to lengthen in geometrical progression. The strain upon me, and, as I could easily see, on the Doctor also, relaxed as she spoke:

"Oh, forgive me, I did not know that you were engaged. I was looking for you, Doctor Winchester, to ask you if I might go to bed to-night with safety, as you will be here. I feel so tired and worn-out that I fear I may break down; and to-night I would certainly not be of any use." Doctor Winchester answered heartily:

"Do! Do go to bed by all means, and get a good night's sleep. God knows! you want it. I am more than glad you have made the suggestion, for I feared when I saw you to-night that I might have you on my hands a patient next."

She gave a sigh of relief, and the tired look seemed to melt from her face. Never shall I forget the deep, earnest look in her great, beautiful black eyes as she said to me:

"You will guard Father to-night, won't you, with Doctor Winchester? I am so anxious about him that every second brings new fears. But I am really worn-out; and if I don't get a good sleep, I think I shall go mad. I will change my room for to-night. I'm afraid that if I stay so close to Father's room I shall multiply every sound into a new terror. But, of course, you will have me waked if there be any cause. I shall be in the bedroom of the little suite next the boudoir off the hall. I had those rooms when first I came to live with Father, and I had no care then. . . . It will be easier to rest there; and perhaps for a few hours I may forget. I shall be all right in the morning. Good-night!"

When I had closed the door behind her and come back to the little table at which we had been sitting, Doctor Winchester said:

"That poor girl is overwrought to a terrible degree. I am delighted that she is to get a rest. It will be life to her; and in the morning she will be all right. Her nervous system is on the verge of a breakdown. Did you notice how fearfully disturbed she was, and how red she got when she came in and found us talking? An ordinary thing like that, in her own house with her own guests, wouldn't under normal circumstances disturb her!"

I was about to tell him, as an explanation in her defence, how her entrance was a repetition of her finding the Detective and myself alone together earlier in the day, when I remembered that that conversation was so private that even an allusion to it might be awkward in evoking curiosity. So I remained silent.

We stood up to go to the sick-room; but as we took our way through the dimly-lighted corridor I could not help thinking, again and again, and again—ay, and for many a day after—how strange it was that she had interrupted me on two such occasions when touching on such a theme.

There was certainly some strange web of accidents, in whose meshes we were all involved.

CHAPTER VII

THE TRAVELLER'S LOSS

THAT night everything went well. Knowing that Miss Trelawny herself was not on guard, Doctor Winchester and I doubled our vigilance. The Nurses and Mrs. Grant kept watch, and the Detectives made their visit each quarter of an hour. All night the patient remained in his trance. He looked healthy, and his chest rose and fell with the easy breathing of a child. But he never stirred; only for his breathing he might have been of marble. Doctor Winchester and I wore our respirators, and irksome they were on that intolerably hot night. Between midnight and three o'clock I felt anxious, and had once more that creepy feeling to which these last few nights had accustomed me; but the grey of the dawn, stealing round the edges of the blinds, came with inexpressible relief. In the cool, hopeful darkness, with the east quickening into pallor, I could breathe freely; the same relief, followed by restfulness, went through the household. During the hot night my ears, strained to every sound, had been almost painfully troubled; as though my brain or sensoria were in anxious touch with them. Every breath of the Nurse or the rustle of her dress; every soft pat of slippered feet, as the Policeman went his rounds ; every moment of watching life, seemed to be a new impetus to guardianship. Something of the same feeling must have been abroad in the house ; now and again I could hear upstairs the sound of restless feet, and more than once downstairs the opening of a window. With the coming of the dawn, however, all this ceased, and the whole household seemed to rest. Doctor Winchester went home when sister Doris came to relieve Mrs. Grant. He was, I think, a little disappointed or chagrined that nothing of an exceptional nature had happened during his long night vigil.

At eight o'clock Miss Trelawny joined us, and I was amazed as well as delighted to see how much good her night's sleep had done her. She was fairly radiant ; just as I had seen her at our first meeting and at the picnic. There was even a suggestion of colour in her cheeks, which, however, looked startlingly white in contrast with her black brows and scarlet lips. With her restored strength, there seemed to have come a tenderness even exceeding that which she had at first shown to her sick father. I could not but be moved by the loving touches as she fixed his pillows and brushed the hair from his forehead.

I was wearied out myself with my long spell of watching ; and now that she was on guard I started off to bed, blinking my tired eyes in the full light and feeling the weariness of a sleepless night on me all at once.

I had a good sleep, and after lunch I was about to start out to walk to Jermyn Street, when I noticed an importunate man at the hall door. The servant in charge was the one called Morris, formerly the "odd man," but since the exodus of the servants promoted to be butler *pro tem.* The stranger was speaking rather loudly, so that there was no difficulty in understanding his grievance. The servant man was respectful in both words and demeanour; but he stood squarely in front of the great double door, so that the other could not enter. The first words which I heard from the visitor sufficiently explained the situation:

"That's all very well, but I tell you I must see Mr. Trelawny! What is the use of your saying I can't, when I tell you I must. You put me off, and off, and off! I came here at nine; you said then that he was not up, and that as he was not well he could not be disturbed. I came at twelve; and you told me again he was not up. I asked then to see any of his household; you told me that Miss Trelawny was not up. Now I come again at three, and you tell me he is still in bed, and is not awake yet. Where is Miss Trelawny? 'She is occupied and must not be disturbed!' Well, she must be disturbed! Or some one must. I am here about Mr. Trelawny's special business; and I have come from a place where servants always begin by saying No. 'No' isn't good enough for me this time! I've had three years of it, waiting outside doors and tents when it took longer to get in than it did into the tombs; and then you would think, too, the men inside were as dead as the mummies. I've had about enough of it, I tell you. And when I come home, and find the door of the man I've been working for barred, in just the same way and with the same old answers, it stirs me up the wrong way. Did Mr. Trelawny leave orders that he would not see me when I should come?"

He paused and excitedly mopped his forehead. The servant answered very respectfully :

"I am very sorry, sir, if in doing my duty I have given any offence. But I have my orders, and must obey them. If you would like to leave any message, I will give it to Miss Trelawny ; and if you will leave your address, she can communicate with you if she wishes." The answer came in such a way that it was easy to see that the speaker was a kind-hearted man, and a just one.

"My good fellow, I have no fault to find with you personally ; and I am sorry if I have hurt your feelings. I must be just, even if I am angry. But it is enough to anger any man to find himself in the position I am. Time is pressing. There is not an hour—not a minute—to lose! And yet here I am, kicking my heels for six hours ; knowing all the time that your master will be a hundred times angrier than I am, when he hears how the time has been fooled away. He would rather be waked out of a thousand sleeps than not see me just at present— and before it is too late. My God! it's simply dreadful, after all I've gone through, to have my work spoiled at the last and be foiled in the very doorway by a stupid flunkey! Is there no one with sense in the house ; or with authority, even if he hasn't got sense? I could mighty soon convince him that your master must be awakened ; even if he sleeps like the Seven Sleepers——"

There was no mistaking the man's sincerity, or the urgency and importance of his business ; from his point of view at any rate. I stepped forward.

"Morris," I said, "you had better tell Miss Trelawny that this gentleman wants to see her particularly. If she is busy, ask Mrs. Grant to tell her."

"Very good, sir!" he answered in a tone of relief, and hurried away.

I took the stranger into the little boudoir across the hall. As we went he asked me:

"Are you the secretary?"

"No! I am a friend of Miss Trelawny's. My name is Ross."

"Thank you very much, Mr. Ross, for your kindness!" he said. "My name is Corbeck. I would give you my card, but they don't use cards where I've come from. And if I had had any, I suppose they, too, would have gone last night——"

He stopped suddenly, as though conscious that he had said too much. We both remained silent; as we waited I took stock of him. A short, sturdy man, brown as a coffee-berry; possibly inclined to be fat, but now lean exceedingly. The deep wrinkles in his face and neck were not merely from time and exposure; there were those unmistakable signs where flesh or fat has fallen away, and the skin has become loose. The neck was simply an intricate surface of seams and wrinkles, and was sun-scarred with the burning of the Desert. The Far East, the Tropic Seasons, and the Desert—each can have its colour mark. But all three are quite different; and an eye which has once known, can thenceforth easily distinguish them. The dusky pallor of one; the fierce red-brown of the other; and of the third, the dark, ingrained burning, as though it had become a permanent colour. Mr. Corbeck had a big head, massive and full; with shaggy, dark red-brown hair, but bald on the temples. His forehead was a fine one, high and broad; with, to use the terms of physiognomy, the frontal sinus boldly marked. The squareness of it showed "ratiocination;" and the fulness under the eyes "language." He had the short, broad nose that marks energy; the square chin—marked despite a thick, unkempt beard—and massive jaw that showed great resolution.

"No bad man for the Desert!" I thought as I looked.

Miss Trelawny came very quickly. When Mr. Corbeck saw her, he seemed somewhat surprised. But his annoyance and excitement had not disappeared; quite enough remained to cover up any such secondary and purely exoteric feeling as surprise. But as she spoke he never took his eyes off her; and I made a mental note that I would find some early opportunity of investigating the cause of his surprise. She began with an apology which quite smoothed down his ruffled feelings:

"Of course, had my Father been well you would not have been kept waiting. Indeed, had not I been on duty in the sick-room when you called the first time, I should have seen you at once. Now will you kindly tell me what is the matter which so presses?" He looked at me and hesitated. She spoke at once:

"You may say before Mr. Ross anything which you can tell me. He has my fullest confidence, and is helping me in my trouble. I do not think you quite understand how serious my Father's condition is. For three days he has not waked, or given any sign of consciousness; and I am in terrible trouble about him. Unhappily I am in great ignorance of my Father and his life. I only came to live with him a year ago; and I know nothing whatever of his affairs. I do not even know who you are, or in what way your business is associated with him." She said this with a little deprecating smile, all conventional and altogether graceful; as though to express in the most genuine way her absurd ignorance.

He looked steadily at her for perhaps a quarter of a minute; then he spoke, beginning at once as though his mind were made up and his confidence established:

"My name is Eugene Corbeck. I am a Master of Arts and Doctor of Laws and Master of Surgery of Cambridge; Doctor of Letters of Oxford; Doctor of Science and Doctor of Languages of London University; Doctor of Philosophy of Berlin; Doctor of Oriental Languages of Paris. I have some other degrees, honorary and otherwise, but I need not trouble you with them. Those I have named will show you that I am sufficiently feathered with diplomas to fly into even a sick-room. Early in life —fortunately for my interests and pleasures, but unfortunately for my pocket—I fell in with Egyptology. I must have been bitten by some powerful scarab, for I took it bad. I went out tomb-hunting; and managed to get a living of a sort, and to learn some things that you can't get out of books. I was in pretty low water when I met your Father, who was doing some explorations on his own account; and since then I haven't found that I have many unsatisfied wants. He is a real patron of the arts; no mad Egyptologist can ever hope for a better chief!"

He spoke with feeling; and I was glad to see that Miss Trelawny coloured up with pleasure at the praise of her father. I could not help noticing, however, that Mr. Corbeck was, in a measure, speaking as if against time. I took it that he wished, while speaking, to study his ground; to see how far he would be justified in taking into confidence the two strangers before him. As he went on, I could see that his confidence kept increasing. When I thought of it afterward, and remembered what he had said, I realised that the measure of the information which he gave us marked his growing trust.

"I have been several times out on expeditions in Egypt for your Father; and I have always found it a delight to work for him. Many of his treasures—and he has some rare ones, I tell you—he has procured through me, either by my exploration or by purchase —or—or—otherwise. Your Father, Miss Trelawny, has a rare knowledge. He sometimes makes up his mind that he wants to find a particular thing, of whose existence—if it still exists—he has become aware; and he will follow it all over the world till he gets it. I've been on just such a chase now."

He stopped suddenly, as suddenly as though his mouth had been shut by the jerk of a string. We waited; when he went on he spoke with a caution that was new to him, as though he wished to forestall our asking any questions:

"I am not at liberty to mention anything of my mission; where it was to, what it was for, or anything at all about it. Such matters are in confidence between Mr. Trelawny and myself; I am pledged to absolute secrecy."

He paused, and an embarrassed look crept over his face. Suddenly he said:

"You are sure, Miss Trelawny, your Father is not well enough to see me to-day?"

A look of wonderment was on her face in turn. But it cleared at once;—she stood up, saying in a tone in which dignity and graciousness were blended:

" Come and see for yourself!" She moved toward
her father's room; he followed, and I brought up the
rear.

Mr. Corbeck entered the sick-room as though he
knew it.   There is an unconscious attitude or bearing
to persons in new surroundings which there is no
mistaking.   Even in his anxiety to see his powerful
friend, he glanced for a moment round the room,
as at a familiar place.   Then all his attention became
fixed on the bed.   I watched him narrowly, for somehow I felt that on this man depended much of our
enlightenment regarding the strange matter in which
we were involved.

It was not that I doubted him.   The man was of
transparent honesty; it was this very quality which
we had to dread.   He was of that courageous, fixed
trueness to his undertaking, that if he should deem
it his duty to guard a secret he would do it to the
last.   The case before us was, at least, an unusual
one; and it would, consequently, require more liberal
recognition of bounds of the duty of secrecy than
would hold under ordinary conditions.   To us,
ignorance was helplessness.   If we could learn anything of the past we might at least form some idea
of the conditions antecedent to the attack; and
might, so, achieve some means of helping the patient
to recovery.   There were curios which might be
removed. . . . My thoughts were beginning to whirl
once again; I pulled myself up sharply and watched.
There was a look of infinite pity on the sun-stained,
rugged face as he gazed at his friend, lying so helpless.   The sternness of Mr. Trelawny's face had not
relaxed in sleep; but somehow it made the helplessness more marked.   It would not have troubled one

to see a weak or an ordinary face under such conditions; but this purposeful, masterful man, lying
before us wrapped in impenetrable sleep, had all the
pathos of a great ruin.   The sight was not a new one
to us; but I could see that Miss Trelawny, like
myself, was moved afresh by it in the presence of
the stranger.   Mr. Corbeck's face grew stern.   All
the pity died away; and in its stead came a grim,
hard look which boded ill for whoever had been the
cause of this mighty downfall.   This look in turn
gave place to one of decision; the volcanic energy of
the man was working to some definite purpose.   He
glanced around at us; and as his eyes lighted on
Nurse Kennedy his eyebrows went up a trifle.   She
noted the look, and glanced interrogatively at Miss
Trelawny, who flashed back a reply with a glance.
She went quietly from the room, closing the door
behind her.   Mr. Corbeck looked first at me, with
a strong man's natural impulse to learn from a man
rather than a woman; then at Miss Trelawny, with a
remembrance of the duty of courtesy, and said:

"Tell me all about it.   How it began and when!"
Miss Trelawny looked at me appealingly; and forthwith I told him all that I knew.   He seemed to make
no motion during the whole time; but insensibly the
bronze face became steel.   When, at the end, I told
him of Mr. Marvin's visit and of the Power of Attorney,
his look began to brighten.   And when, seeing his
interest in the matter, I went more into detail as to
its terms, he spoke:

"Good!   Now I know where my duty lies!"

With a sinking heart I heard him.   Such a phrase,
coming at such a time, seemed to close the door to
my hopes of enlightenment.

" What do you mean ? " I asked, feeling that my question was a feeble one.

His answer emphasized my fears :

" Trelawny knows what he is doing. He had some definite purpose in all that he did ; and we must not thwart him. He evidently expected something to happen, and guarded himself at all points."

" Not at all points ! " I said impulsively. "There must have been a weak spot somewhere, or he wouldn't be lying here like that ! " Somehow his impassiveness surprised me. I had expected that he would find a valid argument in my phrase ; but it did not move him, at least not in the way I thought. Something like a smile flickered over ,is swarthy face as he answered me :

" This is not the end ! Trelawny did not guard himself to no purpose. Doubtless, he expected this too ; or at any rate the possibility of it."

" Do you know what he expected, or from what source ? " The questioner was Miss Trelawny.

The answer came at once : " No ! I know nothing of either. I can guess . . ." He stopped suddenly.

" Guess what ? " The suppressed excitement in the girl's voice was akin to anguish. The steely look came over the swarthy face again ; but there was tenderness and courtesy in both voice and manner as he replied :

" Believe me, I would do anything I honestly could to relieve your anxiety. But in this I have a higher duty."

" What duty ? "

" Silence ! " As he spoke the word, the strong mouth closed like a steel trap.

We all remained silent for a few minutes. In the

intensity of our thinking, the silence became a positive thing; the small sounds of life within and without the house seemed intrusive. The first to break it was Miss Trelawny. I had seen an idea— a hope—flash in her eyes; but she steadied herself before speaking:

"What was the urgent subject on which you wanted to see me, knowing that my Father was— not available?" The pause showed her mastery of her thoughts.

The instantaneous change in Mr. Corbeck was almost ludicrous. His start of surprise, coming close upon his iron-clad impassiveness, was like a panto- mimic change. But all idea of comedy was swept away by the tragic earnestness with which he remem- bered his original purpose.

"My God!" he said, as he raised his hand from the chair back on which it rested, and beat it down with a violence which would in itself have arrested attention. His brows corrugated as he went on: "I quite forgot! What a loss! Now of all times! Just at the moment of success! He lying there helpless, and my tongue tied! Not able to raise hand or foot in my ignorance of his wishes!"

"What is it? Oh, do tell us! I am so anxious about my dear Father! Is it any new trouble? I hope not! oh, I hope not! I have had such anxiety and trouble already! It alarms me afresh to hear you speak so! Won't you tell me something to allay this terrible anxiety and uncertainty?"

He drew his sturdy form up to his full height as he said:

"Alas! I cannot, may not, tell you anything. It is his secret." He pointed to the bed. "And yet—and

yet I came here for his advice, his counsel, his assistance. And he lies there helpless. . . . And time is
flying by us! It may soon be too late!"

"What is it? what is it?" broke in Miss Trelawny
in a sort of passion of anxiety, her face drawn with
pain. "Oh, speak! Say something! This anxiety,
and horror, and mystery are killing me!" Mr.
Corbeck calmed himself by a great effort.

"I may not tell you details; but I have had a great
loss. My mission, in which I have spent three years,
was successful. I discovered all that I sought—and
more; and brought them home with me safely.
Treasures, priceless in themselves, b doubly precious to him by whose wishes and instructions I
sought them. I arrived in London only last night;
and when I woke this morning my precious charge
was stolen. Stolen in some mysterious way. Not a
soul in London knew that I was arriving. No one
but myself knew what was in the shabby portmanteau
that I carried. My room had but one door, and that
I locked and bolted. The room was high in the
house, five stories up, so that no entrance could have
been obtained by the window. Indeed, I had closed
the window myself and shut the hasp, for I wished to
be secure in every way. This morning the hasp was
untouched. . . . And yet my portmanteau was empty.
The lamps were gone! . . . There! it is out. I went
to Egypt to search for a set of antique lamps which
Mr. Trelawny wished to trace. With incredible
labour, and through many dangers, I followed them.
I brought them safe home. . . . And now!" He
turned away much moved. Even his iron nature was
breaking down under the sense of loss.

Miss Trelawny stepped over and laid her hand on

his arm. I looked at her in amazement. All the passion and pain which had so moved her seemed to have taken the form of resolution. Her form was erect, her eyes blazed; energy was manifest in every nerve and fibre of her being. Even her voice was full of nervous power as she spoke. It was apparent that she was a marvellously strong woman, and that her strength could answer when called upon.

"We must act at once! My Father's wishes must be carried out, if it is possible to us. Mr. Ross, you are a lawyer. We have actually in the house a man whom you consider one of the best detectives in London. Surely we can do something. We can begin at once!" Mr. Corbeck took new life from her enthusiasm.

"Good! You are your Father's daughter!" was all he said. But his admiration for her energy was manifested by the impulsive way in which he took her hand. I moved over to the door. I was going to bring Sergeant Daw; and from her look of approval, I knew that Margaret—Miss Trelawny—understood. I was at the door when Mr. Corbeck called me back.

"One moment," he said, "before we bring a stranger on the scene. It must be borne in mind that he is not to know what you know now, that the lamps were the objects of a prolonged and difficult and dangerous search. All I can tell him, all that he must know from any source, is that some of my property has been stolen. I must describe some of the lamps, especially one, for it is of gold; and my fear is lest the thief, ignorant of its historic worth, may, in order to cover up his crime, have it melted. I would willingly pay ten, twenty, a hundred, a thousand times its intrinsic value rather than have it destroyed. I shall tell him only what is necessary. So, please, let me answer any questions he may ask; unless, of course, I ask you or refer to either of you for the answer." We both nodded acquiescence. Then a thought struck me and I said:

"By the way, if it be necessary to keep this matter quiet it will be better to have it if possible a private job for the Detective. If once a thing gets to Scotland Yard it is out of our power to keep it quiet, and further secrecy may be impossible. I shall sound Sergeant Daw before he comes up. If I say nothing, it will mean that he accepts the task and will deal with it privately." Mr. Corbeck answered at once:

"Secrecy is everything. The one thing I dread is that the lamps, or some of them, may be destroyed at once." To my intense astonishment Miss Trelawny spoke out at once, but quietly, in a decided voice:

"They will not be destroyed; nor any of them!" Mr. Corbeck actually smiled in amazement.

"How on earth do you know?" he asked. Her answer was still more incomprehensible:

"I don't know how I know it; but know it I do. I feel it all through me; as though it were a conviction which has been with me all my life!"

CHAPTER VIII

THE FINDING OF THE LAMPS

SERGEANT DAW at first made some demur; but finally agreed to advise privately on a matter which might be suggested to him. He added that I was to remember that he only undertook to advise; for if action were required he might have to refer the matter to headquarters. With this understanding I left him in the study, and brought Miss Trelawny and Mr. Corbeck to him. Nurse Kennedy resumed her place at the bedside before we left the room.

I could not but admire the cautious, cool-headed precision with which the traveller stated his case. He did not seem to conceal anything, and yet he gave the least possible description of the objects missing. He did not enlarge on the mystery of the case; he seemed to look on it as an ordinary hotel theft. Knowing, as I did, that his one object was to recover the articles before their identity could be obliterated, I could see the rare intellectual skill with which he gave the necessary matter and held back all else, though without seeming to do so. "Truly," thought I, "this man has learned the lesson of the Eastern bazaars; and with Western intellect has improved upon his masters!" He quite conveyed his idea to the Detective, who, after thinking the matter over for a few moments, said:

" Pot or scale ? that is the question ! "

"What does that mean ? " asked the other, keenly alert.

"An old thieves' phrase from Birmingham. I thought that in these days of slang everyone knew that. In old times at Brum, which had a lot of small metal industries, the gold- and silver-smiths used to buy metal from almost anyone who came along. And as metal in small quantities could generally be had cheap when they didn't ask where it came from, it got to be a custom to ask only one thing—whether the customer wanted the goods melted, in which case the buyer made the price, and the melting-pot was always on the fire. If it was to be preserved in its present state at the buyer's option, it went into the scale and fetched standard price for old metal.

"There is a good deal of such work done still, and in other places than Brum. When we're looking for stolen watches we often come across the works, and it's not possible to identify wheels and springs out of a heap ; but it's not often that we come across cases that are wanted. Now, in the present instance much will depend on whether the thief is a good man— that's what they call a man who knows his work. A first-class crook will know whether a thing is of more value than merely the metal in it ; and in such case he would put it with someone who could place it later on—in America or France, perhaps. By the way, do you think anyone but yourself could identify your lamps ? "

" No one but myself ! "

" Are there others like them ? "

"Not that I know of," answered Mr. Corbeck ;

"though there may be others that resemble them in many particulars." The Detective paused before asking again: "Would any other skilled person—at the British Museum, for instance, or a dealer, or a collector like Mr. Trelawny, know the value — the artistic value—of the lamps?"

"Certainly! Anyone with a head on his shoulders would see at a glance that the things were valuable."

The Detective's face brightened. "Then there is a chance. If your door was locked and the window shut, the goods were not stolen by the chance of a chambermaid or a boots coming along. Whoever did the job went after it special; and he ain't going to part with his swag without his price. This must be a case of notice to the pawnbrokers. There's one good thing about it, anyhow, that the hue and cry needn't be given. We needn't tell Scotland Yard unless you like; we can work the thing privately. If you wish to keep the thing dark, as you told me at the first, that is our chance." Mr. Corbeck, after a pause, said quietly:

"I suppose you couldn't hazard a suggestion as to how the robbery was effected?" The Policeman smiled the smile of knowledge and experience.

"In a very simple way, I have no doubt, sir. That is how all these mysterious crimes turn out in the long-run. The criminal knows his work and all the tricks of it; and he is always on the watch for chances. Moreover, he knows by experience what these chances are likely to be, and how they usually come. The other person is only careful; he doesn't know all the tricks and pits that may be made for him, and by some little oversight or other he falls into the trap. When we know all about this case,

you will wonder that you did not see the method of
it all along!" This seemed to annoy Mr. Corbeck
a little; there was decided heat in his manner as he
answered:

"Look here, my good friend, there is not anything
simple about this case—except that the things were
taken. The window was closed; the fireplace was
bricked up. There is only one door to the room,
and that I locked and bolted. There is no transom;
I have heard all about hotel robberies through the
transom. I never left my room in the night. I
looked at the things before going to bed; and I
went to look at them again when I woke up. If
you can rig up any kind of simple robbery out of
these facts you are a clever man. That's all I say;
clever enough to go right away and get my things
back." Miss Trelawny laid her hand upon his arm
in a soothing way, and said quietly:

"Do not distress yourself unnecessarily. I am
sure they will turn up." Sergeant Daw turned to
her so quickly that I could not help remembering
vividly his suspicions of her, already formed, as he
said:

"May I ask, miss, on what you base that opinion?"

I dreaded to hear her answer, given to ears already
awake to suspicion; but it came to me as a new pain
or shock all the same:

"I cannot tell you how I know. But I am sure of
it!" The Detective looked at her for some seconds
in silence, and then threw a quick glance at me.

Presently he had a little more conversation with
Mr. Corbeck as to his own movements, the details of
the hotel and the room, and the means of identifying
the goods. Then he went away to commence his

inquiries, Mr. Corbeck impressing on him the necessity for secrecy lest the thief should get wind of his danger and destroy the lamps. Mr. Corbeck promised, when going away to attend to various matters of his own business, to return early in the evening, and to stay in the house.

All that day Miss Trelawny was in better spirits and looked in better strength than she had yet been, despite the new shock and annoyance of the theft which must ultimately bring so much disappointment to her father.

We spent most of the day looking over the curio treasures of Mr. Trelawny. From what I had heard from Mr. Corbeck I began to have some idea of the vastness of his enterprise in the world of Egyptian research; and with this light everything around me began to have a new interest. As I went on, the interest grew; any lingering doubts which I might have had changed to wonder and admiration. The house seemed to be a veritable storehouse of marvels of antique art. In addition to the curios, big and little, in Mr. Trelawny's own room—from the great sarcophagi down to the scarabs of all kinds in the cabinets—the great hall, the staircase landings, the study, and even the boudoir were full of antique pieces which would have made a collector's mouth water.

Miss Trelawny from the first came with me, and looked with growing interest at everything. After having examined some cabinets of exquisite amulets she said to me in quite a naïve way:

"You will hardly believe that I have of late seldom even looked at any of these things. It is only since Father has been ill that I seem to have even any curiosity about them. But now, they grow and grow

on me to quite an absorbing degree. I wonder if it
is that the collector's blood which I have in my veins
is beginning to manifest itself.   If so, the strange
thing is that I have not felt the call of it before.   Of
course I know most of the big things, and have
examined them more or less ; but really, in a sort of
way I have always taken them for granted, as though
they had always been there.   I have noticed the same
thing now and again with family pictures, and the
way they are taken for granted by the family.   If
you will let me examine them with you it will be
delightful ! "

It was a joy to me to hear her talk in such a way ;
and her last suggestion quite thrilled me.   Together
we went round the various rooms and passages,
examining and admiring the magnificent curios.
There was such a bewildering amount and variety
of objects that we could only glance at most of them ;
but as we went along we arranged that we should
take them *seriatim*, day by day, and examine them
more closely.   In the hall was a sort of big frame of
floriated steel work which Margaret said her father
used for lifting the heavy stone lid of the sarcophagi.
It was not heavy and could be moved abou easily
enough.   By aid of this we raised the covers in turn
and looked at the endless series of hieroglyphic pictures cut in most of them.   In spite of her profession
of ignorance Margaret knew a good deal about them ;
her year of life with her father had had unconsciously
its daily and hourly lesson.   She was a remarkably
clever and acute-minded girl, and with a prodigious
memory ; so that her store of knowledge, gathered
unthinkingly bit by bit, had grown to proportions
that many a scholar might have envied.

And yet it was all so naïve and unconscious; so girlish and simple. She was so fresh in her views and ideas, and had so little thought of self, that in her companionship I forgot for the time all the troubles and mysteries which enmeshed the house; and I felt like a boy again. . . .

The most interesting of the sarcophagi were undoubtedly the three in Mr. Trelawny's room. Of these, two were of dark stone, one of porphyry and the other of a sort of ironstone. These were wrought with some hieroglyphs. But the third was strikingly different. It was of some yellow-brown substance of the dominating colour effect of Mexican onyx, which it resembled in many ways, excepting that the natural pattern of its convolutions was less marked. Here and there were patches almost transparent—certainly translucent. The whole chest, cover and all, was wrought with hundreds, perhaps thousands, of minute hieroglyphics, seemingly in an endless series. Back, front, sides, edges, bottom, all had their quota of the dainty pictures, the deep blue of their colouring showing up fresh and sharply edged in the yellow stone. It was very long, nearly nine feet; and perhaps a yard wide. The sides undulated, so that there was no hard line. Even the corners took such excellent curves that they pleased the eye. "Truly," I said, "this must have been made for a giant!"

"Or for a giantess!" said Margaret.

This sarcophagus stood near to one of the windows. It was in one respect different from all the other sarcophagi in the place. All the others in the house, of whatever material—granite, porphyry, ironstone, basalt, slate, or wood—were quite simple in form within. Some of them were plain of interior surface;

others were engraved, in whole or part, with hieroglyphics. But each and all of them had no protuberances or uneven surface anywhere. They might have
been used for baths; indeed, they resembled in many
ways Roman baths of stone or marble which I had
seen. Inside this, however, was a raised space, outlined like a human figure. I asked Margaret if she
could explain it in any way. For answer she said:

"Father never wished to speak about this. It
attracted my attention from the first; but when I
asked him about it he said: 'I shall tell you all about
it some day, little girl—if I live! But not yet! The
story is not yet told, as I hope to tell it to you! Some
day, perhaps soon, I shall know all; and then we
shall go over it together. And a mighty interesting
story you will find it—from first to last!' Once afterward I said, rather lightly I am afraid: 'Is that story
of the sarcophagus told yet, Father?' He shook his
head, and looked at me gravely as he said: 'Not yet,
little girl; but it will be—if I live—if I live!' His
repeating that phrase about his li ing rather frightened
me; I never ventured to ask him again."

Somehow this thrilled me. I could not exactly say
how or why; but it seems like a gleam of light at last.
There are, I think, moments when the mind accepts
something as true; though it can account for neither
the course of the thought, nor, if there be more than
one thought, the connection between them. Hitherto
we had been in such outer darkness regarding Mr.
Trelawny, and the strange visitation which had fallen
on him, that anything which afforded a clue, even of
the faintest and most shadowy kind, had at the outset
the enlightening satisfaction of a certainty. Here
were two lights of our puzzle. The first that Mr.

Trelawny associated with this particular curio a doubt of his own living.   The second that he had some purpose or expectation with regard to it, which he would not disclose, even to his daughter, till complete. Again it was to be borne in mind that this sarcophagus differed internally from all the others.   What meant that odd raised place ?   I said nothing to Miss Trelawny, for I feared lest I should either frighten her or buoy her up with future hopes ; but I made up my mind that I would take an early opportunity for further investigation.

Close beside the sarcophagus was a low table of green stoné with red veins in it, like bloodstone.   The feet were fashioned like the paws of a jackal, and round each leg was twined a full-throated snake wrought exquisitely in pure gold.   On it rested a strange and very beautiful coffer or casket of stone of a peculiar shape.   It was something like a small coffin, except that the longer sides, instead of being cut off square like the upper or level part were continued to a point.   Thus it was an irregular septahedron, there being two planes on each of the two sides, one end and a top and bottom.   The stone, of one piece of which it was wrought, was such as I had never seen before.   At the base it was of a full green, the colour of emerald without, of course, its gleam.   It was not by any means dull, however, either in colour or substance, and was of infinite hardness and fineness of texture.   The surface was almost that of a jewel.   The colour grew lighter as it rose, with gradation so fine as to be imperceptible, changing to a fine yellow almost of the colour of " mandarin " china.   It was quite unlike anything I had ever seen, and did not resemble any stone or gem that I knew.   I took it to be some unique

mother-stone, or matrix of some gem.   It was wrought
all over, except in a few spots, with fine hieroglyphics,
exquisitely done and coloured with the same blue-
green cement or pigment that appeared on the sarcophagus.   In length it was about two feet and a half ;
in breadth about half this, and was nearly a foot high.
The vacant spaces were irregularly distributed about
the top running to the pointed end.   These places
seemed less opaque than the rest of the stone.   I
tried to lift up the lid so that I might see if they were
translucent ; but it was securely fixed.   It fitted so
exactly that the whole coffer seemed like a single
piece of stone mysteriously hollowed from within.
On the sides and edges were some odd-looking protuberances wrought just as finely as any other portion
of the coffer which had been sculptured by manifest
design in the cutting of the stone.   They had queer-
shaped holes or hollows, different in each ; and, like
the rest, were covered with the hieroglyphic figures,
cut finely and filled in with the same blue-green
cement.

On the other side of the great sarcophagus stood
another small table of alabaster, exquisitely chased
with symbolic figures of gods and the signs of the
zodiac.   On this table stood a case of about a foot
square composed of slabs of rock crystal set in a
skeleton of bands of red gold, beautifully engraved
with hieroglyphics, and coloured with a blue green,
very much the tint of the figures on the sarcophagus and the coffer.   The whole work was quite
modern.

But if the case was modern what it held was not.
Within, on a cushion of cloth of gold as fine as
silk, and with the peculiar softness of old gold, rested

a mummy hand, so perfect that it startled one to see it. A woman's hand, fine and long, with slim tapering fingers and nearly as perfect as when it was given to the embalmer thousands of years before. In the embalming it had lost nothing of its beautiful shape; even the wrist seemed to maintain its pliability as the gentle curve lay on the cushion. The skin was of a rich creamy or old ivory colour; a dusky fair skin which suggested heat, but heat in shadow. The great peculiarity of it, as a hand, was that it had in all seven fingers, there being two middle and two index fingers. The upper end of the wrist was jagged, as though it had been broken off, and was stained with a red-brown stain. On the cushion near the hand was a small scarab, exquisitely wrought of emerald.

"That is another of Father's mysteries. When I asked him about it he said that it was perhaps the most valuable thing he had, except one. When I asked him what that one was, he refused to tell me, and forbade me to ask him anything concerning it. 'I will tell you,' he said, 'all about it, too, in good time —if I live!'"

"If I live!" the phrase again. These three things grouped together, the Sarcophagus, the Coffer, and the Hand, seemed to make a trilogy of mystery indeed!

At this time Miss Trelawny was sent for on some domestic matter. I looked at the other curios in the room; but they did not seem to have anything like the same charm for me, now that she was away. Later on in the day I was sent for to the boudoir where she was consulting with Mrs. Grant as to the lodgment of Mr. Corbeck. They were in doubt as to whether he should have a room close to Mr. Trelawny's or quite away from it, and had thought it well to ask my advice on the subject. I came to the conclusion that he had better not be too near ; for the first at all events, he could easily be moved closer if necessary. When Mrs. Grant had gone, I asked Miss Trelawny how it came that the furniture of this room, the boudoir in which we were, was so different from the other rooms of the house.

" Father's forethought ! " she answered. " When I first came, he thought, and rightly enough, that I might get frightened with so many records of death and the tomb everywhere. So he had this room and the little suite off it—that door opens into the sitting-room—where I slept last night, furnished with pretty things. You see, they are all beautiful. That cabinet belonged to the great Napoleon."

" There is nothing Egyptian in these rooms at all then ? " I asked, rather to show interest in what she had said than anything else, for the furnishing of the room was apparent. " What a lovely cabinet ! May I look at it ? "

" Of course ! with the greatest pleasure ! " she answered, with a smile. " Its finishing within and without, Father says, is absolutely complete." I stepped over and looked at it closely. It was made of tulip wood, inlaid in pattern ; and was mounted in ormolu. I pulled open one of the drawers, a deep one where I could see the work to great advantage. As I pulled it, something rattled inside as though rolling ; there was a tinkle as of metal on metal.

" Hullo ! " I said. " There is something in here. Perhaps I had better not open it."

" There is nothing that I know of," she answered.

" Some of the housemaids may have used it to put
something by for the time and forgotten it. Open it
by all means ! "

I pulled open the drawer ; as I did so, both Miss
Trelawny and I started back in amazement.

There before our eyes lay a number of ancient
Egyptian lamps, of various sizes and of strangely varied
shapes.

We leaned over them and looked closely. My own
heart was beating like a trip-hammer ; and I could see
by the heaving of Margaret's bosom that she was
strangely excited.

Whilst we looked, afraid to touch and almost afraid
to think, there was a ring at the front door ; immediately afterwards Mr. Corbeck, followed by Sergeant
Daw, came into the hall. The door of the boudoir
was open, and when they saw us Mr. Corbeck came
running in, followed more slowly by the Detective.
There was a sort of chastened joy in his face and
manner as he said impulsively :

" Rejoice with me, my dear Miss Trelawny, my
luggage has come and all my things are intact ! "
Then his face fell as he added, " Except the lamps.
The lamps that were worth all the rest a thousand
times. . . ." He stopped, struck by the strange pallor
of her face. Then his eyes, following her look and
mine, lit on the cluster of lamps in the drawer. He
gave a sort of cry of surprise and joy as he bent over
and touched them :

" My lamps ! My lamps ! Then they are safe—
safe—safe ! . . . But how, in the name of God—of all
the Gods—did they come here ? "

We all stood silent. The Detective made a deep
sound of in-taking breath. I looked at him, and as he

caught my glance he turned his eyes on Miss Trelawny whose back was toward him.

There was in them the same look of suspicion which had been there when he had spoken to me of her being the first to find her father on the occasions of the attack.

CHAPTER IX

THE NEED OF KNOWLEDGE

MR. CORBECK seemed to go almost off his head at the recovery of the lamps. He took them up one by one and looked them all over tenderly, as though they were things that he loved. In his delight and excitement he breathed so hard that it seemed almost like a cat purring. Sergeant Daw said quietly, his voice breaking the silence like a discord in a melody :

"Are you quite sure those lamps are the ones you had, and that were stolen ? "

His answer was in an indignant tone : "Sure! Of course I'm sure. There isn't another set of lamps like these in the world ! "

"So far as you know!" The Detective's words were smooth enough, but his manner was so exasperating that I was sure he had some motive in it ; so I waited in silence. He went on :

"Of course there may be some in the British Museum ; or Mr. Trelawny may have had these already. There's nothing new under the sun, you know, Mr. Corbeck ; not even in Egypt. These may be the originals, and yours may have been the copies. Are there any points by which you can identify these as yours ? "

Mr. Corbeck was really angry by this time. He

forgot his reserve; and in his indignation poured
forth a torrent of almost incoherent, but enlightening,
broken sentences:

"Identify! Copies of them! British Museum! Rot!
Perhaps they keep a set in Scotland Yard for teaching
idiot policemen Egyptology! Do I know them?
When I have carried them about my body, in the
desert, for three months; and lay awake night after
night to watch them! When I have looked them over
with a magnifying-glass, hour after hour, till my eyes
ached; till every tiny blotch, and chip, and dinge
became as familiar to me as his chart to a captain; as
familiar as they doubtless have been all the time to
every thick-headed area-prowler within the bounds
of mortality. See here, young man, look at these!"
He ranged the lamps in a row on the top of the
cabinet. "Did you ever see a set of lamps of these
shapes—of any one of these shapes? Look at these
dominant figures on them! Did you ever see so
complete a set—even in Scotland Yard; even in Bow
Street? Look! one on each, the seven forms of
Hathor. Look at that figure of the Ka, of a Princess of
the Two Egypts, standing between Ra and Osiris in
the Boat of the Dead, with the Eye of Sleep, supported
on legs, bending before her; and Harmochis rising in
the north. Will you find that in the British Museum—
or Bow Street? Or perhaps your studies in the Gizeh
Museum, or the Fitzwilliam, or Paris, or Leyden, or
Berlin, have shown you that the episode is common in
hieroglyphics; and that this is only a copy. Perhaps
you can tell me what that figure of Ptah-Seker-Ausar
holding the Tet wrapped in the Sceptre of Papyrus
means? Did you ever see it before; even in the
British Museum, or Gizeh, or Scotland Yard?"

He broke off suddenly; and then went on in quite a different way:

"Look here! it seems to me that the thick-headed idiot is myself! I beg your pardon, old fellow, for my rudeness. I quite lost my temper at the suggestion that I do not know these lamps. You don't mind, do you?" The Detective answered heartily:

"Lord, sir, not I. I like to see folks angry when I am dealing with them, whether they are on my side or the other. It is when people are angry that you learn the truth from them. I keep cool; that is my trade! Do you know, you have told me more about those lamps in the past two minutes than when you filled me up with details of how to identify them."

Mr. Corbeck grunted; he was not pleased at having given himself away. All at once he turned to me and said in his natural way:

"Now tell me how you got them back?" I was so surprised that I said without thinking:

"We didn't get them back!" The traveller laughed openly.

"What on earth do you mean?" he asked. "You didn't get them back! Why, there they are before your eyes! We found you looking at them when we came in." By this time I had recovered my surprise and had my wits about me.

"Why, that's just it," I said. "We had only come across them, by accident, that very moment!"

Mr. Corbeck drew back and looked hard at Miss Trelawny and myself; turning his eyes from one to the other as he asked:

"Do you mean to tell me that no one brought them here; that you found them in that drawer? That, so to speak, no one at all brought them back?"

"I suppose someone must have brought them here; they couldn't have come of their own accord. But who it was, or when, or how, neither of us knows. We shall have to make inquiry, and see if any of the servants know anything of it."

We all stood silent for several seconds. It seemed a long time. The first to speak was the Detective, who said in an unconscious way:

"Well, I'm damned! I beg your pardon, miss!" Then his mouth shut like a steel trap.

We called up the servants, one by one, and asked them if they knew anything of some articles placed in a drawer in the boudoir; but none of them could throw any light on the circumstance. We did not tell them what the articles were; or let them see them.

Mr. Corbeck packed the lamps in cotton wool, and placed them in a tin box. This, I may mention incidentally, was then brought up to the detectives' room, where one of the men stood guard over them with a revolver the whole night. Next day we got a small safe into the house, and placed them in it. There were two different keys. One of them I kept myself; the other I placed in my drawer in the Safe Deposit vault. We were all determined that the lamps should not be lost again.

About an hour after we had found the lamps, Doctor Winchester arrived. He had a large parcel with him, which, when unwrapped, proved to be the mummy of a cat. With Miss Trelawny's permission he placed this in the boudoir; and Silvio was brought close to it. To the surprise of us all, however, except perhaps Doctor Winchester, he did not manifest the least annoyance; he took no notice of it whatever. He stood on the table close beside it, purring loudly. Then,

following out his plan, the Doctor brought him into
Mr. Trelawny's room, we all following. Doctor
Winchester was excited; Miss Trelawny anxious. I
was more than interested myself, for I began to have
a glimmering of the Doctor's idea. The Detective
was calmly and coldly superior: but Mr. Corbeck,
who was an enthusiast, was full of eager curiosity..

The moment Doctor Winchester got into the room,
Silvio began to mew and wriggle; and, jumping out
of his arms, ran over to the cat mummy and began
to scratch angrily at it. Miss Trelawny had some
difficulty in taking him away; but so soon as he was
out of the room he became quiet. When she came
back there was a clamour of comments:

"I thought so!" from the Doctor.

"What can it mean?" from Miss Trelawny.

"That's a very strange thing!" from Mr. Corbeck.

"Odd! but it doesn't prove anything!" from the
Detective.

"I suspend my judgment!" from myself, thinking
it advisable to say something.

Then by common consent we dropped the theme
—for the present.

In my room that evening I was making some notes
of what had happened, when there came a low tap
on the door. In obedience to my summons Sergeant
Daw came in, carefully closing the door behind him.

"Well, Sergeant," said I, "sit down. What is it?"

"I wanted to speak to you, sir, about those lamps."
I nodded and waited: he went on: "You know that
that room where they were found opens directly into
the room where Miss Trelawny slept last night?"

"Yes."

"During the night a window somewhere in that

part of the house was opened, and shut again. I
heard it, and took a look round ; but I could see no
sign of anything."

"Yes, I know that!" I said ; "I heard a window
moved myself."

"Does nothing strike you as strange about it, sir?"

"Strange!" I said ; "strange! why it's all the most
bewildering, maddening thing I have ever encoun-
tered. It is all so strange that one seems to wonder,
and simply waits for what will happen next. But
what do you mean by strange?"

The Detective paused, as if choosing his words to
begin ; and then said deliberately :

"You see, I am not one who believes in magic and
such things. I am for facts all the time ; and I
always find in the long-run that there is a reason
and a cause for everything. This new gentleman
says these things were stolen out of his room in
the hotel. The lamps, I take it from some things
he has said, really belong to Mr. Trelawny. His
daughter, the lady of the house, having left the room
she usually occupies, sleeps that night on the ground
floor. A window is heard to open and shut during
the night. When we, who have been during the day
trying to find a clue to the robbery, come to the
house, we find the stolen goods in a room close to
where she slept, and opening out of it!"

He stopped. I felt that same sense of pain and
apprehension, which I had experienced when he had
spoken to me before, creeping, or rather rushing,
over me again. I had to face the matter out, however. My relations with her, and the feeling toward
her which I now knew full well meant a very deep love
and devotion, demanded so much. I said as calmly

as I could, for I knew the keen eyes of the skilful
investigator were on me :

"And the inference?"

He answered with the cool audacity of conviction :

"The inference to me is that there was no robbery
at all. The goods were taken by someone to this
house, where they were received through a window
on the ground floor. They were placed in the cabinet,
ready to be discovered when the proper time should
come !"

Somehow I felt relieved ; the assumption was too
monstrous. I did not want, however, my relief to be
apparent, so I answered as gravely as I could :

"And who do you suppose brought them to the
house ?"

"I keep my mind open as to that. Possibly Mr.
Corbeck himself ; the matter might be too risky to
trust to a third party."

"Then the natural extension of your inference is
that Mr. Corbeck is a liar and a fraud ; and that he is
in conspiracy with Miss Trelawny to deceive someone
or other about those lamps."

"Those are harsh words, Mr. Ross. They're so
plain-spoken that they bring a man up standing, and
make new doubts for him. But I have to go where
my reason points. It may be that there is another
party than Miss Trelawny in it. Indeed, if it hadn't
been for the other matter that set me thinking and
.bred doubts of its own about her, I wouldn't dream
of mixing her up in this. But I'm safe on Corbeck.
Whoever else is in it, he is ! The things couldn't
have been taken without his connivance—if what he
says is true. If it isn't—well ! he is a liar anyhow. I
would think it a bad job to have him stay in the house

with so many valuables, only that it will give me and
my mate a chance of watching him. We'll keep a
pretty good look-out, too, I tell you. He's up in my
room now, guarding those lamps ; but Johnny Wright
is there too. I go on before he comes off ; so there
won't be much chance of another house-breaking. Of
course, Mr. Ross, all this, too, is between you and me."

"Quite so! You may depend on my silence!" I
said ; and he went away to keep a close eye on the
Egyptologist.

It seemed as though all my painful experiences were
to go in pairs, and that the sequence of the previous
day was to be repeated ; for before long I had another
private visit from Doctor Winchester who had now
paid his nightly visit to his patient and was on his
way home. He took the seat which I preferred and
began at once :

"This is a strange affair altogether. Miss Trelawny
has just been telling me about the stolen lamps, and
of the finding of them in the Napoleon cabinet. It
would seem to be another complication of the mystery;
and yet, do you know, it is a relief to me. I have
exhausted all human and natural possibilities of the
case, and am beginning to fall back on superhuman
and supernatural possibilities. Here are such strange
things that, if I am not going mad, I think we must
have a solution before long. I wonder if I might ask
some questions and some help from Mr. Corbeck,
without making further complications and embarrassing us. He seems to know an amazing amount
regarding Egypt and all relating to it. Perhaps he
wouldn't mind translating a little bit of hieroglyphic.
It is child's play to him. What do you think ?"

When I had thought the matter over a few secon'

I spoke. We wanted all the help we could get. For myself, I had perfect confidence in both men ; and any comparing notes, or mutual assistance, might bring good results. Such could hardly bring evil.

"By all means I should ask him. He seems an extraordinarily learned man in Egyptology ; and he seems to me a good fellow as well as an enthusiast. By the way, it will be necessary to be a little guarded as to whom you speak regarding any information which he may give you."

"Of course !" he answered. "Indeed I should not dream of saying anything to anybody, excepting yourself. We have to remember that when Mr. Trelawny recovers he may not like to think that we have been chattering unduly over his affairs."

"Look here !" I said, "why not stay for a while : and I shall ask him to come and have a pipe with us. We can then talk over things."

He acquiesced : so I went to the room where Mr. Corbeck was, and brought him back with me. I thought the detectives were pleased at his going. On the way to my room he said :

"I don't half like leaving those things there, with only those men to guard them. They're a deal sight too precious to be left to the police !"

From which it would appear that suspicion was not confined to Sergeant Daw.

Mr. Corbeck and Doctor Winchester, after a quick glance at each other, became at once on most friendly terms. The traveller professed his willingness to be of any assistance which he could, provided, he added, that it was anything about which he was free to speak. This was not very promising ; but Doctor Winchester began at once :

"I want you, if you will, to translate some hiero-glyphic for me."

"Certainly, with the greatest pleasure, so far as I can. For I may tell you that hieroglyphic writing is not quite mastered yet; though we are getting at it! We are getting at it! What is the inscription?"

"There are two," he answered. "One of them I shall bring here."

He went out, and returned in a minute with the mummy cat which he had that evening introduced to Silvio. The scholar took it; and, after a short examination, said:

"There is nothing especial in this. It is an appeal to Bast, the Lady of Bubastis, to give her good bread and milk in the Elysian Fields. There may be more inside; and if you will care to unroll it, I will do my best. I do not think, however, that there is anything special. From the method of wrapping I should say it is from Delta; and of a late period, when such mummy work was common and cheap. What is the other inscription you wish me to see?"

"The inscription on the mummy cat in Mr. Tre-lawny's room."

Mr. Corbeck's face fell. "No!" he said, "I can-not do that! I am, for the present at all events, practically bound to secrecy regarding any of the things in Mr. Trelawny's room."

Doctor Winchester's comment and my own were made at the same moment. I said only the one word "Checkmate!" from which I think he may have gathered that I guessed more of his idea and purpose than perhaps I had intentionally conveyed to him. He murmured:

"Practically bound to secrecy?"

Mr. Corbeck at once took up the challenge conveyed:

" Do not misunderstand me! I am not bound by any definite pledge of secrecy; but I am bound in honour to respect Mr. Trelawny's confidence, given to me, I may tell you, in a very large measure. Regarding many of the objects in his room he has a definite purpose in view; and it would not be either right or becoming for me, his trusted friend and confidant, to forestall that purpose. Mr. Trelawny, you may know—or rather you do not know or you would not have so construed my remark—is a scholar, a very great scholar. He has worked for years toward a certain end. For this he has spared no labour, no expense, no personal danger or self-denial. He is on the line of a result which will place him amongst the foremost discoverers or investigators of his age. And now, just at the time when any hour might bring him success, he is stricken down ! "

He stopped, seemingly overcome with emotion. After a time he recovered himself and went on :

" Again, do not misunderstand me as to another point. I have said that Mr. Trelawny has made much confidence with me; but I do not mean to lead you to believe that I know all his plans, or his aims or objects. I know the period which he has been studying; and the definite historical individual whose life he has been investigating, and whose records he has been following up one by one with infinite patience. But beyond this I know nothing. That he has some aim or object in the completion of this knowledge I am convinced. What it is I may guess; but I must say nothing. Please to remember, gentlemen, that I have voluntarily accepted the position of recipient of a partial confidence. I have respected that; and I must ask any of my friends to do the same."

He spoke with great dignity; and he grew, moment by moment, in the respect and esteem of both Doctor Winchester and myself. We understood that he had not done speaking; so we waited in silence till he continued:

"I have spoken this much, although I know well that even such a hint as either of you might gather from my words might jeopardise the success of his work. But I am convinced that you both wish to help him—and his daughter," he said this looking me fairly between the eyes, "to the best of your power, honestly and unselfishly. He is so stricken down, and the manner of it is so mysterious that I cannot but think that it is in some way a result of his own work. That he calculated on some set-back is manifest to us all. God knows! I am willing to do what I can, and to use any knowledge I have in his behalf. I arrived in England full of exultation at the thought that I had fulfilled the mission with which he had trusted me. I had got what he said were the last objects of his search; and I felt assured that he would now be able to begin the experiment of which he had often hinted to me. It is too dreadful that at just such a time such a calamity should have fallen on him. Doctor Winchester, you are a physician; and, if your face does not belie you, you are a clever and a bold one. Is there no way which you can devise to wake this man from his unnatural stupor?"

There was a pause; then the answer came slowly and deliberately:

"'There is no ordinary remedy that I know of. There might possibly be some extraordinary one. But there would be no use in trying to find it, except on one condition."

"And that?"

"Knowledge! I am completely ignorant of Egyptian matters, language, writing, history, secrets, medicines, poisons, occult powers—all that go to make up the mystery of that mysterious land. This disease, or condition, or whatever it may be called, from which Mr. Trelawny is suffering, is in some way connected with Egypt. I have had a suspicion of this from the first; and later it grew into a certainty, though without proof. What you have said to-night confirms my conjecture, and makes me believe that a proof is to be had. I do not think that you quite know all that has gone on in this house since the night of the attack—of the finding of Mr. Trelawny's body. Now I propose that we confide in you. If Mr. Ross agrees, I shall ask him to tell you. He is more skilled than I am in putting facts before other people. He can speak by his brief; and in this case he has the best of all briefs, the experience of his own eyes and ears, and the evidence that he has himself taken on the spot from participators in, or spectators of, what has happened. When you know all, you will, I hope, be in a position to judge as to whether you can best help Mr. Trelawny, and further his secret wishes, by your silence or your speech."

I nodded approval. Mr. Corbeck jumped up, and in his impulsive way held out a hand to each.

"Done!" he said. "I acknowledge the honour of your confidence; and on my part I pledge myself that if I find my duty to Mr. Trelawny's wishes will, in his own interest, allow my lips to open on his affairs, I shall speak so freely as I may."

Accordingly I began, and told him, as exactly as I could, everything that had happened from the moment of my waking at the knocking on the door in Jermyn Street. The only reservations I made were as to my own feeling toward Miss Trelawny and the matters of small import to the main subject which followed it; and my conversations with Sergeant Daw, which were in themselves private, and which would have demanded discretionary silence in any case. As I spoke, Mr. Corbeck followed with breathless interest. Sometimes he would stand up and pace about the room in uncontrollable excitement; and then recover himself suddenly, and sit down again. Sometimes he would be about to speak, but would, with an effort, restrain himself. I think the narration helped me to make up my own mind; for even as I talked, things seemed to appear in a clearer light. Things big and little, in relation of their importance to the case, fell into proper perspective. The story up to date became coherent, except as to its cause, which seemed a greater mystery than ever. This is the merit of entire, or collected, narrative. Isolated facts, doubts, suspicions, conjectures, give way to a homogeneity which is convincing.

That Mr. Corbeck was convinced was evident. He did not go through any process of explanation or limitation, but spoke right out at once to the point, and fearlessly, like a man :

" That settles me ! There is in activity some Force that needs special care. If we all go on working in the dark we shall get in one another's way, and by hampering each other, undo the good that any or each of us, working in different directions, might do. It seems to me that the first thing we have to accomplish is to get Mr. Trelawny waked out of that unnatural sleep. That he can be waked is apparent from the way the Nurse has recovered; though what additional harm may have been done to him in the time he has been lying in that room I suppose no one can tell. We must chance that, however. He *has* lain there, and whatever the effect might be, it is there now; and we have, and shall have, to deal with it as a fact. A day more or less won't hurt in the long-run. It is late now; and we shall probably have to-morrow a task before us that will require our energies fresh. You, Doctor, will want to get to your sleep; for I suppose you have other work as well as this to do to-morrow. As for you, Mr. Ross, I understand that you are to have a spell of watching in the sick-room to-night. I shall get you a book which will help to pass the time for you. I shall go and look for it in the library. I know where it was when I was here last; and I don't suppose Mr. Trelawny has used it since. He knew long ago all that was in it which was or might be of interest to him. But it will be necessary, or at least helpful, to understand other things which I shall tell you later. You will be able to tell Doctor Winchester all that would aid him. For I take it that our work will branch out pretty soon. We shall each have our own end to hold up; and it will take each of us all our time and understanding to get through his own tasks. It will not be necessary for you to read the whole book. All that will interest you—with regard to our matter I mean of course, for the whole book is interesting as a record of travel in a country then quite unknown—is the preface, and two or three chapters which I shall mark for you."

He shook hands warmly with Doctor Winchester who had stood up to go.

Whilst he was away I sat lonely, thinking. As I thought, the world around me seemed to be illimitably great. The only little spot in which I was interested seemed like a tiny speck in the midst of a wilderness. Without and around it were darkness and unknown danger, pressing in from every side. And the central figure in our little oasis was one of sweetness and beauty. A figure one could love ; could work for ; could die for . . . !

Mr. Corbeck came back in a very short time with the book ; he had found it at once in the spot where he had seen it three years before. Having placed in it several slips of paper, marking the places where I was to read, he put it into my hands, saying :

"That is what started Mr. Trelawny ; what started me when I read it ; and which will, I have no doubt, be to you an interesting beginning to a special study —whatever the end may be. If, indeed, any of us here may ever see the end."

At the door he paused and said :

"I want to take back one thing. That Detective is a good fellow. What you have told me of him puts him in a new light. The best proof of it is that I can go quietly to sleep to-night, and leave the lamps in his care !"

When he had gone I took the book with me, put on my respirator, and went to my spell of duty in the sick-room !

CHAPTER X

THE VALLEY OF THE SORCERER

I PLACED the book on the little table on which the shaded lamp rested, and moved the screen to one side. Thus I could have the light on my book; and by looking up, see the bed, and the Nurse, and the door. I cannot say that the conditions were enjoyable, or calculated to allow of that absorption in the subject which is advisable for effective study. However, I composed myself to the work as well as I could. The book was one which, on the very face of it, required special attention. It was a folio in Dutch, printed in Amsterdam in 1650. Some one had made a literal translation, writing generally the English word under the Dutch, so that the grammatical differences between the two tongues made even the reading of the translation a difficult matter. One had to dodge backward and forward among the words. This was in addition to the difficulty of deciphering a strange handwriting of two hundred years ago. I found, however, that after a short time I got into the habit of following in conventional English the Dutch construction; and, as I became more familiar with the writing, my task became easier.

At first the circumstances of the room, and the fear lest Miss Trelawny should return unexpectedly

and find me reading the book, disturbed me somewhat. For we had arranged amongst us, before
Doctor Winchester had gone home, that she was not
to be brought into the range of the coming investigation. We considered that there might be some shock
to a woman's mind in matters of apparent mystery ;
and further, that she, being Mr. Trelawny's daughter,
might be placed in a difficult position with him afterward if she took part in, or even had a personal knowledge of, the disregarding of his expressed wishes.
But when I remembered that she did not come on
nursing duty till two o'clock, the fear of interruption
passed away. I had still nearly three hours before
me. Nurse Kennedy sat in her chair by the bedside,
patient and alert. A clock ticked on the landing ;
other clocks in the house ticked ; the life of the city
without manifested itself in the distant hum, now and
again swelling into a roar as a breeze floating west-
ward took the concourse of sounds with it. But still
the dominant idea was of silence. The light on my
book, and the soothing fringe of green silk round the
shade intensified, whenever I looked up, the gloom of
the sick-room. With every line I read, this seemed to
grow deeper and deeper ; so that when my eyes came
back to the page the light seemed to dazzle me. I
stuck to my work, however, and presently began to
get sufficiently into the subject to become interested
in it.

The book was by one Nicholas van Huyn of Hoorn.
In the preface he told how, attracted by the work of
John Greaves of Merton College, *Pyramidographia*, he
himself visited Egypt, where he became so interested
in its wonders that he devoted some years of his life
to visiting strange places, and exploring the ruins of

many temples and tombs. He had come across many
variants of the story of the building of the Pyramids
as told by the Arabian historian, Ibn Abd Alhokin,
some of which he set down. These I did not stop to
read, but went on to the marked pages.

As soon as I began to read these, however, there
grew on me some sense of a disturbing influence.
Once or twice I looked to see if the Nurse had moved,
for there was a feeling as though some one were
near me. Nurse Kennedy sat in her place, as steady
and alert as ever; and I came back to my book again.

The narrative went on to tell how, after passing
for several days through the mountains to the east
of Aswân, the explorer came to a certain place. Here
I give his own words, simply putting the translation
into modern English :

"Toward evening we came to the entrance of a
narrow, deep valley, running east and west. I wished
to proceed through this; for the sun, now nearly
down on the horizon, showed a wide opening beyond
the narrowing of the cliffs. But the fellaheen absolutely refused to enter the valley at such a time,
alleging that they might be caught by the night before
they could emerge from the other end. At first
they would give no reason for their fear. They had
hitherto gone anywhere I wished, and at any time,
without demur. On being pressed, however, they said
that the place was the Valley of the Sorcerer, where
none might come in the night. On being asked to tell
of the Sorcerer, they refused, saying that there was
no name, and that they knew nothing. On the next
morning, however, when the sun was up and shining
down the valley, their fears had somewhat passed
away. Then they told me that a great Sorcerer in

ancient days—'millions of millions of years' was the
term they used—a King or a Queen, they could not
say which, was buried there. They could not give the
name, persisting to the last that there was no name;
and that anyone who should name it would waste
away in life so that at death nothing of him would
remain to be raised again in the Other World. In
passing through the valley they kept together in a
cluster, hurrying on in front of me. None dared to
remain behind. They gave, as their reason for so
proceeding, that the arms of the Sorcerer were long,
and that it was dangerous to be the last. The which
was of little comfort to me who of this necessity took
that honourable post. In the narrowest part of the
valley, on the south side, was a great cliff of rock,
rising sheer, of smooth and even surface. Hereon
were graven certain cabalistic signs, and many figures
of men and animals, fishes, reptiles and birds; suns
and stars; and many quaint symbols. Some of these
latter were disjointed limbs and features, such as arms
and legs, fingers, eyes, noses, ears, and lips. Mysterious symbols which will puzzle the Recording Angel
to interpret at the Judgment Day. The cliff faced
exactly north. There was something about it so
strange, and so different from the other carved rocks
which I had visited, that I called a halt and spent the
day in examining the rock front as well as I could
with my telescope. The Egyptians of my company
were terribly afraid, and used every kind of persuasion
to induce me to pass on. I stayed till late in the
afternoon, by which time I had failed to make out
aright the entry of any tomb, for I suspected that such
was the purpose of the sculpture of the rock. By
this time the men were rebellious; and I had to leave

the valley if I did not wish my whole retinue to
desert.   But I secretly made up my mind to discover
the tomb, and explore it.   To this end I went further
into the mountains, where I met with an Arab Sheik
who was willing to take service with me.   The Arabs
were not bound by the same superstitious fears as the
Egyptians; Sheik Abu Soma and his following were
willing to take a part in the explorations.

"When I returned to the valley with these Bedouins,
I made effort to climb the face of the rock, but failed,
it being of one impenetrable smoothness.   The stone,
generally flat and smooth by nature, had been chiselled
to completeness.   That there had been projecting
steps was manifest, for there remained, untouched by
the wondrous climate of that strange land, the marks
of saw and chisel and mallet where the steps had
been cut or broken away.

"Being thus baffled of winning the tomb from
below, and being unprovided with ladders to scale,
I found a way by much circuitous journeying to the
top of the cliff.   Thence I caused myself to be
lowered by ropes, till I had investigated that portion
of the rock face wherein I expected to find the
opening.   I found that there was an entrance, closed
however by a great stone slab.   This was cut in the
rock more than a hundred feet up, being two-thirds
the height of the cliff.   The hieroglyphic and cabalistic symbols cut in the rock were so managed as to
disguise it.   The cutting was deep, and was continued
through the rock and the portals of the doorway, and
through the great slab which formed the door itself.
This was fixed in place with such incredible exactness
that no stone chisel or cutting implement which I
had with me could find a lodgment in the interstices.

I used much force, however; and by many heavy strokes won a way into the tomb, for such I found it to be. The stone door having fallen into the entrance I passed over it into the tomb, noting as I went a long iron chain which hung coiled on a bracket close to the doorway.

"The tomb I found to be complete, after the manner of the finest Egyptian tombs, with chamber and shaft leading down to the corridor, ending in the Mummy Pit. It had the table of pictures, which seems some kind of record—whose meaning is now for ever lost—graven in a wondrous colour on a wondrous stone.

"All the walls of the chamber and the passage were carved with strange writings in the uncanny form mentioned. The huge stone coffin or sarcophagus in the deep pit was marvellously graven throughout with signs. The Arab chief and two others who ventured into the tomb with me, and who were evidently used to such grim explorations, managed to take the cover from the sarcophagus without breaking it. At which they wondered; for such good fortune, they said, did not usually attend such efforts. Indeed they seemed not over careful; and did handle the various furniture of the tomb with such little concern that, only for its great strength and thickness, even the coffin itself might have been injured. Which gave me much concern, for it was very beautifully wrought of rare stone, such as I had no knowledge of. Much I grieved that it were not possible to carry it away. But time and desert journeyings forbade such; I could only take with me such small matters as could be carried on the person.

"Within the sarcophagus was a body, manifestly
of a woman, swathed with many wrappings of linen,
as is usual with all mummies. From certain em-
broiderings thereon, I gathered that she was of high
rank. Across the breast was one hand, unwrapped.
In the mummies which I had seen, the arms and
hands are within the wrappings, and certain adornments of wood, shaped and painted to resemble arms
and hands, lie outside the enwrapped body.

"But this hand was strange to see, for it was the
real hand of her who lay enwrapped there ; the arm
projecting from the cerements being of flesh, seemingly made as like marble in the process of embalming.
Arm and hand were of dusky white, being of the hue
of ivory that hath lain long in air. The skin and the
nails were complete and whole, as though the body
had been placed for burial over night. I touched the
hand and moved it, the arm being something flexible
as a live arm ; though stiff with long disuse, as are
the arms of those faqueers which I have seen in
the Indees. There was, too, an added wonder that
on this ancient hand were no less than seven fingers,
the same all being fine and long, and of great beauty.
Sooth to say, it made me shudder and my flesh creep
to touch that hand that had lain there undisturbed
for so many thousands of years, and yet was like unto
living flesh. Underneath the hand, as though guarded
by it, lay a huge jewel of ruby ; a great stone of
wondrous bigness, for the ruby is in the main a
small jewel. This one was of wondrous colour,
being as of fine blood whereon the light shineth.
But its wonder lay not in its size or colour, though
these were, as I have said, of priceless rarity ; but
in that the light of it shone from seven stars, each

of seven points, as clearly as though the stars were
in reality there imprisoned. When that the hand
was lifted, the sight of that wondrous stone lying
there struck me with a shock almost to momentary
paralysis. I stood gazing on it, as did those with
me, as though it were that fabled head of the Gorgon
Medusa with the snakes in her hair, whose sight
struck into stone those who beheld. So strong was
the feeling that I wanted to hurry away from the
place. So, too, those with me; therefore, taking
this rare jewel, together with certain amulets of
strangeness and richness being wrought of jewel-
stones, I made haste to depart. I would have
remained longer, and made further research in the
wrappings of the mummy, but that I feared so to do.
For it came to me all at once that I was in a desert
place, with strange men who were with me because
they were not over-scrupulous. That we were in a
lone cavern of the dead, an hundred feet above the
ground, where none could find me were ill done to
me, nor would any ever seek. But in secret I determined that I would come again, though with more
secure following. Moreover, was I tempted to seek
further, as in examining the wrappings I saw many
things of strange import in that wondrous tomb;
including a casket of eccentric shape made of some
strange stone, which methought might have contained
other jewels, inasmuch as it had secure lodgment in
the great sarcophagus itself. There was in the tomb
also another coffer which, though of rare proportion
and adornment, was more simply shaped. It was
of ironstone of great thickness; but the cover was
lightly cemented down with what seemed gum and
Paris plaster, as though to insure that no air could

penetrate. The Arabs with me so insisted in its opening, thinking that from its thickness much treasure was stored therein, that I consented thereto. But their hope was a false one, as it proved. Within, closely packed, stood four jars finely wrought and carved with various adornments. Of these one was the head of a man, another of a dog, another of a jackal, and another of a hawk. I had before known that such burial urns as these were used to contain the entrails and other organs of the mummied dead ; but on opening these, for the fastening of wax, though complete, was thin, and yielded easily, we found that they held but oil. The Bedouins, spilling most of the oil in the process, groped with their hands in the jars lest treasure should have been there concealed. But their searching was of no avail ; no treasure was there. I was warned of my danger by seeing in the eyes of the Arabs certain covetous glances. Whereon, in order to hasten their departure, I wrought upon those fears of superstition which even in these callous men were apparent. The chief of the Bedouins ascended from the Pit to give the signal to those above to raise us ; and I, not caring to remain with the men whom I mistrusted, follo ed him immediately. The others did not come at o. ce ; from which I feared that they were rifling the tomb afresh on their own account. I refrained to speak of it, however, lest worse should befall. At last they came. One of them, who ascended first, in landing at the top of the cliff lost his foothold and fell below. He was instantly killed. The other followed, but in safety. The chief came next, and I came last. Before coming away I pulled into its place again, as well as I could, the slab of stone that covered the entrance to the tomb. I wished, if possible, to preserve it for my own examination should I come again.

"When we all stood on the hill above the cliff, the burning sun that was bright and full of glory was good to see after the darkness and strange mystery of the tomb. Even was I glad that the poor Arab who fell down the cliff and lay dead below, lay in the sunlight and not in that gloomy cavern. I would fain have gone with my companions to seek him and give him sepulture of some kind; but the Sheik made light of it, and sent two of his men to see to it whilst we went on our way.

"That night as we camped, one of the men only returned, saying that a lion of the desert had killed his companion after that they had buried the dead man in a deep sand without the valley, and had covered the spot where he lay with many great rocks, so that jackals or other preying beasts might not dig him up again as is their wont.

"Later, in the light of the fire round which the men sat or lay, I saw him exhibit to his fellows something white which they seemed to regard with special awe and reverence. So I drew near silently, and saw that it was none other than the white hand of the mummy which had lain protecting the Jewel in the great sarcophagus. I heard the Bedouin tell how he had found it on the body of him who had fallen from the cliff. There was no mistaking it, for there were the seven fingers which I had noted before. This man must have wrenched it off the dead body whilst his chief and I were otherwise engaged; and from the awe of the others I doubted not that he had hoped to use it as an Amulet, or charm. Whereas if powers it had, they were not for him who had taken it from the dead; since his death followed hard upon his theft. Already his Amulet had had an awesome baptism; for the wrist of the dead hand was stained with red as though it had been dipped in recent blood.

" That night I was in certain fear lest there should be some violence done to me; for if the poor dead hand was so valued as a charm, what must be the worth in such wise of the rare Jewel which it had guarded. Though only the chief knew of it, my doubt was perhaps even greater; for he could so order matters as to have me at his mercy when he would. I guarded myself, therefore, with wakefulness so well as I could, determined that at my earliest opportunity I should leave this party, and complete my journeying home, first to the Nile bank, and then down its course by boat to Alexandria; with other guides who knew not what strange matters I had with me.

" At last there came over me a disposition of sleep, so potent that I felt it would be resistless. Fearing attack, or that being searched in my sleep the Bedouin might find the Star Jewel which he had seen me place with others in my dress, I took it out unobserved and held it in my hand. It seemed to give back the light of the flickering fir and the light of the stars—for there was no moon—with equal fidelity; and I could note that on its reverse it was graven deeply with certain signs such as I had seen in the tomb. As I sank into the unconsciousness of sleep, the graven Star Jewel was hidden in the hollow of my clenched hand.

" I waked out of sleep with the light of the morning sun on my face. I sat up and looked around me.

The fire was out, and the camp was desolate; save
for one figure which lay prone close to me. It was
that of the Arab chief, who lay on his back, dead.
His face was almost black; and his eyes were open,
and staring horribly up at the sky, as though he saw
there some dreadful vision. He had evidently been
strangled; for on looking, I found on his throat the
red marks where fingers had pressed. There seemed
so many of these marks that I counted them. There
were seven; and all parallel, except the thumb mark,
as though made with one hand. This thrilled me as
I thought of the mummy hand with the seven fingers.

"Even there, in the open desert, it seemed as if
there could be enchantments!

"In my surprise, as I bent over him, I opened
my right hand, which up to now I had held shut
with the feeling, instinctive even in sleep, of keeping
safe that which it held. As I did so, the Star Jewel
held there fell out and struck the dead man on the
mouth. *Mirabile dictu* there came forth at once from
the dead mouth a great gush of blood, in which the
red jewel was for the moment lost. I turned the
dead man over to look for it, and found that he lay
with his right hand bent under him as though he
had fallen on it; and in it he held a great knife, keen
of point and edge, such as Arabs carry at the belt.
It may have been that he was about to murder me
when vengeance came on him, whether from man
or God, or the Gods of Old, I know not. Suffice it,
that when I found my Ruby Jewel, which shone up
as a living star from the mess of blood wherein it
lay, I paused not, but fled from the place. I journeyed
on alone through the hot desert, till, by God's grace,
I came upon an Arab tribe camping by a well, who

gave me salt. With them I rested till they had set me on my way.

"I know not what became of the mummy hand, or of those who had it. What strife, or suspicion, or disaster, or greed went with it I know not; but some such cause there must have been, since those who had it fled with it. It doubtless is used as a charm of potence by some desert tribe.

"At the earliest opportunity I made examination of the Star Ruby, as I wished to try to understand what was graven on it. The symbols—whose meaning, however, I could not understand—were as follows . . ."

Twice, whilst I had been reading this engrossing narrative, I had thought that I had seen across the page streaks of shade, which the weirdness of the subject had made to seem like the shadow of a hand. On the first of these occasions I found that the illusion came from the fringe of green silk around the lamp; but on the second I had looked up, and my eyes had lit on the mummy hand across the room on which the starlight was falling under the edge of the blind. It was of little wonder that I had connected it with such a narrative; for if my eyes told me truly, here, in this room with me, was the very hand of which the traveller Van Huyn had written. I looked over at the bed; and it comforted me to think that the Nurse still sat there, calm and wakeful. At such a time, with such surroundings, during such a narrative, it was well to have assurance of the presence of some living person.

I sat looking at the book on the table before me; and so many strange thoughts crowded on me that my mind began to whirl. It was almost as if th

light on the white fingers in front of me was beginning to have some hypnotic effect. All at once, all
thoughts seemed to stop; and for an instant the
world and time stood still.

There lay a real hand across the book! What was
there to so overcome me, as was the case? I knew
the hand that I saw on the book — and loved it.
Margaret Trelawny's hand was a joy to me to see—
to touch; and yet at that moment, coming after other
marvellous things, it had a strangely moving effect on
me. It was but momentary, however, and had passed
even before her voice had reached me.

"What disturbs you? What are you staring at the
book for? I thought for an instant that you must
have been overcome again!" I jumped up.

"I was reading," I said, "an old book from the
library." As I spoke I closed it and put it under
my arm. "I shall now put it back, as I understand
that your Father wishes all things, especially books,
kept in their proper places." My words were intentionally misleading; for I did not wish her to
know what I was reading, and thought it best not
to wake her curiosity by leaving the book about. I
went away, but not to the library; I left the book
in my room where I could get it when I had had
my sleep in the day. When I returned Nurse
Kennedy was ready to go to bed; so Miss Trelawny
watched with me in the room. I did not want any
book whilst she was present. We sat close together
and talked in a whisper whilst the moments flew by.
It was with surprise that I noted the edge of the
curtains changing from grey to yellow light. What
we talked of had nothing to do with the sick man,
except in so far that all which concerned his daughter

must ultimately concern him. But it had nothing to say to Egypt, or mummies, or the dead, or caves, or Bedouin chiefs. I could well take note in the growing light that Margaret's hand had not seven fingers, but five; for it lay in mine.

When Doctor Winchester arrived in the morning and had made his visit to his patient, he came to see me as I sat in the dining-room having a little meal—breakfast or supper, I hardly knew which it was—before I went to lie down. Mr. Corbeck came in at the same time; and we resumed our conversation where we had left it the night before. I told Mr. Corbeck that I had read the chapter about the find-ing of the tomb, and that I thought Doctor Winchester should read it, too. The latter said that, if he might, he would take it with him; he had that morning to make a railway journey to Ipswich, and would read it on the train. He said he would bring it back with him when he came again in the evening. I went up to my room to bring it down; but I could not find it anywhere. I had a distinct recollection of having left it on the little table beside my bed, when I had come up after Miss Trelawny's going on duty into the sick-room. It was very strange; for the book was not of a kind that any of the servants would be likely to take. I had to come back and explain to the others that I could not find it.

When Doctor Winchester had gone, Mr. Corbeck, who seemed to know the Dutchman's work by heart, talked the whole matter over with me. I told him that I was interrupted by a change of nurses, just as I had come to the description of the ring. He smiled as he said:

"So far as that is concerned, you need not be disappointed. Not in Van Huyn's time, nor for nearly two centuries later, could the meaning of that engraving have been understood. It was only when the work was taken up and followed by Young and Champollion, by Birch and Lepsius and Rosellini and Salvolini, by Mariette Bey and by Wallis Budge and Flinders Petrie and the other scholars of their times that great results ensued, and that the true meaning of hieroglyphic was known.

"Later, I shall explain to you, if Mr. Trelawny does not explain it himself, or if he does not forbid me to, what it means in that particular place. I think it will be better for you to know what followed Van Huyn's narrative; for with the description of the stone, and the account of his bringing it to Holland at the termination of his travels, the episode ends. Ends so far as his book is concerned. The chief thing about the book is that it sets others thinking — and acting. Amongst them were Mr. Trelawny and myself. Mr. Trelawny is a good linguist of the Orient, but he does not know Northern tongues. As for me I have a faculty for learning languages; and when I was pursuing my studies in Leyden I learned Dutch so that I might more easily make references in the library there. Thus it was, that at the very time when Mr. Trelawny, who, in making his great collection of works on Egypt, had, through a booksellers' catalogue, acquired this volume with the manuscript translation, was studying it, I was reading another copy, in original Dutch, in Leyden. We were both struck by the description of the lonely tomb in the rock; cut so high up as to be inaccessible to ordinary seekers: with all means of reaching it carefully obliterated; and yet with such an elaborate ornamentation of the smoothed surface of the cliff as Van Huyn has described. It also struck us both as an odd thing—for in the years between Van Huyn's time and our own the general knowledge of Egyptian curios and records has increased marvellously—that in the case of such a tomb, made in such a place, and which must have cost an immense sum of money, there was no seeming record or effigy to point out who lay within. Moreover, the very name of the place, "the Valley of the Sorcerer," had, in a prosaic age, attractions of its own. When we met, which we did through his seeking the assistance of other Egyptologists in his work, we talked over this as we did over many other things; and we determined to make search for the mysterious valley. Whilst we were waiting to start on the travel, for many things were required which Mr. Trelawny undertook to see to himself, I went to Holland to try if I could by any traces verify Van Huyn's narrative. I went straight to Hoorn, and set patiently to work to find the house of the traveller and his descendants, if any. I need not trouble you with details of my seeking—and finding. Hoorn is a place that has not changed much since Van Huyn's time, except that it has lost the place which it held amongst commercial cities. Its externals are such as they had been then; in such a sleepy old place a century or two does not count for much. I found the house, and discovered that none of the descendants were alive. I searched records; but only to one end—death and extinction. Then I set me to work to find what had become of his treasures; for that such a traveller must have had great treasures was apparent. I traced a good many to museums in Leyden, Utrecht, and Amsterdam; and some few to the private houses of rich collectors. At last, in the shop of an old watchmaker and jeweller at Hoorn, I found what he considered his chiefest treasure: a great ruby, carven like a scarab, with seven stars, and engraven with hieroglyphics. The old man did not know hieroglyphic character, and in his old-world, sleepy life, the philological discoveries of recent years had not reached him. He did not know anything of Van Huyn, except that such a person had been, and that his name was, during two centuries, venerated in the town as a great traveller. He valued the jewel as only a rare stone, spoiled in part by the cutting; and though he was at first loth to part with such an unique gem, he became amenable ultimately to commercial reason. I had a full purse, since I bought for Mr. Trelawny, who is, as I suppose you know, immensely wealthy. I was shortly on my way back to London, with the Star Ruby safe in my pocket-book; and in my heart a joy and exultation which knew no bounds.

"For here we were with proof of Van Huyn's wonderful story. The jewel was put in security in Mr. Trelawny's great safe; and we started out on our journey of exploration in full hope.

"Mr. Trelawny was, at the last, loth to leave his young wife whom he dearly loved; but she, who loved him equally, knew his longing to prosecute the search. So keeping to herself, as all good women do, all her anxieties—which in her case were special— she bade him follow out his bent.

CHAPTER XI

A QUEEN'S TOMB

" MR. TRELAWNY'S hope was at least as great as my
own. He is not so volatile a man as I am, prone to
ups and downs of hope and despair; but he has a
fixed purpose which crystallises hope into belief. At
times I had feared that there might have been two
such stones, or that the adventures of Van Huyn
were traveller's fictions, based on some ordinary
acquisition of the curio in Alexandria or Cairo, or
London or Amsterdam. But Mr. Trelawny never
faltered in his belief. We had many things to distract
our minds from belief or disbelief. This was soon
after Arabi Pasha, and Egypt was no safe place for
travellers, especially if they were English. But Mr.
Trelawny is a fearless man; and I almost come to
think at times that I am not a coward myself. We
got together a band of Arabs whom one or other of
us had known in former trips to the desert, and whom
we could trust; that is, we did not distrust them as
much as others. We were numerous enough to pro-
tect ourselves from chance marauding bands, and we
took with us large impedimenta. We had secured
the consent and passive co-operation of the officials
still friendly to Britain; in the acquiring of which
consent I need hardly say that Mr. Trelawny's riches

were of chief importance. We found our way in dhahabiyehs to Aswân; whence, having got some Arabs from the Sheik and having given our usual backsheesh, we set out on our journey through the desert.

"Well, after much wandering and trying every winding in the interminable jumble of hills, we came at last at nightfall on just such a valley as Van Huyn had described. A valley with high, steep cliffs; narrowing in the centre, and widening out to the eastern and western ends. At daylight we were opposite the cliff and could easily note the opening high up in the rock, and the hieroglyphic figures which were evidently intended originally to conceal it.

"But the signs which had baffled Van Huyn and those of his time—and later, were no secrets to us. The host of scholars who have given their brains and their lives to this work, had wrested open the mysterious prison-house of Egyptian language. On the hewn face of the rocky cliff we, who had learned the secrets, could read what the Theban priesthood had had there inscribed nearly fifty centuries before.

"For that the external inscription was the work of the priesthood—and a hostile priesthood at that—there could be no living doubt. The inscription on the rock, written in hieroglyphic, ran thus:

"'Hither the Gods come not at any summons. The "Nameless One" has insulted them and is for ever alone. Go not nigh, lest their vengeance wither you away!'

"The warning must have been a terribly potent one at the time it was written and for thousands of years afterwards; even when the language in which it was given had become a dead mystery to the people of the land. The tradition of such a terror lasts longer than its cause. Even in the symbols used there was an added significance of alliteration. 'For ever' is given in the hieroglyphics as 'millions of years.' This symbol was repeated nine times, in three groups of three; and after each group a symbol of the Upper World, the Under World, and the Sky. So that for this Lonely One there could be, through the vengeance of all the Gods, resurrection in neither the World of Sunlight, in the World of the Dead, or for the soul in the region of the Gods.

"Neither Mr. Trelawny nor I dared to tell any of our people what the writing meant. For though they did not believe in the religion whence the curse came, or in the Gods whose vengeance was threatened, yet they were so superstitious that they would probably, had they known of it, have thrown up the whole task and run away.

"Their ignorance, however, and our discretion preserved us. We made an encampment close at hand; but behind a jutting rock a little further along the valley, so that they might not have the inscription always before them. For even that traditional name of the place: 'The Valley of the Sorcerer,' had a fear for them; and for us through them. With the timber which we had brought, we made a ladder up the face of the rock. We hung a pulley on a beam fixed to project from the top of the cliff. We found the great slab of rock, which formed the door, placed clumsily in its place and secured by a few stones. Its own weight kept it in safe position. In order to enter, we had to push it in; and we passed over it. We found the great coil of chain which Van Huyn had described

fastened into the rock.   There were, however, abun-
dant evidences amid the wreckage of the great stone
door, which had revolved on iron hinges at top and
bottom, that ample provision had been originally
made for closing and fastening it from within.

"Mr. Trelawny and I went alone into the tomb.
We had brought plenty of lights with us; and we
fixed them as we went along. We wished to get a
complete survey at first, and then make examination
of all in detail. As we went on, we were filled with
ever-increasing wonder and delight. The tomb was
one of the most magnificent and beautiful which
either of us had ever seen. From the elaborate nature
of the sculpture and painting, and the perfection of
the workmanship, it was evident that the tomb was
prepared during the lifetime of her for whose resting-
place it was intended. The drawing of the hieroglyphic pictures was fine, and the colouring superb;
and in that high cavern, far away from even the damp
of the Nile-flood, all was as fresh as when the artists
had laid down their palettes. There was one thing
which we could not avoid seeing. That although the
cutting on the outside rock was the work of the
priesthood, the smoothing of the cliff face was probably a part of the tomb-builder's original design.
The symbolism of the painting and cutting within all
gave the same idea. The outer cavern, partly natural
and partly hewn, was regarded architecturally as only
an ante-chamber. At the end of it, so that it would
face the east, was a pillared portico, hewn out of the
solid rock. The pillars were massive and were seven-
sided, a thing which we had not come across in any
other tomb. Sculptured on the architrave was the
Boat of the Moon, containing Hathor, cow-headed

and bearing the disk and plumes, and the dog-headed Hapi, the God of the North. It was steered by Harpocrotes towards the north, represented by the Pole Star surrounded by Draco and Ursa Major. In the latter the stars that form what we call the ' Plough ' were cut larger than any of the other stars ; and were filled with gold so that, in the light of torches, they seemed to flame with a special significance. Passing within the portico, we found two of the architectural features of a rock tomb, the Chamber, or Chapel, and the Pit, all complete as Van Huyn had noticed, though in his day the names given to these parts by the Egyptians of old were unknown.

"The Stele, or record, which had its place low down on the western wall, was so remarkable that we examined it minutely, even before going on our way to find the mummy which was the object of our search. This Stele was a great slab of lapis lazuli, cut all over with hieroglyphic figures of small size and of much beauty. The cutting was filled in with some cement of exceeding fineness, and of the colour of pure vermilion. The inscription began :

"'Tera, Queen of the Egypts, daughter of Antef, Monarch of the North and the South.' 'Daughter of the Sun,' 'Queen of the Diadems.'

"It then set out, in full record, the history of her life and reign.

"The signs of sovereignty were given with a truly feminine profusion of adornment. The united Crowns of Upper and Lower Egypt were, in especial, cut with exquisite precision. It was new to us both to find the Hejet and the Desher—the White and the Red crowns of Upper and Lower Egypt—on the Stele of a queen ; for it was a rule, without excep-

tion in the records, that in ancient Egypt either
crown was worn only by a king; though they are
to be found on goddesses. Later on we found an
explanation, of which I shall say more presently.

"Such an inscription was in itself a matter so
startling as to arrest attention from anyone anywhere at any time; but you can have no conception
of the effect which it had upon us. Though our
eyes were not the first which had seen it, they were
the first which could see it with understanding since
first the slab of rock was fixed in the cliff opening
nearly five thousand years before. To us was given
to read this message from the dead. This message
of one who had warred against the Gods of Old, and
claimed to have controlled them at a time when the
hierarchy professed to be the only means of exciting
their fears or gaining their good will.

"The walls of the upper chamber of the Pit and
the sarcophagus Chamber were profusely inscribed;
all the inscriptions, except that on the Stele, being
coloured with bluish-green pigment. The effect when
seen sideways as the eye caught the green facets, was
that of an old, discoloured Indian turquoise.

"We descended the Pit by the aid of the tackle we
had brought with us. Trelawny went first. It was a
deep pit, more than seventy feet; but it had never
been filled up. The passage at the bottom sloped
up to the sarcophagus Chamber, and was longer than
is usually found. It had not been walled up.

"Within, we found a great sarcophagus of yellow
stone. But that I need not describe; you have seen
it in Mr. Trelawny's chamber. The cover of it lay
on the ground; it had not been cemented, and was
just as Van Huyn had described it. Needless to say,

we were excited as we looked within. There must, however, be one sense of disappointment. I could not help feeling how different must have been the sight which met the Dutch traveller's eyes when he looked within and found that white hand lying lifelike above the shrouding mummy cloths. It is true that a part of the arm was there, white and ivory like.

"But there was a thrill to us which came not to Van Huyn!

"The end of the wrist was covered with dried blood! It was as though the body had bled after death! The jagged ends of the broken wrist were rough with the clotted blood; through this the white bone, sticking out, looked like the matrix of opal. The blood had streamed down and stained the brown wrappings as with rust. Here, then, was full confirmation of the narrative. With such evidence of the narrator's truth before us, we could not doubt the other matters which he had told, such as the blood on the mummy hand, or marks of the seven fingers on the throat of the strangled Sheik.

"I shall not trouble you with details of all we saw, or how we learned all we knew. Part of it was from knowledge common to scholars; part we read on the Stele in the tomb, and in the sculptures and hieroglyphic paintings on the walls.

"Queen Tera was of the Eleventh, or Theban Dynasty of Egyptian Kings which held sway between twenty-ninth and twenty-fifth centuries before Christ. She succeeded as the only child of her father, Antef. She must have been a girl of extraordinary character as well as ability, for she was but a young girl when her father died. Her youth and sex encouraged the

ambitious priesthood, which had then achieved immense power. By their wealth and numbers and
learning they dominated all Egypt, more especially
the Upper portion. They were then secretly ready
to make an effort for the achievement of their bold
and long-considered design, that of transferring the
governing power from a Kingship to a Hierarchy.
But King Antef had suspected some such movement,
and had taken the precaution of securing to his
daughter the allegiance of the army. He had also had
her taught statecraft, and had even made her learned
in the lore of the very priests themselves. He had
used those of one cult against the other ; each being
hopeful of some present gain on its own part by the
influence of the King, or of some ultimate gain from
its own influence over his daughter. Thus, the
Princess had been brought up amongst scribes, and
was herself no mean artist. Many of these things
were told on the walls in picture or in hieroglyphic
writing of great beauty ; and we came to the conclusion that not a few of them had been done by
the Princess herself. It was not without cause that
she was inscribed on the Stele as 'Protector of the
Arts.'

"But the King had gone to further lengths, and had
had his daughter taught magic, by which she had
power over Sleep and Will. This was real magic—
'black' magic ; not the magic of the temples, which,
I may explain, was of the harmless or 'white' order,
and was intended to impress rather than to effect.
She had been an apt pupil ; and had gone further
than her teachers. Her power and her resources had
given her great opportunities, of which she had availed
herself to the full. She had won secrets from nature

in strange ways; and had even gone to the length of
going down into the tomb herself, having been swathed
and coffined and left as dead for a whole month. The
priests had tried to make out that the real Princess
Tera had died in the experiment, and that another
girl had been substituted; but she had conclusively
proved their error. All this was told in pictures of
great merit. It was probably in her time that the
impulse was given in the restoring the artistic great-
ness of the Fourth Dynasty which had found its perfection in the days of Chufu.

" In the Chamber of the sarcophagus were pictures
and writings to show that she had achieved victory
over Sleep. Indeed, there was everywhere a symbolism, wonderful even in a land and an age of
symbolism. Prominence was given to the fact that
she, though a Queen, claimed all the privileges of
kingship and masculinity. In one place she was
pictured in man's dress, and wearing the White and
Red Crowns. In the following picture she was in
female dress, but still wearing the Crowns of Upper
and Lower Egypt, while the discarded male raiment
lay at her feet. In every picture where hope, or aim,
or resurrection was expressed there was the added
symbol of the North; and in many places—always
in representations of important events, past, present,
or future—was a grouping of the stars of the Plough.
She evidently regarded this constellation as in some
way peculiarly associated with herself.

" Perhaps the most remarkable statement in the
records, both on the Stele and in the mural writings,
was that Queen Tera had power to compel the Gods.
This, by the way, was not an isolated belief in
Egyptian history; but was different in its cause. She

had engraved on a ruby, carved like a scarab, and having seven stars of seven points, Master Words to compel all the Gods, both of the Upper and the Under Worlds.

"In the statement it was plainly set forth that the hatred of the priests was, she knew, stored up for her, and that they would after her death try to suppress her name. This was a terrible revenge, I may tell you, in Egyptian mythology ; for without a name no one can after death be introduced to the Gods, or have prayers said for him. Therefore, she had intended her resurrection to be after long time and in a more northern land, under the constellation whose seven stars had ruled her birth. To this end, her hand was to be in the air—'unwrapped'—and in it the Jewel of Seven Stars, so that wherever was air she might move even as her Ka could move! This, after thinking it over, Mr. Trelawny and I agreed meant that her body could become astral at command, and so move, particle by particle, and become whole again when and where required. Then there was a piece of writing in which allusion was made to a chest or casket in which were contained all the Gods, and Will, and Sleep, the two latter being personified by symbols. The box was mentioned as with seven sides. It was not much of a surprise to us when, underneath the feet of the mummy, we found the seven-sided casket, which you have also seen in Mr. Trelawny's room. On the underneath part of the wrapping-linen of the left foot was painted, in the same vermilion colour as that used in the Stele, the hieroglyphic symbol for much water :〰, and underneath the right foot the symbol of the earth : Ⅱ We made out the symbolism to be that her body, immortal and transferable at will, ruled both the land and water, air and fire—the latter being exemplified by the light of the Jewel Stone, and further by the flint and iron which lay outside the mummy wrappings.

"As we lifted the casket from the sarcophagus, we noticed on its sides the strange protuberances which you have already seen; but we were unable at the time to account for them. There were a few amulets in the sarcophagus, but none of any special worth or significance. We took it that if there were such, they were within the wrappings; or more probably in the strange casket underneath the mummy's feet. This, however, we could not open. There were signs of there being a cover; certainly the upper portion and the lower were each in one piece. The fine line, a little way from the top, appeared to be where the cover was fixed; but it was made with such exquisite fineness and finish that the joining could hardly be seen. Certainly the top could not be moved. We took it, that it was in some way fastened from within. I tell you all this in order that you may understand things with which you may be in contact later. You must suspend your judgment entirely. Such strange things have happened regarding this mummy and all around it, that there is a necessity for new belief somewhere. It is absolutely impossible to reconcile certain things which have happened with the ordinary currents of life or knowledge.

"We stayed around the Valley of the Sorcerer, till we had copied roughly all the drawings and writings on the walls, ceiling, and floor. We took with us the Stele of lapis lazuli, whose graven record was coloured with vermilion pigment. We took the sarcophagus and the mummy; the stone chest with the alabaster jars ; the tables of bloodstone and alabaster and onyx and carnelian ; and the ivory pillow whose arch rested on 'buckles,' round each of which was twisted an uræus wrought in gold. We took all the articles which lay in the Chapel, and the Mummy Pit ; the wooden boats with crews and the ushaptiu figures, and the symbolic amulets.

"When coming away we took down the ladders, and at a distance buried them in the sand under a cliff, which we noted so that if necessary we might find them again. Then with our heavy baggage, we set out on our laborious journey back to the Nile. It was no easy task, I tell you, to bring the case with that great sarcophagus over the desert. We had a rough cart and sufficient men to draw it ; but the progress seemed terribly slow, for we were anxious to get our treasures into a place of safety. The night was an anxious time with us, for we feared attack from some marauding band. But more still we feared some of those with us. They were, after all, but predatory, unscrupulous men ; and we had with us a considerable bulk of precious things. They, or at least the dangerous ones amongst them, did not know why it was so precious ; they took it for granted that it was material treasure of some kind that we carried. We had taken the mummy from the sarcophagus, and packed it for safety of travel in a separate case. During the first night two attempts were made to steal things from the cart ; and two men were found dead in the morning.

"On the second night there came on a violent storm, one of those terrible simoons of the desert which makes one feel his helplessness. We were overwhelmed with the drifting sand. Some of our Bedouins had fled before the storm, hoping to find shelter; the rest of us, wrapped in our bournous, endured with what patience we could. In the morning, when the storm had passed, we recovered from under the piles of sand what we could of our impedimenta. We found the case in which the mummy had been packed all broken, but the mummy itself could nowhere be found. We searched everywhere around, and dug up the sand which had piled around us; but in vain. We did not know what to do, for Trelawny had his heart set on taking home that mummy. We waited a whole day in hopes that the Bedouins, who had fled, would return; we had a blind hope that they might have in some way removed the mummy from the cart, and would restore it. That night, just before dawn, Mr. Trelawny woke me up and whispered in my ear:

"'We must go back to the tomb in the Valley of the Sorcerer. Show no hesitation in the morning when I give the orders! If you ask any questions as to where we are going it will create suspicion, and will defeat our purpose.'

"'All right!' I answered. 'But why shall we go there?' His answer seemed to thrill through me as though it had struck some chord ready tuned within:

"'We shall find the mummy there! I am sure of it!' Then anticipating doubt or argument he added:

"'Wait, and you shall see!' and he sank back into his blanket again.

"The Arabs were surprised when we retraced our steps; and some of them were not satisfied. There was a good deal of friction, and there were several desertions; so that it was with a diminished following that we took our way eastward again. At first the Sheik did not manifest any curiosity as to our definite destination; but when it became apparent that we were again making for the Valley of the Sorcerer, he too showed concern. This grew as we drew near; till finally at the entrance of the valley he halted and refused to go further. He said he would await our return if we chose to go on alone. That he would wait three days; but if by that time we had not returned he would leave. No offer of money would tempt him to depart from this resolution. The only concession he would make was that he would find the ladders and bring them near the cliff. This he did; and then, with the rest of the troop, he went back to wait at the entrance of the valley.

" Mr. Trelawny and I took ropes and torches, and again ascended to the tomb. It was evident that some-one had been there in our absence, for the stone slab which protected the entrance to the tomb was lying flat inside, and a rope was dangling from the cliff summit. Within, there was another rope hanging into the shaft of the Mummy Pit. We looked at each other; but neither said a word. We fixed our own rope, and as arranged Trelawny descended first, I following at once. It was not till we stood together at the foot of the shaft that the thought flashed across me that we might be in some sort of a trap; that some-one might descend the rope from the cliff, and by cutting the rope by which we had lowered ourselves into the Pit, bury us there alive. The thought was horrifying; but it was too late to do anything. I remained silent. We both had torches, so that there was ample light as we passed through the passage and entered the Chamber where the sarcophagus had stood. The first thing noticeable was the emptiness of the place. Despite all its magnificent adornment, the tomb was made a desolation by the absence of the great sarcophagus, to hold which it was hewn in the rock; of the chest with the alabaster jars; of the tables which had held the implements and food for the use of the dead, and the ushaptiu figures.

"It was made more infinitely desolate still by the shrouded figure of the mummy of Queen Tera which lay on the floor where the great sarcophagus had stood! Beside it lay, in the strange contorted attitudes of violent death, three of the Arabs who had deserted from our party. Their faces were black, and their hands and necks were smeared with blood which had burst from mouth and nose and eyes.

"On the throat of each were the marks, now blackening, of a hand of seven fingers.

"Trelawny and I drew close, and clutched each other in awe and fear as we looked.

"For, most wonderful of all, across the breast of the mummied Queen lay a hand of seven fingers, ivory white, the wrist only showing a scar like a jagged red line, from which seemed to depend drops of blood.

CHAPTER XII

THE MAGIC COFFER

"WHEN we recovered our amazement, which seemed to last unduly long, we did not lose any time carrying the mummy through the passage, and hoisting it up the Pit shaft. I went first, to receive it at the top. As I looked down, I saw Mr. Trelawny lift the severed hand and put it in his breast, manifestly to save it from being injured or lost. We left the dead Arabs where they lay. With our ropes we lowered our precious burden to the ground; and then took it to the entrance of the valley where our escort was to wait. To our astonishment we found them on the move. When we remonstrated with the Sheik, he answered that he had fulfilled his contract to the letter; he had waited the three days as arranged. I thought that he was lying to cover up his base intention of deserting us; and I found when we compared notes that Trelawny had the same suspicion. It was not till we arrived at Cairo that we found he was correct. It was the 3rd of November 1884 when we entered the Mummy Pit for the second time; we had reason to remember the date.

"We had lost three whole days of our reckoning —out of our lives—whilst we had stood wondering in that chamber of the dead. Was it strange, then, that we had a superstitious feeling with regard to the dead Queen Tera and all belonging to her ? Is it any wonder that it rests with us now, with a bewildering sense of some power outside ourselves or our comprehension ? Will it be any wonder if it go down to the grave with us at the appointed time ? If, indeed, there be any graves for us who have robbed the grave!" He was silent for quite a minute before he went on :

"We got to Cairo all right, and from there to Alexandria, where we were to take ship by the Messagerie service to Marseilles, and go thence by express to London. But

> ' The best-laid schemes o' mice and men
>   Gang aft agley.'

At Alexandria, Trelawny found waiting a cable stating that Mrs. Trelawny had died in giving birth to a daughter.

"Her stricken husband hurried off at once by the Orient Express ; and I had to bring the treasures alone to the desolate house. I got to London all safe ; there seemed to be some special good fortune to our journey. When I got to this house, the funeral had long been over. The child had been put out to nurse, and Mr. Trelawny had so far recovered from the shock of his loss that he had set himself to take up again the broken threads of his life and his work. That he had had a shock, and a bad one, was apparent. The sudden grey in his black hair was proof enough in itself ; but in addition, the strong cast of his features had become set and stern. Since he received that cable in the shipping office at Alexandria I have never seen a happy smile on his face.

"Work is the best thing in such a case; and to his work he devoted himself heart and soul. The strange tragedy of his loss and gain—for the child was born after the mother's death—took place during the time that we stood in that trance in the Mummy Pit of Queen Tera. It seemed to have become in some way associated with his Egyptian studies, and more especially with the mysteries connected with the Queen. He told me very little about his daughter; but that two forces struggled in his mind regarding her was apparent. I could see that he loved, almost idolised her. Yet he could never forget that her birth had cost her mother's life. Also, there was something whose existence seemed to wring his father's heart, though he would never tell me what it was. Again, he once said in a moment of relaxation of his purpose of silence:

"'She is unlike her mother; but in both feature and colour she has a marvellous resemblance to the pictures of Queen Tera.'

"He said that he had sent her away to people who would care for her as he could not; and that till she became a woman she should have all the simple pleasures that a young girl might have, and that were best for her. I would often have talked with him about her; but he would never say much. Once he said to me: 'There are reasons why I should not speak more than is necessary. Some day you will know—and understand!' I respected his reticence; and beyond asking after her on my return after a journey, I have never spoken of her again. I had never seen her till I did so in your presence.

"Well, when the treasures which we had—ah!— taken from the tomb had been brought here, Mr.

Trelawny arranged their disposition himself. The mummy, all except the severed hand, he placed in the great ironstone sarcophagus in the hall. This was wrought for the Theban High Priest Uni, and is, as you may have remarked, all inscribed with wonderful invocations to the old Gods of Egypt. The rest of the things from the tomb he disposed about his own room, as you have seen. Amongst them he placed, for special reasons of his own, the mummy hand. I think he regards this as the most sacred of his possessions, with perhaps one exception. That is the carven ruby which he calls the 'Jewel of Seven Stars,' which he keeps in that great safe which is locked and guarded by various devices, as you know.

"I dare say you find this tedious; but I have had to explain it, so that you should understand all up to the present. It was a long time after my return with the mummy of Queen Tera when Mr. Trelawny re-opened the subject with me. He had been several times to Egypt, sometimes with me and sometimes alone; and I had been several trips, on my own account or for him. But in all that time, nearly sixteen years, he never mentioned the subject, unless when some pressing occasion suggested, if it did not necessitate, a reference.

"One morning early he sent for me in a hurry; I was then studying in the British Museum, and had rooms in Hart Street. When I came, he was all on fire with excitement. I had not seen him in such a glow since before the news of his wife's death. He took me at once into his room. The window blinds were down and the shutters closed; not a ray of daylight came in. The ordinary lights in the room were not lit, but there were a lot of powerful electric lamps, fifty candle-power at least, arranged on one side of the room. The little bloodstone table on which the heptagonal coffer stands was drawn to the centre of the room. The coffer looked exquisite in the glare of light which shone on it. It actually seemed to glow as if lit in some way from within.

"'What do you think of it?' he asked.

"'It is like a jewel,' I answered. 'You may well call it the "Sorcerer's Magic Coffer," if it often looks like that. It almost seems to be alive.'

"'Do you know why it seems so?'

"'From the glare of the light, I suppose?'

"'Light of course,' he answered, 'but it is rather the disposition of light.' As he spoke he turned up the ordinary lights of the room and switched off the special ones. The effect on the stone box was surprising; in a second it lost all its glowing effect. It was still a very beautiful stone, as always; but it was stone and no more.

"'Do you notice anything in the arrangement of the lamps?' he asked.

"'No!'

"'They were in the shape of the stars in the Plough, as the stars are in the ruby!' The statement came to me with a certain sense of conviction. I do not know why, except that there had been so many mysterious associations with the mummy and all belonging to it that any new one seemed enlightening. I listened as Trelawny went on to explain:

"'For sixteen years I have never ceased to think of that adventure, or to try to find a clue to the mysteries which came before us; but never until last night did I seem to find a solution. I think I must have dreamed of it, for I woke all on fire about it.

I jumped out of bed with a determination of doing
something, before I quite knew what it was that I
wished to do. Then, all at once, the purpose was
clear before me. There were allusions in the writing
on the walls of the tomb to the seven stars of the
Great Bear that go to make up the Plough; and the
North was again and again emphasized. The same
symbols were repeated with regard to the " Magic
Box" as we called it. We had already noticed those
peculiar translucent spaces in the stone of the box.
You remember the hieroglyphic writing had told that
the jewel came from the heart of an aerolite, and that
the coffer was cut from it also. It might be, I thought,
that the light of the seven stars, shining in the right
direction, might have some effect on the box, or something within it. I raised the blind and looked out.
The Plough was high in the heavens, and both its
stars and the Pole Star were straight opposite the
window. I pulled the table with the coffer out into
the light, and shifted it until the translucent patches
were in the direction of the stars. Instantly the
box began to glow, as you saw it under the lamps,
though but slightly. I waited and waited; but the
sky clouded over, and the light died away. So I got
wires and lamps—you know how often I use them in
experiments—and tried the effect of electric light. It
took me some time to get the lamps properly placed,
so that they would correspond to the parts of the
stone, but the moment I got them right the whole
thing began to glow as you have seen it.

"'I could get no further, however. There was evidently something wanting. All at once it came to me
that if light could have some effect there should be in
the tomb some means of producing light; for there

could not be starlight in the Mummy Pit in the cavern.
Then the whole thing seemed to become clear.   On
the bloodstone table, which has a hollow carved in its
top, into which the bottom of the coffer fits, I laid the
Magic Coffer ; and I at once saw that the odd protuberances so carefully wrought in the substance of
the stone corresponded in a way to the stars in the
constellation.   These, then, were to hold lights.

"'*Eureka!*' I cried. 'All we want now is the lamps.'
I tried placing the electric lights on, or close to, the
protuberances.   But the glow never came to the stone.
So the conviction grew on me that there were special
lamps made for the purpose.   If we could find them,
a step on the road to solving the mystery should be
gained.

"'But what about the lamps ?' I asked. 'Where
are they ?   When are we to discover them ?   How
are we to know them if we do find them ?   What——'

" He stopped me at once :

"'One thing at a time!' he said quietly. 'Your
first question contains all the rest.   Where are these
lamps ?   I shall tell you : In the tomb !'

"'In the tomb!' I repeated in surprise.   'Why
you and I searched the place ourselves from end to
end ; and there was not a sign of a lamp.   Not a
sign of anything remaining when we came away
the first time ; or on the second, except the bodies
of the Arabs.'

" Whilst I was speaking, he had uncoiled some large
sheets of paper which he had brought in his hand
from his own room.   These he spread out on the
great table, keeping their edges down with books and
weights.   I knew them at a glance ; they were the
careful copies which he had made of our first tran-

scripts from the writing in the tomb. When he had all ready, he turned to me and said slowly :

"' Do you remember wondering, when we examined the tomb, at the lack of one thing which is usually found in such a tomb ?'

"' Yes! There was no serdâb.'

"The Serdâb, I may perhaps explain," said Mr. Corbeck to me, "is a sort of niche built or hewn in the wall of a tomb. Those which have as yet been examined bear no inscriptions, and contain only effigies of the dead for whom the tomb was made." Then he went on with his narrative :

"Trelawny, when he saw that I had caught his meaning, went on speaking with something of his old enthusiasm :

"' I have come to the conclusion that there must be a serdâb—a secret one. We were dull not to have thought of it before. We might have known that the maker of such a tomb—a woman, who had shown in other ways such a sense of beauty and completeness, and who had finished every detail with a feminine richness of elaboration—would not have neglected such an architectural feature. Even if it had not its own special significance in ritual, she would have had it as an adornment. Others had had it, and she liked her own work to be complete. Depend upon it, there was—there is— a serdâb; and that in it, when it is discovered, we shall find the lamps. Of course, had we known then what we now know or at all events surmise, that there were lamps, we might have suspected some hidden spot, some caçhet. I am going to ask you to go out to Egypt again ; to seek the tomb ; to find the serdâb; and to bring back the lamps !'

"'And if I find there is no serdâb; or if discovering it I find no lamps in it, what then?' He smiled grimly with that saturnine smile of his, so rarely seen for years past, as he spoke slowly:

"'Then you will have to hustle till you find them!'

"'Good!' I said. He pointed to one of the sheets.

"'Here are the transcripts from the Chapel at the south and the east. I have been looking over the writings again; and I find that in seven places round this corner are the symbols of the constellation which we call the Plough, which Queen Tera held to rule her birth and her destiny. I have examined them carefully, and I notice that they are all representations of the grouping of the stars, as the constellation appears in different parts of the heavens. They are all astronomically correct; and as in the real sky the Pointers indicate the Pole Star, so these all point to one spot in the wall where usually the serdâb is to be found!'

"'Bravo!' I shouted, for such a piece of reasoning demanded applause. He seemed pleased as he went on:

"'When you are in the tomb, examine this spot. There is probably some spring or mechanical contrivance for opening the receptacle. What it may be, there is no use guessing. You will know what best to do, when you are on the spot.'

"I started the next week for Egypt; and never rested till I stood again in the tomb. I had found some of our old following; and was fairly well provided with help. The country was now in a condition very different to that in which it had been sixteen years before; there was no need for troops or armed men.

" I climbed the rock face alone. There was no difficulty, for in that fine climate the woodwork of the ladder was still dependable. It was easy to see that in the years that had elapsed there had been other visitors to the tomb ; and my heart sank within me when I thought that some of them might by chance have come across the secret place. It would be a bitter discovery indeed to find that they had forestalled me; and that my journey had been in vain.

" The bitterness was realised when I lit my torches, and passed between the seven-sided columns to the Chapel of the tomb.

" There, in the very spot where I had expected to find it, was the opening of a serdâb. And the serdâb was empty.

" But the Chapel was not empty; for the dried-up body of a man in Arab dress lay close under the opening, as though he had been stricken down. I examined all round the walls to see if Trelawny's surmise was correct ; and I found that in all the positions of the stars as given, the Pointers of the Plough indicated a spot to the left hand, or south side, of the opening of the serdâb, where was a single star in gold.

" I pressed this, and it gave way. The stone which had marked the front of the serdâb, and which lay back against the wall within, moved slightly. On further examining the other side of the opening, I found a similar spot, indicated by other represen-tations of the constellation ; but this was itself a figure of the seven stars, and each was wrought in burnished gold. I pressed each star in turn ; but without result. Then it struck me that if the opening spring was on the left, this on the right might have been intended for the simultaneous pressure of all the stars by one hand of seven fingers. By using both my hands, I managed to effect this.

"With a loud click, a metal figure seemed to dart from close to the opening of the serdâb; the stone slowly swung back to its place, and shut with a click. The glimpse which I had of the descending figure appalled me for the moment. It was like that grim guardian which, according to the Arabian historian Ibn Abd Alhokin, the builder of the Pyramids, King Saurid Ibn Salhouk placed in the Western Pyramid to defend its treasure: 'A marble figure, upright, with lance in hand; with on his head a serpent wreathed. When any approached, the serpent would bite him on one side, and twining about his throat and killing him, would return again to his place.'

"I knew well that such a figure was not wrought to pleasantry; and that to brave it was no child's play. The dead Arab at my feet was proof of what could be done! So I examined again along the wall; and found here and there chippings as if someone had been tapping with a heavy hammer. This then had been what happened: The grave-robber more expert at his work than we had been, and suspecting the presence of a hidden serdâb, had made essay to find it. He had struck the spring by chance; had released the avenging 'Treasurer,' as the Arabian writer designated him. The issue spoke for itself. I got a piece of wood, and, standing at a safe distance, pressed with the end of it upon the star.

"Instantly the stone flew back. The hidden figure within darted forward and thrust out its lance. Then it rose up and disappeared. I thought I might now safely press on the seven stars; and did so. Again the stone rolled back; and the 'Treasurer' flashed by to his hidden lair.

"I repeated both experiments several times; with always the same result. I should have liked to examine the mechanism of that figure of such malignant mobility; but it was not possible without such tools as could not easily be had. It might be necessary to cut into a whole section of the rock. Some day I hope to go back, properly equipped, and attempt it.

"Perhaps you do not know that the entrance to a serdâb is almost always very narrow; sometimes a hand can hardly be inserted. Two things I learned from this serdâb. The first was that the lamps, if lamps at all there had been, could not have been of large size; and secondly, that they would be in some way associated with Hathor, whose symbol, the hawk in a square with the right top corner forming a smaller square, was cut in relief on the wall within, and coloured the bright vermilion which we had found on the Stele. Hathor is the goddess who in Egyptian mythology answers to Venus of the Greeks, in as far as she is the presiding deity of beauty and pleasure. In the Egyptian mythology, however, each God has many forms; and in some aspects Hathor has to do with the idea of resurrection. There are seven forms or variants of the Goddess; why should not these correspond in some way to the seven lamps! That there had been such lamps, I was convinced. The first grave-robber had met his death; the second had found the contents of the serdâb. The first attempt had been made years since; the state of the body proved this. I had no clue to the second attempt. It might have been long ago ; or it might have been recently.   If, however, others had been to the tomb, it was probable that the lamps had been taken long ago.   Well ! all the more difficult would be my search; for undertaken it must be !

"That was nearly three years ago ; and for all that time I have been like the man in the Arabian Nights, seeking old lamps, not for new, but for cash.   I dared not say what I was looking for, or attempt to give any description ; for such would have defeated my purpose. But I had in my own mind at the start a vague idea of what I must find.   In process of time this grew more and more clear ; till at last I almost overshot my mark by searching for something which might have been wrong.

"The disappointments I suffered, and the wild-goose chases I made, would fill a volume ; but I persevered.   At last, not two months ago, I was shown by an old dealer in Mossul one lamp such as I had looked for.   I had been tracing it for nearly a year, always suffering disappointment, but always buoyed up to further endeavour by a growing hope that I was on the track.

"I do not know how I restrained myself when I realised that, at last, I was at least close to success.   I was skilled, however, in the finesse of Eastern trade ; and the Jew-Arab-Portugee trader met his match.   I wanted to see all his stock before buying ; and one by one he produced, amongst masses of rubbish, seven different lamps.   Each of them had a distinguishing mark ; and each and all was some form of the symbol of Hathor.   I think I shook the imperturbability of my swarthy friend by the magnitude of my purchases ; for in order to prevent him guessing what form of goods I sought, I nearly cleared out his shop. At the end he nearly wept, and said I had ruined him ; for now he had nothing to sell. He would have torn his hair had he known what price I should ultimately have given for some of his stock, that perhaps he valued least.

" I parted with most of my merchandise at normal price as I hurried home. I did not dare to give it away, or even lose it, lest I should incur suspicion. My burden was far too precious to be risked by any foolishness now. I got on as fast as it is possible to travel in such countries ; and arrived in London with only the lamps and certain portable curios and papyri which I had picked up on my travels.

" Now, Mr. Ross, you know all I know ; and I leave it to your discretion how much, if any of it, you will tell Miss Trelawny."

As he finished a clear young voice said behind us :

" What about Miss Trelawny ?   She is here ! "

We turned, startled ; and looked at each other inquiringly.   Miss Trelawny stood in the doorway. We did not know how long she had been present, or how much she had heard.

CHAPTER XIII

AWAKING FROM THE TRANCE

THE first unexpected words may always startle a hearer; but when the shock is over, the listener's reason has asserted itself, and he can judge of the manner, as well as of the matter, of speech. Thus it was on this occasion. With intelligence now alert, I could not doubt of the simple sincerity of Margaret's next question.

"What have you two men been talking about all this time, Mr. Ross? I suppose, Mr. Corbeck has been telling you all his adventures in finding the lamps. I hope you will tell me too, some day, Mr. Corbeck; but that must not be till my poor Father is better. He would like, I am sure, to tell me all about these things himself; or to be present when I heard them." She glanced sharply from one to the other. "Oh, that was what you were saying as I came in? All right! I shall wait; but I hope it won't be long. The continuance of Father's condition is, I feel, breaking me down. A little while ago I felt that my nerves were giving out; so I determined to go out for a walk in the Park. I am sure it will do me good. I want you, if you will, Mr. Ross, to be with Father whilst I am away. I shall feel secure then."

I rose with alacrity, rejoicing that the poor girl

was going out, even for half an hour. She was looking terribly wearied and haggard; and the sight of her pale cheeks made my heart ache. I went to the sick-room; and sat down in my usual place. Mrs. Grant was then on duty; we had not found it necessary to have more than one person in the room during the day. When I came in, she took occasion to go about some household duty. The blinds were up, but the north aspect of the room softened the hot glare of the sunlight without.

I sat for a long time thinking over all that Mr. Corbeck had told me; and weaving its wonders into the tissue of strange things which had come to pass since I had entered the house. At times I was inclined to doubt; to doubt everything and every one; to doubt even the evidences of my own senses. The warnings of the skilled detective kept coming back to my mind. He had put down Mr. Corbeck as a clever liar, and a confederate of Miss Trelawny. Of Margaret! That settled it! Face to face with such a proposition as that, doubt vanished. Each time when her image, her name, the merest thought of her, came before my mind, each event stood out stark as a living fact. My life upon her faith!

I was recalled from my reverie, which was fast becoming a dream of love, in a startling manner. A voice came from the bed; a deep, strong, masterful voice. The first note of it called up like a clarion my eyes and my ears. The sick man was awake and speaking!

"Who are you? What are you doing here?"

Whatever ideas any of us had ever formed of his waking, I am quite sure that none of us expected to see him start up all awake and full master of himself. I was so surprised that I answered almost mechanically:

"Ross is my name. I have been watching by you!"
He looked surprised for an instant, and then I could see that his habit of judging for himself came into play.

"Watching by me! How do you mean? Why watching by me?" His eye had now lit on his heavily bandaged wrist. He went on in a different tone; less aggressive, more genial, as of one accepting facts:

"Are you a doctor?" I felt myself almost smiling as I answered; the relief from the long pressure of anxiety regarding his life was beginning to tell:

"No, sir!"

"Then why are you here? If you are not a doctor, what are you?" His tone was again more dictatorial. Thought is quick; the whole train of reasoning on which my answer must be based flooded through my brain before the words could leave my lips. Margaret! I must think of Margaret! This was her father, who as yet knew nothing of me; even of my very existence. He would be naturally curious, if not anxious, to know why I amongst men had been chosen as his daughter's friend on the occasion of his illness. Fathers are naturally a little jealous in such matters as a daughter's choice, and in the undeclared state of my love for Margaret I must do nothing which could ultimately embarrass her.

"I am a Barrister. It is not, however, in that capacity I am here; but simply as a friend of your daughter. It was probably her knowledge of my being a lawyer which first determined her to ask me to come when she thought you had been murdered. Afterwards she was good enough to consider me to be a friend, and to allow me to remain in accordance with your expressed wish that someone should remain to watch."

Mr. Trelawny was manifestly a man of quick thought, and of few words. He gazed at me keenly as I spoke, and his piercing eyes seemed to read my thought. To my relief he said no more on the subject just then, seeming to accept my words in simple faith. There was evidently in his own mind some cause for the acceptance deeper than my own knowledge. His eyes flashed, and there was an unconscious movement of the mouth—it could hardly be called a twitch—which betokened satisfaction. He was following out some train of reasoning in his own mind. Suddenly he said :

"She thought I had been murdered! Was that last night ? "

"No! four days ago." He seemed surprised. Whilst he had been speaking the first time he had sat up in bed ; now he made a movement as though he would jump out. With an effort, however, he restrained himself ; leaning back on his pillows he said quietly :

"Tell me all about it! All you know! Every detail! Omit nothing! But stay ; first lock the door! I want to know, before I see anyone, exactly how things stand."

Somehow his last words made my heart leap. "Anyone !" He evidently accepted me, then, as an exception. In my present state of feeling for his daughter, this was a comforting thought. I felt exultant as I went over to the door and softly turned the key. When I came back I found him sitting up again. He said :

"Go on!"

Accordingly, I told him every detail, even of the slightest which I could remember, of what had happened from the moment of my arrival at the house. Of course I said nothing of my feeling towards Margaret, and spoke only concerning those things already within his own knowledge. With regard to Corbeck, I simply said that he had brought back some lamps of which he had been in quest. Then I proceeded to tell him fully of their loss, and of their re-discovery in the house.

He listened with a self-control which, under the circumstances, was to me little less than marvellous. It was not impassiveness, for at times his eyes would flash or blaze, and the strong fingers of his uninjured hand would grip the sheet, pulling it into far-extending wrinkles. This was most noticeable when I told him of the return of Corbeck, and the finding of the lamps in the boudoir. At times he spoke, but only a few words, and as if unconsciously in emotional comment. The mysterious parts, those which had most puzzled us, seemed to have no special interest for him; he seemed to know them already. The utmost concern he showed was when I told him of Daw's shooting. His muttered comment: "Stupid ass!" together with a quick glance across the room at the injured cabinet, marked the measure of his disgust. As I told him of his daughter's harrowing anxiety for him, of her unending care and devotion, of the tender love which she had shown, he seemed much moved. There was a sort of veiled surprise in his unconscious whisper:

"Margaret! Margaret!"

When I had finished my narration, bringing matters

up to the moment when Miss Trelawny had gone
out for her walk—I thought of her as "Miss Trelawny," not as "Margaret" now, in the presence of
her father—he remained silent for quite a long time.
It was probably two or three minutes; but it seemed
interminable. All at once he turned and said to me
briskly:

"Now tell me all about yourself!" This was something of a floorer; I felt myself grow red-hot. Mr.
Trelawny's eyes were upon me; they were now calm
and inquiring, but never ceasing in their soul-search-
ing scrutiny. There was just a suspicion of a smile
on the mouth which, though it added to my embarrassment, gave me a certain measure of relief. I was,
however, face to face with difficulty; and the habit
of my life stood me in good stead. I looked him
straight in the eyes as I spoke:

"My name, as I told you, is Ross, Malcolm Ross.
I am by profession a Barrister. I was made a Q.C.
in the last year of the Queen's reign. I have been
fairly successful in my work." To my relief he
said:

"Yes, I know. I have always heard well of you!
Where and when did you meet Margaret?"

"First at the Hay's in Belgrave Square, ten days
ago. Then at a picnic up the river with Lady
Strathconnell. We went from Windsor to Cookham.
Mar—Miss Trelawny was in my boat. I scull a
little, and I had my own boat at Windsor. We had
a good deal of conversation—naturally."

"Naturally!" there was just a suspicion of something sardonic in the tone of acquiescence; but there
was no other intimation of his feeling. I began to
think that as I was in the presence of a strong man,

I should show something of my own strength.   My
friends, and sometimes my opponents, say that I am
a strong man.   In my present circumstances, not to
be absolutely truthful would be to be weak.   So I
stood up to the difficulty before me; always bearing
in mind, however, that my words might effect Margaret's happiness through her love for her father.   I
went on :

"In conversation at a place and time and amid
surroundings so pleasing, and in a solitude inviting
to confidence, I got a glimpse of her inner life.
Such a glimpse as a man of my years and experience
may get from a young girl!"   The father's face grew
graver as I went on ; but he said nothing.   I was
committed now to a definite line of speech, and went
on with such mastery of my mind as I could exercise.
The occasion might be fraught with serious conse-
quences to me too.

"I could not but see that there was over her spirit
a sense of loneliness which was habitual to her.   I
thought I understood it; I am myself an only child.
I ventured to encourage her to speak to me freely ;
and was happy enough to succeed.   A sort of confidence became established between us."   There was
something in the father's face which made me add
hurriedly :

"Nothing was said by her, sir, as you can well
imagine, which was not right and proper.   She only
told me in the impulsive way of one longing to give
voice to thoughts long carefully concealed, of her
yearning to be closer to the father whom she loved ;
more *en rapport* with him ; more in his confidence ;
closer within the circle of his sympathies.   Oh, believe
me, sir, that it was all good !   All that a father's heart

could hope or wish for! It was all loyal! That she spoke it to me was perhaps because I was almost a stranger with whom there was no previous barrier to confidence."

Here I paused. It was hard to go on; and I feared lest I might, in my zeal, do Margaret a disservice. The relief of the strain came from her father.

"And you?"

"Sir, Miss Trelawny is very sweet and beautiful! She is young; and her mind is like crystal! Her sympathy is a joy! I am not an old man, and my affections were not engaged. They never had been till then. I hope I may say as much, even to a father!" My eyes involuntary dropped. When I raised them again Mr. Trelawny was still gazing at me keenly. All the kindliness of his nature seemed to wreathe itself in a smile as he held out his hand and said:

"Malcolm Ross, I have always heard of you as a fearless and honourable gentleman. I am glad my girl has such a friend! Go on!"

My heart leaped. The first step to the winning of Margaret's father was gained. I dare say I was somewhat more effusive in my words and my manner as I went on. I certainly felt that way.

"One thing we gain as we grow older: to use our age judiciously! I have had much experience. I have fought for it and worked for it all my life; and I felt that I was justified in using it. I ventured to ask Miss Trelawny to count on me as a friend; to let me serve her should occasion arise. She promised me that she would. I had little idea that my chance of serving her should come so soon or

in such a way; but that very night you were stricken
down. In her desolation and anxiety she sent for
me!" I paused. He continued to look at me as
I went on:

"When your letter of instructions was found, I
offered my services. They were accepted, as you
know."

"And these days, how did they pass for you?"
The question startled me. There was in it something of Margaret's own voice and manner; something so greatly resembling her lighter moments that
it brought out all the masculinity in me. I felt more
sure of my ground now as I said:

"These days, sir, despite all their harrowing anxiety,
despite all the pain they held for the girl whom I
grew to love more and more with each passing hour,
have been the happiest of my life!" He kept silence
for a long time; so long that, as I waited for him
to speak, with my heart beating, I began to wonder
if my frankness had been too effusive. At last he
said:

"I suppose it is hard to say so much vicariously.
Her poor mother should have heard you; it would
have made her heart glad!" Then a shadow swept
across his face; and he went on more hurriedly.

"But are you quite sure of all this?"

"I know my own heart, sir; or, at least, I think
I do!"

"No!' no!" he answered, "I don't mean you.
That is all right! But you spoke of my girl's
affection for me . . . and yet. . . ! And yet she
has been living here, in my house, a whole year.
. . . Still, she spoke to you of her loneliness—her
desolation. I never—it grieves me to say it, but it

is true—I never saw sign of such affection towards myself in all the year! . . ." His voice trembled away into sad, reminiscent introspection.

"Then, sir," I said, "I have been privileged to see more in a few days than you in her whole lifetime!" My words seemed to call him up from himself; and I thought that it was with pleasure as well as surprise that he said:

"I had no idea of it. I thought that she was indifferent to me. That what seemed the neglect of her youth was revenging itself on me. That she was cold of heart. . . . It is a joy unspeakable to me that her mother's daughter loves me too!" Unconsciously he sank back upon his pillow, lost in memories of the past.

How he must have loved her mother! It was the love of her mother's child, rather than the love of his own daughter, that appealed to him. My heart went out to him in a great wave of sympathy and kindliness. I began to understand. To understand the passion of these two great, silent, reserved natures, that successfully concealed the burning hunger for the other's love! It did not surprise me when presently he murmured to himself:

"Margaret, my child! Tender, and thoughtful, and strong, and true, and brave! Like her dear mother! like her dear mother!"

And then to the very depths of my heart I rejoiced that I had spoken frankly.

Presently Mr. Trelawny said:

"Four days! The sixteenth! Then this is the twentieth of July?" I nodded affirmation; he went on:

"So I have been lying in a trance for four days.

It is not the first time. I was in a trance once under strange conditions for three days; and never even suspected it till I was told of the lapse of time. I shall tell you all about it some day, if you care to hear."

That made me thrill with pleasure. That he, Margaret's father, would so take me into his confidence made it possible. . . . The business-like, every-day alertness of his voice as he spoke next quite recalled me:

"I had better get up now. When Margaret comes in, tell her yourself that I am all right. It will avoid any shock! And will you tell Corbeck that I would like to see him as soon as I can. I want to see those lamps, and hear all about them!"

His attitude towards me filled me with delight. There was a possible father-in-law aspect that would have raised me from a death-bed. I was hurrying away to carry out his wishes; when, however, my hand was on the key of the door, his voice recalled me:

"Mr. Ross!"

I did not like to hear him say "Mr." After he knew of my friendship with his daughter he had called me Malcolm Ross; and this obvious return to formality not only pained, but filled me with apprehension. It must be something about Margaret. I thought of her as "Margaret" and not as "Miss Trelawny," now that there was danger of losing her. I know now what I felt then : that I was determined to fight for her rather than lose her. I came back, unconsciously holding myself erect. Mr. Trelawny, the keen observer of men, seemed to read my thought; his face, which was set in a new anxiety, relaxed as he said:

"Sit down a minute; it is better that we speak now than later. We are both men, and men of the world. All this about my daughter is very new to me, and very sudden; and I want to know exactly how and where I stand. Mind, I am making no objection; but as a father I have duties which are grave, and may prove to be painful. I—I "—he seemed slightly at a loss how to begin, and this gave me hope—"I suppose I am to take it, from what you have said to me of your feelings towards my girl, that it is in your mind to be a suitor for her hand, later on ? " I answered at once:

"Absolutely! Firm and fixed; it was my intention the evening after I had been with her on the river, to seek you, of course after a proper and respectful interval, and to ask you if I might approach her on the subject. Events forced me into closer relationship more quickly than I had dared to hope would be possible; but that first purpose has remained fresh in my heart, and has grown in intensity, and multiplied itself with every hour which has passed since then." His face seemed to soften as he looked at me; the memory of his own youth was coming back to him instinctively. After a pause he said:

"I suppose I may take it, too, Malcolm Ross "— the return to the familiarity of address swept through me with a glorious thrill—"that as yet you have not made any protestation to my daughter ? "

"Not in words, sir." The *arrière pensée* of my phrase struck me, not by its own inherent humour, but through the grave, kindly smile on the father's face. There was a pleasant sarcasm in his comment:

"Not in words! That is dangerous! She might have doubted words, or even disbelieved them."

"I felt myself blushing to the roots of my hair as I went on:

"The duty of delicacy in her defenceless position; my respect for her father—I did not know you then, sir, as yourself, but only as her father—restrained me. But even had not these barriers existed, I should not have dared in the presence of such grief and anxiety to have declared myself. Mr. Trelawny, I assure you on my word of honour that your daughter and I are as yet, on her part, but friends and nothing more!" Once again he held out his hands, and we clasped each other warmly. Then he said heartily:

"I am satisfied, Malcolm Ross. Of course, I take it that until I have seen her and have given you permission, you will not make any declaration to my daughter—in words," he added, with an indulgent smile. But his face became stern again as he went on:

"Time presses; and I have to think of some matters so urgent and so strange that I dare not lose an hour. Otherwise I should not have been prepared to enter, at so short a notice and to so new a friend, on the subject of my daughter's settlement in life, and of her future happiness." There was a dignity and a certain proudness in his manner which impressed me much.

"I shall respect your wishes, sir!" I said as I went back and opened the door. I heard him lock it behind me.

When I told Mr. Corbeck that Mr. Trelawny had quite recovered, he began to dance about like a wild man. But he suddenly stopped, and asked me to be careful not to draw any inferences, at all events at first, when in the future speaking of the finding of the

lamps, or of the first visits to the tomb.   This was in
case Mr. Trelawny should speak to me on the subject;
"as, of course, he will," he added, with a sidelong
look at me which meant knowledge of the affairs of
my heart.   I agreed to this, feeling that it was quite
right.   I did not quite understand why; but I knew
that Mr. Trelawny was a peculiar man.   In no case
could one make a mistake by being reticent.   Reticence
is a quality which a strong man always respects.

The manner in which the others of the house took
the news of the recovery varied much.   Mrs. Grant
wept with emotion; then she hurried off to see if she
could do anything personally, and to set the house in
order for "Master," as she always called him.   The
Nurse's face fell: she was deprived of an interesting
case.   But the disappointment was only momentary;
and she rejoiced that the trouble was over.   She was
ready to come to the patient the moment she should
be wanted; but in the meantime she occupied herself
in packing her portmanteau.

I took Sergeant Daw into the study, so that we
should be alone when I told him the news.   It surprised even his iron self-control when I told him the
method of the waking.   I was myself surprised in turn
by his first words:

"And how did he explain the first attack?   He was
unconscious when the second was made."

Up to that moment the nature of the attack, which
was the cause of my coming to the house, had never
even crossed my mind, except when I had simply
narrated the various occurrences in sequence to Mr.
Trelawny.   The Detective did not seem to think
much of my answer:

"Do you know, it never occurred to me to ask

him!" The professional instinct was strong in the man, and seemed to supersede everything else.

"That is why so few cases are ever followed out," he said, "unless our people are in them. Your amateur detective never hunts down to the death. As for ordinary people, the moment things begin to mend, and the strain of suspense is off them, they drop the matter in hand. It is like sea-sickness," he added philosophically after a pause ; "the moment you touch the shore you never give it a thought, but run off to the buffet to feed! Well, Mr. Ross, I'm glad the case is over; for over it is, so far as I am concerned. I suppose that Mr. Trelawny knows his own business; and that now he is well again, he will take it up himself. Perhaps, however, he will not do anything. As he seemed to expect something to happen, but did not ask for protection from the police in any way, I take it that he don't want them to interfere with an eye to punishment. We'll be told officially, I suppose, that it was an accident, or sleep-walking, or something of the kind, to satisfy the conscience of our Record Department; and that will be the end. As for me, I tell you frankly, sir, that it will be the saving of me. I verily believe I was beginning to get dotty over it all. There were too many mysteries, that aren't in my line, for me to be really satisfied as to either facts or the causes of them. Now, I'll be able to wash my hands of it, and get back to clean, wholesome, criminal work. Of course, sir, I'll be glad to know if you ever do light on a cause of any kind. And I'll be grateful if you can ever tell me how the man was dragged out of bed when the cat bit him, and who used the knife the second time. For master Silvio could never have done it by himself. But there! I keep thinking of it still. I must look out and keep a check on myself, or I shall think of it when I have to keep my mind on other things!"

When Margaret returned from her walk, I met her in the hall. She was still pale and sad; somehow, I had expected to see her radiant after her walk. The moment she saw me her eyes brightened, and she looked at me keenly.

"You have some good news for me?" she said. "Is Father better?"

"He is! Why did you think so?"

"I saw it in your face. I must go to him at once." She was hurrying away when I stopped her.

"He said he would send for you the moment he was dressed."

"He said he would send for me!" she repeated in amazement. "Then he is awake again, and conscious? I had no idea he was so well as that! O Malcolm!"

She sat down on the nearest chair and began to cry. I felt overcome myself. The sight of her joy and emotion, the mention of my own name in such a way and at such a time, the rush of glorious possibilities all coming together, quite unmanned me. She saw my emotion, and seemed to understand. She put out her hand. I held it hard, and kissed it. Such moments as these, the opportunities of·lovers, are gifts of the gods! Up to this instant, though I knew I loved her, and though I believe she returned my affection, I had had only hope. Now, however, the self-surrender manifest in her willingness to let me squeeze her hand, the ardour of her pressure in return, and the glorious flush of love in her beautiful, deep, dark eyes as she lifted them to mine, were all the eloquences which the most impatient or exacting lover could expect or demand.

No word was spoken; none was needed. Even had I not been pledged to verbal silence, words would have been poor and dull to express what we felt. Hand in hand, like two little children, we went up the staircase and waited on the landing, till the summons from Mr. Trelawny should come.

I whispered in her ear—it was nicer than speaking aloud and at a greater distance—how her father had awakened, and what he had said; and all that had passed between us, except when she herself had been the subject of conversation.

Presently a bell rang from the room. Margaret slipped from me, and looked back with warning finger on lip. She went over to her father's door and knocked softly.

"Come in!" said the strong voice.

"It is I, Father!" The voice was tremulous with love and hope.

There was a quick step inside the room; the door was hurriedly thrown open, and in an instant Margaret, who had sprung forward, was clasped in her father's arms. There was little speech; only a few broken phrases.

"Father! Dear, dear Father!"

"My child! Margaret! My dear, dear child!"

"O Father, Father! At last! At last!"

Here the father and daughter went into the room together, and the door closed.

CHAPTER XIV

THE BIRTH-MARK

DURING my waiting for the summons to Mr. Trelawny's room, which I knew would come, the time
was long and lonely. After the first few moments of
emotional happiness at Margaret's joy, I somehow
felt apart and alone; and for a little time the selfish-
ness of a lover possessed me. But it was not for long.
Margaret's happiness was all in all to me; and in the
conscious sense of it I lost my baser self. Margaret's
last words as the door closed on them gave the key to
the whole situation, as it had been and as it was
These two proud, strong people, though father and
daughter, had only come to know each other when
the girl was grown up. Margaret's nature was of
that kind which matures early.

The pride and strength of each, and the reticence
which was their corollary, made a barrier at the
beginning. Each had respected the other's reticence
too much thereafter; and the misunderstanding grew
to habit. And so these two loving hearts, each of
which yearned for sympathy from the other, were
kept apart. But now all was well, and in my heart of
hearts I rejoiced that at last Margaret was happy.
Whilst I was still musing on the subject, and dreaming dreams of a personal nature, the door was opened,
and Mr. Trelawny beckoned to me.

"Come in, Mr. Ross!" he said cordially, but with a certain formality which I dreaded. I entered the room, and he closed the door again. He held out his hand, and I put mine in it. He did not let it go, but still held it as he drew me over toward his daughter. Margaret looked from me to him, and back again; and her eyes fell. When I was close to her, Mr. Trelawny let go my hand, and, looking his daughter straight in the face, said:

"If things are as I fancy, we shall not have any secrets between us. Malcolm Ross knows so much of my affairs already, that I take it he must either let matters stop where they are and go away in silence, or else he must—know more. Margaret! are you willing to let Mr. Ross see your wrist?"

She threw one swift look of appeal in his eyes; but even as she did so she seemed to make up her mind. Without a word she raised her right hand, so that the bracelet of spreading wings which covered the wrist fell back, leaving the flesh bare. Then an icy chill shot through me.

On her wrist was a thin red jagged line, from which seemed to hang red stains like drops of blood!

She stood there, a veritable figure of patient pride.

Oh! but she looked proud! Through all her sweetness, all her dignity, all the high-souled negation of self which I had known, and which never seemed more marked than now—through all the fire that seemed to shine from the dark depths of her eyes into my very soul, pride shone conspicuously. The pride that has faith; the pride that is born of conscious purity; the pride of a veritable queen of Old Time, when to be royal was to be the first and greatest and bravest in all high things. As we stood thus for some seconds, the deep, grave voice of her father seemed to sound a challenge in my ears:

"What do you say now?"

My answer was not in words. I caught Margaret's right hand in mine as it fell, and, holding it tight, whilst with the other I pushed back the golden cincture, stooped and kissed the wrist. As I looked up at her, but never letting go her hand, there was a look of joy on her face such as I dream of when I think of heaven. Then I faced her father.

"You have my answer, sir!" His strong face looked gravely sweet. He only said one word as he laid his hand on our clasped ones, whilst he bent over and kissed his daughter:

"Good!"

We were interrupted by a knock at the door. In answer to an impatient "Come in!" from Mr. Tre-lawny, Mr. Corbeck entered. When he saw us grouped he would have drawn back; but in an instant Mr. Trelawny had sprung forth and dragged him forward. As he shook him by both hands, he seemed a trans-formed man. All the enthusiasm of his youth, of which Mr. Corbeck had told us, seemed to have come back to him in an instant.

"So you have got the lamps!" he almost shouted. "My reasoning was right after all. Come to the library, where we will be alone, and tell me all about it! And while he does it, Ross," said he, turning to me, "do you, like a good fellow, get the key from the safe deposit, so that I may have a look at the lamps!"

Then the three of them, the daughter lovingly hold-ing her father's arm, went into the library, whilst I hurried off to Chancery Lane.

When I returned with the key, I found them still

engaged in the narrative ; but Doctor Winchester, who had arrived soon after I left, was with them. Mr. Trelawny, on hearing from Margaret of his great attention and kindness, and how he had, under much pressure to the contrary, steadfastly obeyed his written wishes, had asked him to remain and listen. " It will interest you, perhaps," he said, "to learn the end of the story ! "

We all had an early dinner together. We sat after it a good while, and then Mr. Trelawny said :

" Now, I think we had all better separate and go quietly to bed early. We may have much to talk about to-morrow ; and to-night I want to think."

Doctor Winchester went away, taking, with a courteous forethought, Mr. Corbeck with him, and leaving me behind. When the others had gone Mr. Trelawny said :

" I think it will be well if you, too, will go home for to-night. I want to be quite alone with my daughter ; there are many things I wish to speak of to her, and to her alone. Perhaps, even to-morrow, I will be able to tell you also of them ; but in the meantime there will be less distraction to us both if we are alone in the house." I quite understood and sympathised with his feelings ; but the experiences of the last few days were strong on me, and with some hesitation I said :

" But may it not be dangerous ? If you knew as we do——" To my surprise Margaret interrupted me :

" There will be no danger, Malcolm. I shall be with Father ! " As she spoke she clung to him in a protective way. I said no more, but stood up to go at once. Mr. Trelawny said heartily :

"Come as early as you please, Ross. Come to breakfast. After it, you and I will want to have a word together." He went out of the room quietly, leaving us together. I clasped and kissed Margaret's hands, which she held out to me, and then drew her close to me, and our lips met for the first time.

I did not sleep much that night. Happiness on the one side of my bed and Anxiety on the other kept sleep away. But if I had anxious care, I had also happiness which had not equal in my life—or ever can have. The night went by so quickly that the dawn seemed to rush on me, not stealing as is its wont.

Before nine o'clock I was at Kensington. All anxiety seemed to float away like a cloud as I met Margaret, and saw that already the pallor of her face had given way to the rich bloom which I knew. She told me that her father had slept well, and that he would be with us soon.

"I do believe," she whispered, "that my dear and thoughtful Father has kept back on purpose, so that I might meet you first, and alone!"

After breakfast Mr. Trelawny took us into the study, saying as he passed in:

"I have asked Margaret to come too." When we were seated, he said gravely:

"I told you last night that we might have something to say to each other. I dare say that you may have thought that it was about Margaret and yourself. Isn't that so?"

"I thought so."

"Well, my boy, that is all right. Margaret and I have been talking, and I know her wishes." He held out his hand. When I had wrung it, and had kissed

Margaret, who drew her chair close to mine, so that we could hold hands as we listened, he went on, but with a certain hesitation—it could hardly be called nervousness—which was new to me :

"You know a good deal of my hunt after this mummy and her belongings; and I dare say you have guessed a good deal of my theories. But these at any rate I shall explain later, concisely and categorically, if it be necessary. What I want to consult you about now is this: Margaret and I disagree on one point. I am about to make an experiment; the experiment which is to crown all that I have devoted twenty years of research, and danger, and labour to prepare for. Through it we may learn things that have been hidden from the eyes and the knowledge of men for centuries; for scores of centuries. I do not want my daughter to be present; for I cannot blind myself to the fact that there may be danger in it—great danger, and of an unknown kind. I have, however, already faced very great dangers, and of an unknown kind; and so has that brave scholar who has helped me in the work. As to myself, I am willing to run any risk. For science, and history, and philosophy may benefit; and we may turn one old page of a wisdom unknown in this prosaic age. But for my daughter to run such a risk I am loth. Her young bright life is too precious to throw lightly away; now especially when she is on the very threshold of new happiness. I do not wish to see her life given, as her dear mother's was——"

He broke down for a moment, and covered his eyes with his hands. In an instant Margaret was beside him, clasping him close, and kissing him, and comforting him with loving words. Then, standing erect, with one hand on his head, she said :

"Father! mother did not bid you stay beside her, even when you wanted to go on that journey of unknown danger to Egypt; though that country was then upset from end to end with war and the dangers that follow war. You have told me how she left you free to go as you wished; though that she thought of danger for you and feared it for you, is proved by this!" She held up her wrist with the scar that seemed to run blood. "Now, mother's daughter does as mother would have done herself!" Then she turned to me :

"Malcolm, you know I love you! But love is trust; and you must trust me in danger as well as in joy. You and I must stand beside Father in this unknown peril. Together we shall come through it; or together we shall fail; together we shall die. That is my wish; my first wish to my husband that is to be! Do you not think that, as a daughter, I am right? Tell my Father what you think!"

She looked like a Queen stooping to plead. My love for her grew and grew. I stood up beside her; and took her hand and said :

"Mr. Trelawny! in this Margaret and I are one!"

He took both our hands and held them hard. Presently he said with deep emotion :

"It is as her mother would have done!"

Mr. Corbeck and Doctor Winchester came exactly at the time appointed, and joined us in the library. Despite my great happiness I felt our meeting to be a very solemn function. For I could never forget the strange things that had been; and the idea of the strange things which might be, was with me like a cloud, pressing down on us all. From the gravity of my companions I gathered that each of them also was ruled by some such dominating thought.

Instinctively we gathered our chairs into a circle round Mr. Trelawny, who had taken the great arm-chair near the window. Margaret sat by him on his right, and I was next to her. Mr. Corbeck was on his left, with Doctor Winchester on the other side. After a few seconds of silence Mr. Trelawny said to Mr. Corbeck:

"You have told Doctor Winchester all up to the present, as we arranged?

"Yes," he answered; so Mr. Trelawny said:

"And I have told Margaret, so we all know!" Then, turning to the Doctor, he asked:

"And am I to take it that you, knowing all as we know it who have followed the matter for years, wish to share in the experiment which we hope to make?" His answer was direct and uncompromising:

"Certainly! Why, when this matter was fresh to me, I offered to go on with it to the end. Now that it is of such strange interest, I would not miss it for anything which you could name. Be quite easy in your mind, Mr. Trelawny. I am a scientist and an investigator of phenomena. I have no one belonging to me or dependent on me. I am quite alone, and free to do what I like with my own—including my life!" Mr. Trelawny bowed gravely, and turning to Mr. Corbeck said:

"I have known your ideas for many years past, old friend; so I need ask you nothing. As to Margaret and Malcolm Ross, they have already told me their wishes in no uncertain way." He paused a few seconds, as though to put his thoughts or his words in order; then he began to explain his views and intentions. He spoke very carefully, seeming always to bear in mind that some of us who listened were ignorant of the very root and nature of some things touched upon, and explaining them to us as he went on :

"The experiment which is before us is to try whether or no there is any force, any reality, in the old Magic. There could not possibly be more favourable conditions for the test ; and it is my own desire to do all that is possible to make the original design effective. That there is some such existing power I firmly believe. It might not be possible to create, or arrange, or organise such a power in our own time; but I take it that if in Old Time such a power existed, it may have some exceptional survival. After all, the Bible is not a myth ; and we read there that the sun stood still at a man's command, and that an ass—not a human one —spoke. And if the Witch at Endor could call up to Saul the spirit of Samuel, why may not there have been others with equal powers ; and why may not one among them survive ? Indeed, we are told in the Book of Samuel that the Witch of Endor was only one of many, and her being consulted by Saul was a matter of chance. He only sought one among the many whom he had driven out of Israel; 'all those that had Familiar Spirits, and the Wizards.' This Egyptian Queen, Tera, who reigned nearly two thousand years before Saul, had a Familiar, and was a Wizard too. See how the priests of her time, and those after it tried to wipe out her name from the face of the earth, and put a curse over the very door of her tomb so that none might ever discover the lost name. Ay, and they succeeded so well that even Manetho, the historian of the Egyptian Kings, writing in the tenth century before Christ, with all the lore of the priesthood for forty centuries behind him, and with possibility of access to every existing record, could not even find her name. Did it strike any of you, in thinking of the late events, who or what her Familiar was?" There was an interruption, for Doctor Winchester struck one hand loudly on the other as he ejaculated:

"The cat! The mummy cat! I knew it!" Mr. Trelawny smiled over at him.

"You are right! There is every indication that the Familiar of the Wizard Queen was that cat which was mummied when she was, and was not only placed in her tomb, but was laid in the sarcophagus with her. That was what bit into my wrist, what cut me with sharp claws." He paused. Margaret's comment was a purely girlish one:

"Then my poor Silvio is acquitted. I am glad!" Her father stroked her hair and went on:

"This woman seems to have had an extraordinary foresight. Foresight far, far beyond her age and the philosophy of her time. She seems to have seen through the weakness of her own religion, and even prepared for emergence into a different world. All her aspirations were for the North, the point of the compass whence blew the cool invigorating breezes that make life a joy. From the first, her eyes seem to have been attracted to the seven stars of the Plough from the fact, as recorded in the hieroglyphics in her tomb, that at her birth a great aerolite fell, from whose heart was finally extracted that Jewel of Seven Stars which she regarded as the talisman of her life. It seems to have so far ruled her destiny that all her thought and care circled round it. The Magic Coffer, so wondrously wrought with seven sides, we learn from the same source, came from the aerolite. Seven was to her a magic number ; and no wonder. With seven fingers on one hand, and seven toes on one foot. With a talisman of a rare ruby with seven stars in the same position as in that constellation which ruled her birth, each star of the seven having seven points—in itself a geological wonder—it would have been odd if she had not been attracted by it. Again, she was born, we learn in the Stele of her tomb, in the seventh month of the year—the month beginning with the Inundation of the Nile. Of which month the presiding Goddess was Hathor, the Goddess of her own house, of the Antefs of the Theban line—the Goddess who in various forms symbolises beauty, and pleasure, and resurrection. Again, in this seventh month—which, by later Egyptian astronomy began on October 28th, and ran to the 27th of our November —on the seventh day the Pointer of the Plough just rises above the horizon of the sky at Thebes.

"In a marvellously strange way, therefore, are grouped into this woman's life these various things. The number seven ; the Pole Star, with the constella-tion of seven stars ; the God of the month, Hathor, who was her own particular God, the God of her family, the Antefs of the Theban Dynasty, whose Kings' symbol it was, and whose seven forms ruled love and the delights of life and resurrection. If ever there was ground for magic ; for the power of symbolism carried into mystic use ; for a belief in finite spirits in an age which knew not the Living God, it is here.

" Remember, too, that this woman was skilled in all

the science of her time. Her wise and cautious father took care of that, knowing that by her own wisdom she must ultimately combat the intrigues of the Hierarchy. Bear in mind that in old Egypt the science of Astronomy began and was developed to an extraordinary height; and that Astrology followed Astronomy in its progress. And it is possible that in the later developments of science with regard to light rays, we may yet find that Astrology is on a scientific basis. Our next wave of scientific thought may deal with this. I shall have something special to call your minds to on this point presently. Bear in mind also that the Egyptians knew sciences, of which to-day, despite all our advantages, we are profoundly ignorant. Acoustics, for instance, an exact science with the builders of the temples of Karnak, of Luxor, of the Pyramids, is to-day a mystery to Bell, and Kelvin, and Edison, and Marconi. Again, these old miracle-workers probably understood some practical way of using other forces, and amongst them the forces of light that at present we do not dream of. But of this matter I shall speak later. That Magic Coffer of Queen Tera is probably a magic box in more ways than one. It may—possibly it does—contain forces that we wot not of. We cannot open it; it must be closed from within. How then was it closed? It is a coffer of solid stone, of amazing hardness, more like a jewel than an ordinary marble, with a lid equally solid; and yet all is so finely wrought that the finest tool made to-day cannot be inserted under the flange. How was it wrought to such perfection? How was the stone so chosen that those translucent patches match the relations of the seven stars of the constellation? How is it, or from what cause, that when the starlight shines on it, it glows from within—that when I fix the lamps in similar form the glow grows greater still ; and yet the box is irresponsive to ordinary light however great ?   I tell you that that box hides some great mystery of science.   We shall find that the light will open it in some way : either by striking on some substance, sensitive in a peculiar way to its effect, or in releasing some greater power.   I only trust that in our ignorance we may not so bungle things as to do harm to its mechanism ; and so deprive the knowledge of our time of a lesson handed down, as by a miracle, through nearly five thousand years.

" In another way, too, there may be hidden in that box secrets which, for good or ill, may enlighten the world.   We know from their records, and inferentially also, that the Egyptians studied the properties of herbs and minerals for magic purposes—white magic as well as black.   We know that some of the wizards of old could induce from sleep dreams of any given kind. That this purpose was mainly effected by hypnotism, which was another art or science of Old Nile, I have little doubt.   But still, they must have had a mastery of drugs that is far beyond anything we know.   With our own pharmacopœia we can, to a certain extent, induce dreams.   We may even differentiate between good and bad—dreams of pleasure, or disturbing and harrowing dreams.   But these old practitioners seemed to have been able to command at will any form or colour of dreaming ; could work round any given subject or thought in almost any way required.   In that coffer, which you have seen, may rest a very armoury of dreams.   Indeed, some of the forces that lie within it may have been already used in my

household." Again there was an interruption from
Doctor Winchester.

"But if in your case some of these imprisoned
forces were used, what set them free at the opportune
time, or how? Besides, you and Mr. Corbeck were
once before put into a trance for three whole days,
when you were in the Queen's tomb for the second
time. And then, as I gathered from Mr. Corbeck's
story, the coffer was not back in the tomb, though the
mummy was. Surely in both these cases there must
have been some active intelligence awake, and with
some other power to wield." Mr. Trelawny's answer
was equally to the point:

"There was some active intelligence awake. I am
convinced of it. And it wielded a power which it
never lacks. I believe that on both those occasions
hypnotism was the power wielded."

"And wherein is that power contained? What view
do you hold on the subject?" Doctor Winchester's
voice vibrated with the intensity of his excitement as
he leaned forward, breathing hard, and with eyes
staring. Mr. Trelawny said solemnly:

"In the mummy of the Queen Tera! I was coming
to that presently. Perhaps we had better wait till I
clear the ground a little. What I hold is, that the
preparation of that box was made for a special occasion; as indeed were all the preparations of the tomb
and all belonging to it. Queen Tera did not trouble
herself to guard against snakes and scorpions, in that
rocky tomb cut in the sheer cliff face a hundred feet
above the level of the valley, and fifty down from
the summit. Her precautions were against the dis-
turbances of human hands; against the jealousy and
hatred of the priests, who, had they known of her real

aims, would have tried to baffle them.   From her
point of view, she made all ready for the time of
resurrection, whenever that might be.   I gather from
the symbolic pictures in the tomb that she so far
differed from the belief of her time that she looked
for a resurrection in the flesh.   It was doubtless this
that intensified the hatred of the priesthood, and gave
them an acceptable cause for obliterating the very
existence, present and future, of one who had outraged their theories and blasphemed their gods.   All
that she might require, either in the accomplishment
of the resurrection or after it, were contained in that
almost hermetically sealed suite of chambers in the
rock.   In the great sarcophagus, which as you know
is of a size quite unusual even for kings, was the
mummy of her Familiar, the cat, which from its great
size I take to be a sort of tiger-cat.   In the tomb, also
in a strong receptacle, were the canopic jars usually
containing those internal organs which are separately
embalmed, but which in this case had no such contents.   So that, I take it, there was in her case a
departure in embalming; and that the organs were
restored to the body, each in its proper place—if,
indeed, they had ever been removed.   If this surmise
be true, we shall find that the brain of the Queen
either was never extracted in the usual way, or, if so
taken out, that it was duly replaced, instead of being
enclosed within the mummy wrappings.   Finally, in
the sarcophagus there was the Magic Coffer on which
her feet rested.   Mark you also, the care taken in the
preservance of her power to control the elements.
According to her belief, the open hand outside the
wrappings controlled the Air, and the strange Jewel
Stone with the shining stars controlled Fire.   The

symbolism inscribed on the soles of her feet gave sway over Land and Water. About the Star Stone I shall tell you later ; but whilst we are speaking of the sarcophagus, mark how she guarded her secret in case of grave-wrecking or intrusion. None could open her Magic Coffer without the lamps, for we know now that ordinary light will not be effective. The great lid of the sarcophagus was not sealed down as usual, because she wished to control the air. But she hid the lamps, which in structure belong to the Magic Coffer, in a place where none could find them, except by following the secret guidance which she had prepared for only the eyes of wisdom. And even here she had guarded against chance discovery, by preparing a bolt of death for the unwary discoverer. To do this she had applied the lesson of the tradition of the avenging guard of the treasures of the pyramid, built by her great predecessor of the Fourth Dynasty of the throne of Egypt.

" You have noted, I suppose, how there were, in the case of her tomb, certain deviations from the usual rules. For instance, the shaft of the Mummy Pit, which is usually filled up solid with stones and rubbish, was left open. Why was this ? I take it that she had made arrangements for leaving the tomb when, after her resurrection, she should be a new woman, with a different personality, and less inured to the hardships that in her first existence she had suffered. So far as we can judge of her intent, all things needful for her exit into the world had been thought of, even to the iron chain, described by Van Huyn, close to the door in the rock, by which she might be able to lower herself to the ground. That she expected a long period to elapse was shown in the choice of material. An ordinary rope would be rendered weaker or unsafe in process of time, but she imagined, and rightly, that the iron would endure.

"What her intentions were when once she trod the open earth afresh we do not know, and we never shall, unless her own dead lips can soften and speak.

CHAPTER XV

THE PURPOSE OF QUEEN TERA

"Now, as to the Star Jewel! This she manifestly regarded as the greatest of her treasures. On it she had engraven words which none of her time dared to speak.

"In the old Egyptian belief it was held that there were words, which, if used properly—for the method of speaking them was as important as the words themselves—could command the Lords of the Upper and the Lower Worlds. The 'hekau,' or word of power, was all-important in certain ritual. On the Jewel of Seven Stars, which, as you know, is carved into the image of a scarab, are graven in hieroglyphic two such hekau, one above, the other underneath. But you will understand better when you see it! Wait here! Do not stir!"

As he spoke, he rose and left the room. A great fear for him came over me; but I was in some strange way relieved when I looked at Margaret. Whenever there had been any possibility of danger to her father, she had shown great fear for him; now she was calm and placid. I said nothing, but waited.

In two or three minutes Mr. Trelawny returned. He held in his hand a little golden box. This, as he resumed his seat, he placed before him on the table. We all leaned forward as he opened it.

On a lining of white satin lay a wondrous ruby of immense size, almost as big as the top joint of Margaret's little finger. It was carven—it could not possibly have been its natural shape, but jewels do not show the working of the tool—into the shape of a scarab, with its wings folded, and its legs and feelers pressed back to its sides. Shining through

its wondrous "pigeon's blood" colour were seven different stars, each of seven points, in such position that they reproduced exactly the figure of the Plough. There could be no possible mistake as to this in the mind of anyone who had ever noted the constellation. On it were some hieroglyphic figures, cut with the most exquisite precision, as I could see when it came to my turn to use the magnifying-glass, which Mr. Trelawny took from his pocket and handed to us.

When we all had seen it fully, Mr. Trelawny turned it over so that it rested on its back in a cavity made to hold it in the upper half of the box. The reverse was no less wonderful than the upper, being carved to resemble the under side of the beetle. It, too, had some hieroglyphic figures cut on it. Mr. Trelawny resumed his lecture as we all sat with our heads close to this wonderful jewel:

"As you see, there are two words, one on the top, the other underneath. The symbols on the top represent a single word, composed of one syllable prolonged, with its determinatives. You know, all of you, I suppose, that the Egyptian language was phonetic, and that the hieroglyphic symbol represented the sound. The first symbol here, the hoe, means 'mer,' and the two pointed ellipses the prolongation of the final r: mer-r-r. The sitting figure with the hand to its face is what we call the 'determinative' of 'thought'; and the roll of papyrus that of 'abstraction.' Thus we get the word 'mer,' love, in its abstract, general, and fullest sense. This is the hekau which can command the Upper World."

Margaret's face was a glory as she said in a deep, low, ringing tone:

"Oh, but it is true. How the old wonder-workers guessed at almighty Truth!" Then a hot blush swept her face, and her eyes fell. Her father smiled at her lovingly as he resumed:

"The symbolisation of the word on the reverse is simpler, though the meaning is more abstruse. The first symbol means 'men,' 'abiding,' and the second, 'ab,' 'the heart.' So that we get 'abiding of heart,' or in our own language 'patience.' And this is the hekau to control the Lower World!"

He closed the box, and motioning us to remain as we were, he went back to his room to replace the

Jewel in the safe. When he had returned and resumed his seat, he went on :

"That Jewel, with its mystic words, and which Queen Tera held under her hand in the sarcophagus, was to be an important factor—probably the most important—in the working out of the act of her resurrection. From the first I seemed by a sort of instinct to realise this. I kept the Jewel within my great safe, whence none could extract it ; not even Queen Tera herself with her astral body."

"Her 'astral body'? What is that, Father? What does that mean?" There was a keenness in Margaret's voice as she asked the question which surprised me a little ; but Trelawny smiled a sort of indulgent parental smile, which came through his grim solemnity like sunshine through a rifted cloud, as he spoke :

"The astral body, which is a part of Buddhist belief, long subsequent to the time I speak of, and which is an accepted fact of modern mysticism, had its rise in Ancient Egypt; at least, so far as we know. It is that the gifted individual can at will, quick as thought itself, transfer his body whithersoever he chooses, by the dissolution and reincarnation of particles. In the ancient belief there were several parts of a human being. You may as well know them ; so that you will understand matters relative to them or dependent on them as they occur.

"First there is the 'Ka,' or 'Double,' which, as Doctor Budge explains, may be defined as 'an abstract individuality of personality' which was imbued with all the characteristic attributes of the individual it represented, and possessed an absolutely independent existence. It was free to move from place to place on earth at will; and it could enter into heaven and hold converse with the gods. Then there was the 'Ba,' or 'soul,' which dwelt in the 'Ka,' and had the power of becoming corporeal or incorporeal at will; 'it had both substance and form. . . . It had power to leave the tomb . . . It could revisit the body in the tomb . . . and could reincarnate it and hold converse with it.' Again there was the 'Khu,' the 'spiritual intelligence,' or spirit. It took the form of 'a shining, luminous, intangible shape of the body.' . . . Then, again, there was the 'Sekhem,' or 'power' of a man, his strength or vital force personified. These were the 'Khaibit,' or 'shadow,' the 'Ren,' or 'name,' the 'Khat,' or 'physical body,' and 'Ab,' the 'heart,' in which life was seated, went to the full making up of a man.

"Thus you will see, that if this division of functions, spiritual and bodily, ethereal and corporeal, ideal and actual, be accepted as exact, there are all the possibilities and capabilities of corporeal transference, guided always by an unimprisonable will or intelligence." As he paused I murmured the lines from Shelley's "Prometheus Unbound":

"'The Magnus Zoroaster . . .
Met his own image walking in the garden.'"

Mr. Trelawny was not displeased. "Quite so!" he said, in his quiet way. "Shelley had a better conception of ancient beliefs than any of our poets." With a voice changed again he resumed his lecture, for so it was to some of us:

"There is another belief of the ancient Egyptian which you must bear in mind; that regarding the ushaptiu figures of Osiris, which were placed with the dead to do its work in the Under World. The enlargement of this idea came to a belief that it was possible to transmit, by magical formulæ, the soul and qualities of any living creature to a figure made in its image. This would give a terrible extension of power to one who held the gift of magic.

"It is from a union of these various beliefs, and their natural corollaries, that I have come to the conclusion that Queen Tera expected to be able to effect her own resurrection, when, and where, and how, she would. That she may have held before her a definite time for making her effort is not only possible but likely. I shall not stop now to explain it, but shall enter upon the subject later on. With a soul with the Gods, a spirit which could wander the earth at will, and a power of corporeal transference, or an astral body, there need be no bounds or limits to her ambition. The belief is forced upon us that for these forty or fifty centuries she lay dormant in her tomb—waiting. Waiting with that "patience" which could rule the Gods of the Under World, for that "love" which could command those of the Upper World. What she may have dreamt we know not; but her dream must have been broken when the Dutch explorer entered her sculptured cavern, and his follower violated the sacred privacy of her tomb by his rude outrage in the theft of her hand.

"That theft, with all that followed, proved to us one thing, however: that each part of her body, though separated from the rest, can be a central point or rallying place for the items or particles of her astral body. That hand in my room could ensure her instantaneous presence in the flesh, and its equally rapid dissolution.

"Now comes the crown of my argument. The purpose of the attack on me was to get the safe open, so that the sacred Jewel of Seven Stars could be extracted. That immense door of the safe could not keep out her astral body, which, or any part of it, could gather itself as well within as without the safe. And I doubt not that in the darkness of the night that mummied hand sought often the Talisman Jewel, and drew new inspiration from its touch. But despite all its power, the astral body could not remove the Jewel through the chinks of the safe. The Ruby is not astral; and it could only be moved in the ordinary way by the opening of the doors. To this end, the Queen used her astral body and the fierce force of her Familiar, to bring to the keyhole of the safe the master key which debarred her wish. For years I have suspected, nay, have believed as much; and I, too, guarded myself against powers of the Nether World. I, too, waited in patience till I should have gathered together all the factors required for the opening of the Magic Coffer and the resurrection of the mummied Queen!" He paused, and his daughter's voice came out sweet and clear, and full of intense feeling:

"Father, in the Egyptian belief, was the power of resurrection of a mummied body a general one, or was it limited? That is: could it achieve resurrection many times in the course of ages; or only once, and that one final?"

"There was but one resurrection," he answered. "There were some who believed that this was to be a definite resurrection of the body into the real world.

But in the common belief, the Spirit found joy in the Elysian Fields, where there was plenty of food and no fear of famine. Where there was moisture and deep-rooted reeds, and all the joys that are to be expected by the people of an arid land and burning clime."

Then Margaret spoke with an earnestness which showed the conviction of her inmost soul:

"To me, then, it is given to understand what was the dream of this great and far-thinking and high-souled lady of old; the dream that held her soul in patient waiting for its realisation through the passing of all those tens of centuries. The dream of a love that might be; a love that she felt she might, even under new conditions, herself evoke. The love that is the dream of every woman's life; of the Old and of the New; Pagan or Christian; under whatever sun; in whatever rank or calling; however may have been the joy or pain of her life in other ways. Oh! I know it! I know it! I am a woman, and I know a woman's heart. What were the lack of food or the plenitude of it; what were feast or famine to this woman, born in a palace, with the shadow of the Crown of the Two Egypts on her brows! What were reedy morasses or the tinkle of running water to her whose barges could sweep the great Nile from the mountains to the sea. What were petty joys and absence of petty fears to her, the raising of whose hand could hurl armies, or draw to the water-stairs of her palaces the commerce of the world! At whose word rose temples filled with all the artistic beauty of the Times of Old which it was her aim and pleasure to restore! Under whose guidance the solid rock yawned into the sepulchre that she designed!

"Surely, surely, such a one had nobler dreams!
I can feel them in my heart; I can see them with
my sleeping eyes!"

As she spoke she seemed to be inspired; and her
eyes had a far-away look as though they saw something beyond mortal sight. And then the deep eyes
filled up with unshed tears of great emotion. The
very soul of the woman seemed to speak in her voice;
whilst we who listened sat entranced.

"I can see her in her loneliness and in the silence
of her mighty pride, dreaming her own dream of
things far different from those around her. Of some
other land, far, far away under the canopy of the
silent night, lit by the cool, beautiful light of the stars.
A land under that Northern star, whence blew the
sweet winds that cooled the feverish desert air. A
land of wholesome greenery, far, far away. Where
were no scheming and malignant priesthood; whose
ideas were to lead to power through gloomy temples
and more gloomy caverns of the dead, through an
endless ritual of death! A land where love was not
base, but a divine possession of the soul! Where
there might be some one kindred spirit which could
speak to hers through mortal lips like her own;
whose being could merge with hers in a sweet
communion of soul to soul, even as their breaths
could mingle in the ambient air! I know the feeling,
for I have shared it myself. I may speak of it now,
since the blessing has come into my own life. I
may speak of it since it enables me to interpret the
feelings, the very longing soul, of that sweet and
lovely Queen, so different from her surroundings,
so high above her time! Whose nature, put into a
word, could control the forces of the Under World;

and the name of whose aspiration, though but graven
on a star-lit jewel, could command all the powers in
the Pantheon of the High Gods.

"And in the realisation of that dream she will surely
be content to rest!"

We men sat silent, as the young girl gave her
powerful interpretation of the design or purpose of
the woman of old. Her every word and tone carried
with it the conviction of her own belief. The loftiness
of her thoughts seemed to uplift us all as we listened.
Her noble words, flowing in musical cadence and
vibrant with internal force, seemed to issue from some
great instrument of elemental power. Even her tone
was new to us all; so that we listened as to some new
and strange being from a new and strange world. Her
father's face was full of delight. I knew now its cause.
I understood the happiness that had come into his
life, on his return to the world that he knew, from that
prolonged sojourn in the world of dreams. To find
in his daughter, whose nature he had never till now
known, such a wealth of affection, such a splendour
of spiritual insight, such a scholarly imagination, such
. . . The rest of his feeling was of hope!

The two other men were silent unconsciously. One
man had had his dreaming; for the other, his dreams
were to come.

For myself, I was like one in a trance. Who was
this new, radiant being who had won to existence out
of the mist and darkness of our fears. Love has
divine possibilities for the lover's heart! The wings
of the soul may expand at any time from the shoulders
of the loved one, who then may sweep into angel
form. I knew that in my Margaret's nature were
divine possibilities of many kinds. When under the

shade of the overhanging willow-tree on the river, I
had gazed into the depths of her beautiful eyes, I had
thenceforth a strict belief in the manifold beauties
and excellences of her nature ; but this soaring and
understanding spirit was, indeed, a revelation. My
pride, like her father's, was outside myself ; my joy
and rapture were complete and supreme :

When we had all got back to earth again in our
various ways, Mr. Trelawny, holding his daughter's
hand in his, went on with his discourse :

" Now, as to the time at which Queen Tera intended
her resurrection to take place ! We are in contact
with some of the higher astronomical calculations in
connection with true orientation. As you know, the
stars shift their relative positions in the heavens ; but
though the real distances traversed are beyond all
ordinary comprehension, the effects as we see them
are small. Nevertheless, they are susceptible of
measurement, not by years, indeed, but by centuries.
It was by this means that Sir John Herschel arrived
at the date of the building of the Great Pyramid—a
date fixed by the time necessary to change the star
of the true north from Draconis to the Pole Star, and
since then verified by later discoveries. From the
above there can be no doubt whatever that astronomy
was an exact science with the Egyptians at least a
thousand years before the time of Queen Tera. Now,
the stars that go to make up a constellation change in
process of time their relative positions, and the Plough
is a notable example. The changes in the position of
stars in even forty centuries is so small as to be
hardly noticeable by an eye not trained to minute
observances, but they can be measured and verified.
Did you, or any of you, notice how exactly the stars

in the Ruby correspond to the position of the stars in
the Plough ; or how the same holds with regard to
the translucent places in the Magic Coffer ? "

We all assented. He went on :

" You are quite correct. They correspond exactly.
And yet when Queen Tera was laid in her tomb,
neither the stars in the Jewel nor the translucent places
in the Coffer corresponded to the position of the stars
in the Constellation as they then were ! '

We looked at each other as he paused : a new light
was breaking upon us. With a ring of mastery in his
voice he went on :

" Do you not see the meaning of this ? Does it not
throw a light on the intention of the Queen ? She,
who was guided by augury, and magic, and superstition, naturally chose a time for her resurrection which
seemed to have been pointed out by the High Gods
themselves, who had sent their message on a thunder-
bolt from other worlds. When such a time was fixed by
supernal wisdom, would it not be the height of human
wisdom to avail itself of it ? Thus it is "—here his voice
deepened and trembled with the intensity of his feeling
—" that to us and our time is given the opportunity
of this wondrous peep into the old world, such as has
been the privilege of none other of our time ; which
may never be again.

" From first to last the cryptic writing and symbolism
of that wondrous tomb of that wondrous woman is
full of guiding light ; and the key of the many mysteries
lies in that most wondrous Jewel which she held in
her dead hand over the dead heart, which she hoped
and believed would beat again in a newer and nobler
world !

" There are only loose ends now to consider. Margaret has given us the true inwardness of the feeling of the other Queen!" He looked at her fondly, and stroked her hand as he said it. "For my own part I sincerely hope she is right; for in such case it will be a joy, I am sure, to all of us to assist at such a realisation of hope. But we must not go too fast, or believe too much in our present state of knowledge. The voice that we hearken for comes out of times strangely other than our own; when human life counted for little, and when the morality of the time made little account of the removing of obstacles in the way to achievement of desire. We must keep our eyes fixed on the scientific side, and wait for the developments on the psychical side.

"Now, as to this stone box, which we call the Magic Coffer. As I have said, I am convinced that it opens only in obedience to some principle of light, or the exercise of some of its forces at present unknown to us. There is here much ground for conjecture and for experiment; for as yet the scientists have not thoroughly differentiated the kinds, and powers, and degrees of light. Without analysing various rays we may, I think, take it for granted that there are different qualities and powers of light; and this great field of scientific investigation is almost virgin soil. We know as yet so little of natural forces, that imagination need set no bounds to its flights in considering the possibilities of the future. Within but a few years we have made such discoveries as two centuries ago would have sent the discoverers to the flames. The liquefaction of oxygen; the existence of radium, of helium, of polonium, of argon; the different powers of Röntgen and Cathode and Becquerel rays. And as we may finally prove that there are different kinds and qualities of light, so we may find that combustion may have its own powers of differentiation; that there are qualities in some flames non-existent in others. It may be that some of the essential conditions of substance are continuous, even in the destruction of their bases. Last night I was thinking of this, and reasoning that as there are are certain qualities in some oils which are not in others, so there may be certain similar or corresponding qualities or powers in the combinations of each. I suppose we have all noticed some time or other that the light of colza oil is not quite the same as that of paraffin, or that the flames of coal gas and whale oil are different. They find it so in the light-houses! All at once it occurred to me that there might be some special virtue in the oil which had been found in the jars when Queen Tera's tomb was opened. These had not been used to preserve the intestines as usual, so they must have been placed there for some other purpose. I remembered that in Van Huyn's narrative he had commented on the way the jars were sealed. This was lightly, though effectually; they could be opened without force. The jars were themselves preserved in a sarcophagus which, though of immense strength and hermetically sealed, could be opened easily. Accordingly, I went at once to examine the jars. A little—very little of the oil still remained, but it had grown thick in the two and a half centuries in which the jars had been open. Still, it was not rancid; and on examining it I found it was cedar oil, and that it still exhaled something of its original aroma. This gave me the idea that it was to be used to fill the lamps.

Whoever had placed the oil in the jars, and the jars in the sarcophagus, knew that there might be shrinkage in process of time, even in vases of alabaster, and fully allowed for it; for each of the jars would have filled the lamps half a dozen times. With part of the oil remaining I made some experiments, therefore, which may give useful results. You know, Doctor, that cedar oil, which was much used in the preparation and ceremonials of the Egyptian dead, has a certain refractive power which we do not find in other oils. For instance, we use it on the lenses of our microscopes to give additional clearness of vision. Last night I put some in one of the lamps, and placed it near a translucent part of the Magic Coffer. The effect was very great; the glow of light within was fuller and more intense than I could have imagined, where an electric light similarly placed had little, if any, effect. I should have tried others of the seven lamps, but that my supply of oil ran out. This, however, is on the road to rectification. I have sent for more cedar oil, and expect to have before long an ample supply. Whatever may happen from other causes, our experiment shall not, at all events, fail from this. We shall see! We shall see!"

Doctor Winchester had evidently been following the logical process of the other's mind, for his comment was:

"I do hope that when the light is effective in opening the box, the mechanism will not be impaired or destroyed."

His doubt as to this gave anxious thought to some of us.

I

CHAPTER XVI

THE CAVERN

IN the evening Mr. Trelawny took again the whole party into the study. When we were all attention he began to unfold his plans :

" I have come to the conclusion that for the proper carrying out of what we will call our Great Experiment we must have absolute and complete isolation. Isolation not merely for a day or two, but for as long as we may require. Here such a thing would be impossible ; the needs and habits of a great city with its ingrained possibilities of interruption, would, or might, quite upset us. Telegrams, registered letters, or express messengers would alone be sufficient ; but the great army of those who want to get something would make disaster certain. In addition, the occurrences of the last week have drawn police attention to this house. Even if special instructions to keep an eye on it have not been issued from Scotland Yard or the District Station, you may be sure that the individual policeman on his rounds will keep it well under observation. Besides, the servants who have discharged themselves will before long begin to talk. They must ; for they have, for the sake of their own characters, to give some reason for the termination of a service which has I should say a position in the neighbourhood. The servants of the neighbours will begin to talk, and, perhaps the neighbours themselves. Then the active and intelligent Press will, with its usual zeal for the enlightenment of the public and its eye to increase of circulation, get hold of the matter. When the reporter is after us we shall not have much chance of privacy. Even if we were to bar ourselves in, we should not be free from interruption, possibly from intrusion. Either would ruin our plans, and so we must take measures to effect a retreat, carrying all our impedimenta with us. For this I am prepared. For a long time past I have foreseen such a possibility, and have made preparation for it. Of course, I had no foreknowledge of what has happened; but I knew something would, or might, happen. For more than two years past my house in Cornwall has been made ready to receive all the curios which are preserved here. When Corbeck went off on his search for the lamps I had the old house at Kyllion made ready; it is fitted with electric light all over, and all the appliances for manufacture of the light are complete. I had perhaps better tell you, for none of you, not even Margaret, knows anything of it, that the house is absolutely shut out from public access or even from view. It stands on a little rocky promontory behind a steep hill, and except from the sea cannot be seen. Of old it was fenced in by a high stone wall, for the house which it succeeded was built by an ancestor of mine in the days when a great house far away from a centre had to be prepared to defend itself. Here, then, is a place so well adapted to our needs that it might have been prepared on purpose. I shall explain it to you when we are all there. This will not be long, for already our movement is in train. I have sent word to Marvin to have all preparation for our transport ready. He is to have a special train, which is to run at night so as to avoid notice. Also a number of carts and stone-wagons, with sufficient men and appliances to take all our packing-cases to Paddington. We shall be away before the Argus-eyed Pressman is on the watch. We shall to-day begin our packing up; and I dare say that by to-morrow night we shall be ready. In the outhouses I have all the packing-cases which were used for bringing the things from Egypt, and I am satisfied that as they were sufficient for the journey across the desert and down the Nile to Alexandria and thence on to London, they will serve without fail between here and Kyllion. We four men, with Margaret to hand us such things as we may require, will be able to get the things packed safely; and the carrier's men will take them to the trucks.

" To-day the servants go to Kyllion, and Mrs. Grant will make such arrangements as may be required. She will take a stock of necessaries with her, so that we will not attract local attention by our daily needs; and will keep us supplied with perishable food from London. Thanks to Margaret's wise and generous treatment of the servants who decided to remain, we have got a staff on which we can depend. They have been already cautioned to secrecy, so that we need not fear gossip from within. Indeed, as the servants will be in London after their preparations at Kyllion are complete, there will not be much subject for gossip, in detail at any rate.

" As, however, we should commence the immediate work of packing at once, we will leave over the after proceedings till later when we have leisure."

Accordingly we set about our work. Under Mr. Trelawny's guidance, and aided by the servants, we took from the outhouses great packing-cases. Some of these were of enormous strength, fortified by many thicknesses of wood, and by iron bands and rods with screw-ends and nuts. We placed them throughout the house, each close to the object which it was to contain. When this preliminary work had been effected, and there had been placed in each room and in the hall great masses of new hay, cotton-waste and paper, the servants were sent away. Then we set about packing.

No one, not accustomed to packing, could have the slightest idea of the amount of work involved in such a task as that in which we were engaged. For my own part I had had a vague idea that there were a large number of Egyptian objects in Mr. Trelawny's house; but until I came to deal with them *seriatim* I had little idea of either their importance, the size of some of them, or of their endless number. Far into the night we worked. At times we used all the strength which we could muster on a single object; again we worked separately, but always under Mr. Trelawny's immediate direction. He himself, assisted by Margaret, kept an exact tally of each piece.

It was only when we sat down, utterly wearied, to a long-delayed supper that we began to realise that a large part of the work was done. Only a few of the packing-cases, however, were closed; for a vast amount of work still remained. We had finished some of the cases, each of which held only one of the great sarcophagi. The cases which held many objects could not be closed till all had been differentiated and packed.

I slept that night without movement or without dreams; and on our comparing notes in the morning, I found that each of the others had had the same experience.

By dinner-time next evening the whole work was complete, and all was ready for the carriers who were to come at midnight. A little before the appointed time we heard the rumble of carts; then we were shortly invaded by an army of workmen, who seemed by sheer force of numbers to move without effort, in an endless procession, all our prepared packages. A little over an hour sufficed them, and when the carts had rumbled away, we all got ready to follow them to Paddington. Silvio was of course to be taken as one of our party.

Before leaving we went in a body over the house, which looked desolate indeed. As the servants had all gone to Cornwall there had been no attempt at tidying-up; every room and passage in which we had worked, and all the stairways, were strewn with paper and waste, and marked with dirty feet.

The last thing which Mr. Trelawny did before coming away was to take from the great safe the Ruby with the Seven Stars. As he put it safely into his pocket-book, Margaret, who had all at once seemed to grow deadly tired and stood beside her father pale and rigid, suddenly became all aglow, as though the sight of the Jewel had inspired her. She smiled at her father approvingly as she said:

"You are right, Father. There will not be any more trouble to-night. She will not wreck your arrangements for any cause. I would stake my life upon it."

"She—or something—wrecked us in the desert

when we had come from the tomb in the Valley of
the Sorcerer!" was the grim comment of Corbeck,
who was standing by. Margaret answered him like
a flash:

"Ah! she was then near her tomb from which for
thousands of years her body had not been moved.
She must know that things are different now."

"How must she know?" asked Corbeck keenly.

"If she has that astral body that Father spoke of,
surely she must know! How can she fail to, with an
invisible presence and an intellect that can roam
abroad even to the stars and the worlds beyond us!"
She paused, and her father said solemnly:

"It is on that supposition that we are proceeding.
We must have the courage of our convictions, and
act on them—to the last!"

Margaret took his hand and held it in a dreamy
kind of way as we filed out of the house. She was
holding it still when he locked the hall door, and
when we moved up the road to the gateway, whence
we took a cab to Paddington.

When all the goods were loaded at the station, the
whole of the workmen went on to the train; this took
also some of the stone-wagons used for carrying the
cases with the great sarcophagi. Ordinary carts and
plenty of horses were to be found at Westerton, which
was our station for Kyllion. Mr. Trelawny had ordered
a sleeping-carriage for our party; as soon as the train
had started we all turned into our cubicles.

That night I slept sound. There was over me a
conviction of security which was absolute and supreme.
Margaret's definite announcement: "There will not
be any trouble to-night!" seemed to carry assurance
with it. I did not question it; nor did anyone else.

It was only afterwards that I began to think as to how she was so sure. The train was a slow one, stopping many times and for considerable intervals. As Mr. Trelawny did not wish to arrive at Westerton before dark, there was no need to hurry; and arrangements had been made to feed the workmen at certain places on the journey. We had our own hamper with us in the private car.

All that afternoon we talked over the Great Experiment, which seemed to have become a definite entity in our thoughts. Mr. Trelawny became more and more enthusiastic as the time wore on; hope was with him becoming certainty. Doctor Winchester seemed to become imbued with some of his spirit, though at times he would throw out some scientific fact which would either make an *impasse* to the other's line of argument, or would come as an arresting shock. Mr. Corbeck, on the other hand, seemed slightly antagonistic to the theory. It may have been that whilst the opinions of the others advanced, his own stood still; but the effect was an attitude which appeared negative, if not wholly one of negation.

As for Margaret, she seemed to be in some way overcome. Either it was some new phase of feeling with her, or else she was taking the issue more seriously than she had yet done. She was generally more or less *distraite*, as though sunk in a brown study; from this she would recover herself with a start. This was usually when there occurred some marked episode in the journey, such as stopping at a station, or when the thunderous rumble of crossing a viaduct woke the echoes of the hills or cliffs around us. On each such occasion she would plunge into the conversation, taking such a part in it as to show that, whatever had been her abstracted thought, her senses had taken in fully all that had gone on around her. Towards myself her manner was strange. Sometimes it was marked by a distance, half shy, half haughty, which was new to me. At other times there were moments of passion in look and gesture and voice which almost made me dizzy with delight. Little, however, of a marked nature transpired during the journey. There was but one episode which had in it any element of alarm, but as we were all asleep at the time it did not disturb us. We only learned it from a communicative guard in the morning. Whilst running between Dawlish and Teignmouth the train was stopped by a warning given by someone who moved a torch to and fro right on the very track. The driver had found on pulling up that just ahead of the train a small landslip had taken place, some of the red earth from the high bank having fallen away. It did not however reach to the metals; and the driver had resumed his way, none too well pleased at the delay. To use his own words, the guard thought "there was too much bally caution on this 'ere line!"

We arrived at Westerton about nine o'clock in the evening. Carts and horses were in waiting, and the work of unloading the train began at once. Our own party did not wait to see the work done, as it was in the hands of competent people. We took the carriage which was in waiting, and through the darkness of the night sped on to Kyllion.

We were all impressed by the house as it appeared in the bright moonlight. A great grey stone mansion of the Jacobean period; vast and spacious, standing high over the sea on the very verge of a high cliff. When we had swept round the curve of the avenue cut through the rock, and come out on the high plateau on which the house stood, the crash and murmur of waves breaking against rock far below us came with an invigorating breath of moist sea air. We understood then in an instant how well we were shut out from the world on that rocky shelf above the sea.

Within the house we found all ready. Mrs. Grant and her staff had worked well, and all was bright and fresh and clean. We took a brief survey of the chief rooms, and then separated to have a wash and to change our clothes after our long journey of more than four-and-twenty hours.

We had supper in the great dining-room on the south side, the walls of which actually hung over the sea. The murmur came up muffled, but it never ceased. As the little promontory stood well out into the sea, the northern side of the house was open ; and the due north was in no way shut out by the great mass of rock, which, reared high above us, shut out the rest of the world. Far off across the bay we could see the trembling lights of the castle, and here and there along the shore the faint light of a fisher's window. For the rest the sea was a dark blue plain with an occasional flicker of light as the gleam of star-light fell on the slope of a swelling wave.

When supper was over we all adjourned to the room which Mr. Trelawny had set aside as his study, his bedroom being close to it. As we entered, the first thing I noticed was a great safe, somewhat similar to that which stood in his room in London. When we were in the room Mr. Trelawny went over to the table, and, taking out his pocket-book, laid it on the table. As he did so he pressed down on it with the palm of his hand. A strange pallor came over his face. With fingers that trembled he opened the book, saying as he did so :

" Its bulk does not seem the same ; I hope nothing has happened ! "

All three of us men crowded round close. Margaret alone remained calm ; she stood erect and silent, and still as a statue. She had a far-away look in her eyes, as though she did not either know or care what was going on around her.

With a despairing gesture Trelawny threw open the pouch of the pocket-book wherein he had placed the Jewel of Seven Stars. As he sank down on the chair which stood close to him, he said in a hoarse voice :

" My God ! it is gone. Without it the Great Experiment can come to nothing ! "

His words seemed to wake Margaret from her introspective mood. An agonised spasm swept her face ; but almost on the instant she was calm. She almost smiled as she said :

" You may have left it in your room, Father. Perhaps it has fallen out of the pocket-book whilst you were changing." Without a word we all hurried into the next room through the open door between the study and the bedroom. And then a sudden calm fell on us like a cloud of fear.

There ! on the table, lay the Jewel of Seven Stars, shining and sparkling with lurid light, as though each of the seven points of each of the seven stars gleamed through blood !

Timidly we each looked behind us, and then at each other. Margaret was now like the rest of us. She had lost her statuesque calm. All the introspective rigidity had gone from her; and she clasped her hands together till the knuckles were white.

Without a word Mr. Trelawny raised the Jewel, and hurried with it into the next room. As quietly as he could he opened the door of the safe with the key fastened to his wrist and placed the Jewel within. When the heavy doors were closed and locked he seemed to breathe more freely.

Somehow this episode, though a disturbing one in many ways, seemed to bring us back to our old selves. Since we had left London we had all been overstrained; and this was a sort of relief. Another step in our strange enterprise had been effected.

The change back was more marked in Margaret than in any of us. Perhaps it was that she was a woman, whilst we were men; perhaps it was that she was younger than the rest; perhaps both reasons were effective, each in its own way. At any rate the change was there, and I was happier than I had been through the long journey. All her buoyancy, her tenderness, her deep feeling seemed to shine forth once more; now and again as her father's eyes rested on her, his face seemed to light up.

Whilst we waited for the carts to arrive, Mr. Trelawny took us through the house, pointing out and explaining where the objects which we had brought with us were to be placed. In one respect only did he withhold confidence. The positions of all those things which had connection with the Great Experiment were not indicated. The cases containing them were to be left in the outer hall, for the present.

By the time we had made the survey, the carts began to arrive; and the stir and bustle of the previous night were renewed. Mr. Trelawny stood in the hall beside the massive ironbound door, and gave directions as to the placing of each of the great packing-cases. Those containing many items were placed in the inner hall where they were to be unpacked.

In an incredibly short time the whole consignment was delivered; and the men departed with a *douceur* for each, given through their foreman, which made them effusive in their thanks. Then we all went to our own rooms. There was a strange confidence over us all. I do not think that any one of us had a doubt as to the quiet passing of the remainder of the night.

The faith was justified, for on our re-assembling in the morning we found that all had slept well and peaceably.

During that day all the curios, except those required for the Great Experiment, were put into the places designed for them. Then it was arranged that all the servants should go back with Mrs. Grant to London on the next morning.

When they had all gone Mr. Trelawny, having seen the doors locked, took us into the study.

"Now," said he when we were seated, "I have a secret to impart; but, according to an old promise which does not leave me free, I must ask you each to give me a solemn promise not to reveal it. For three hundred years at least such a promise has been exacted from everyone to whom it was told, and more than once life and safety were secured through loyal observance of the promise. Even as it is, I am breaking the letter, if not the spirit of the tradition; for I should only tell it to the immediate members of my family."

We all gave the promise required. Then he went on :

"There is a secret place in this house, a cave, natural originally but finished by labour, underneath this house. I will not undertake to say that it has always been used according to the law. During the Bloody Assize more than a few Cornishmen found refuge in it ; and later, and earlier, it formed, I have no doubt whatever, a useful place for storing contraband goods. 'Tre Pol and Pen,' I suppose you know, have always been smugglers ; and their relations and friends and neighbours have not held back from the enterprise. For all such reasons a safe hiding-place was always considered a valuable possession ; and as the heads of our House have always insisted on preserving the secret, I am in honour bound to it. Later on, if all be well, I shall of course tell you, Margaret, and you too, Ross, under the conditions that I am bound to make."

He rose up, and we all followed him. Leaving us in the outer hall, he went away alone for a few minutes ; and returning, beckoned us to follow him.

In the inside hall we found a whole section of an outstanding angle moved away, and from the cavity saw a great hole dimly dark, and the beginning of a rough staircase cut in the rock. As it was not pitch dark there was manifestly some means of lighting it naturally, so without pause we followed our host as he descended. After some forty or fifty steps cut in a winding passage, we came to a great cave whose further end tapered away into blackness. It was a huge place, dimly lit by a few irregular long slits of eccentric shape. Manifestly these were faults in the rock which would readily allow the windows to

be disguised. Close to each of them was a hanging
shutter which could be easily swung across by means
of a dangling rope. The sound of the ceaseless beat
of the waves came up muffled from far below. Mr.
Trelawny at once began to speak:

"This is the spot which I have chosen, as the best
I know, for the scene of our Great Experiment. In
a hundred different ways it fulfils the conditions
which I am led to believe are primary with regard
to success. Here, we are, and shall be, as isolated
as Queen Tera herself would have been in her rocky
tomb in the Valley of the Sorcerer, and still in a
rocky cavern. For good or ill we must here stand
by our chances, and abide by results. If we are
successful we shall be able to let in on the world
of modern science such a flood of light from the
Old World as will change every condition of thought
and experiment and practice. If we fail, then even
the knowledge of our attempt will die with us. For
this, and all else which may come, I believe we are
prepared!" He paused. No one spoke, but we all
bowed our heads gravely in acquiescence. He resumed, but with a certain hesitancy:

"It is not yet too late! If any of you have a
doubt or a misgiving, for God's sake speak it now!
Whoever it may be, can go hence without let or
hindrance. The rest of us can go on our way
alone!"

Again he paused, and looked keenly at us in turn.
We looked at each other; but no one quailed. For
my own part, if I had had any doubt as to going
on, the look on Margaret's face would have reassured
me. It was fearless; it was intense; it was full of a
divine calm.

Mr. Trelawny took a long breath, and in a more cheerful, as well as in a more decided tone, went on :

"As we are all of one mind, the sooner we get the necessary matters in train the better. Let me tell you that this place, like all the rest of the house, can be lit with electricity. We could not join the wires to the mains lest our secret should become known, but I have a cable here which we can attach in the hall and complete the circuit!" As he was speaking, he began to ascend the steps. From close to the entrance he took the end of a cable ; this he drew forward and attached to a switch in the wall. Then, turning on a tap, he flooded the whole vault and staircase below with light. I could now see from the volume of light streaming up into the hallway that the hole beside the staircase went direct into the cave. Above it was a pulley and a mass of strong tackle with multiplying blocks of the Smeaton order. Mr. Trelawny, seeing me looking at this, said, correctly interpreting my thoughts :

"Yes! it is new. I hung it myself there on purpose. I knew we should have to lower great weights; and as I did not wish to take too many into my confidence, I arranged a tackle which I could work alone if necessary."

We set to work at once ; and before nightfall had lowered, unhooked, and placed in the positions designated for each by Trelawny, all the great sarcophagi and all the curios and other matters which we had taken with us.

It was a strange and weird proceeding the placing of those wonderful monuments of a bygone age in that green cavern, which represented in its cutting and purpose and up-to-date mechanism and electric lights both the old world and the new. But as time went on I grew more and more to recognise the wisdom and correctness of Mr. Trelawny's choice. I was much disturbed when Silvio, who had been brought into the cave in the arms of his mistress, and who was lying asleep on my coat which I had taken off, sprang up when the cat mummy had been unpacked, and flew at it with the same ferocity which he had previously exhibited. The incident showed Margaret in a new phase, and one which gave my heart a pang. She had been standing quite still at one side of the cave leaning on a sarcophagus, in one of those fits of abstraction which had of late come upon her; but on hearing the sound, and seeing Silvio's violent onslaught, she seemed to fall into a positive fury of passion. Her eyes blazed, and her mouth took a hard, cruel tension which was new to me. Instinctively she stepped towards Silvio as if to interfere in the attack. But I too had stepped forward; and as she caught my eye a strange spasm came upon her, and she stopped. Its intensity made me hold my breath; and I put up my hand to clear my eyes. When I had done this, she had on the instant recovered her calm, and there was a look of brief wonder on her face. With all her old grace and sweetness she swept over and lifted Silvio, just as she had done on former occasions, and held him in her arms, petting him and treating him as though he were a little child who had erred.

As I looked a strange fear came over me. The Margaret that I knew seemed to be changing; and in my inmost heart I prayed that the disturbing cause might soon come to an end. More than ever I longed at that moment that our terrible Experiment should come to a prosperous termination.

When all had been arranged in the room as Mr. Trelawny wished he turned to us, one after another, till he had concentrated the intelligence of us all upon him. Then he said:

"All is now ready in this place. We must only await the proper time to begin."

We were silent for a while. Doctor Winchester was the first to speak:

"What is the proper time? Have you any approximation, even if you are not satisfied as to the exact day." He answered at once:

"After the most anxious thought I have fixed on July 31!"

"May I ask why that date?" He spoke his answer slowly:

"Queen Tera was ruled in great degree by mysticism, and there are so many evidences that she looked for resurrection that naturally she would choose a period ruled over by a God specialised to such a purpose. Now, the fourth month of the season of Inundation was ruled by Harmachis, this being the name for 'Ra' the Sun-God, at his rising in the morning, and therefore typifying the awakening or arising. This arising is manifestly to physical life, since it is of the mid-world of human daily life. Now as this month begins on our 25th July, the seventh day would be July 31st, for you may be sure that the mystic Queen would not have chosen any day but the seventh or some power of seven.

"I dare say that some of you have wondered why our preparations have been so deliberately undertaken. This is why! We must be ready in every possible way when the time comes ; but there was no use in having to wait round for a needless number of days."

And so we waited only for the 31st of July, the next day but one, when the Great Experiment would be made.

CHAPTER XVII

DOUBTS AND FEARS

WE learn of great things by little experiences. The history of ages is but an indefinite repetition of the history of hours. The record of a soul is but a multiple of the story of a moment. The Recording Angel writes in the Great Book in no rainbow tints; his pen is dipped in no colours but light and darkness. For the eye of infinite wisdom there is no need of shading. All things, all thoughts, all emotions, all experiences, all doubts and hopes and fears, all intentions, all wishes seen down to the lower strata of their concrete and multitudinous elements, are finally resolved into direct opposites.

Did any human being wish for the epitome of a life wherein were gathered and grouped all the experiences that a child of Adam could have, the history, fully and frankly written, of my own mind during the next forty-eight hours would afford him all that could be wanted. And the Recorder could have wrought as usual in sunlight and shadow, which may be taken to represent the final expressions of Heaven and Hell. For in the highest Heaven is Faith; and Doubt hangs over the yawning blackness of Hell.

There were of course times of sunshine in those two days; moments when, in the realisation of

Margaret's sweetness· and her love for me, all doubts
were dissipated like morning mist before the sun.
But the balance of the time—and an overwhelming
balance it was—gloom hung over me like a pall.
The hour, in whose coming I had acquiesced, was
approaching so quickly and was already so near
that the sense of finality was bearing upon me!
The issue was perhaps life or death to any of us;
but for this we were all prepared. Margaret and
I were one as to the risk. The question of the
moral aspect of the case, which involved the re-
ligious belief in which I had been reared, was not
one to trouble me; for the issues, and the causes
that lay behind them, were not within my power
even to comprehend. The doubt of the success of
the Great Experiment was such a doubt as exists in
all enterprises which have great possibilities. To
me, whose life was passed in a series of intellectual
struggles, this form of doubt was a stimulus, rather
than deterrent. What then was it that made for
me a trouble, which became an anguish when my
thoughts dwelt long on it?

I was beginning to doubt Margaret!

What it was that I doubted I knew not. It was not
her love, or her honour, or her truth, or her kindness,
or her zeal. What then was it?

It was herself!

Margaret was changing! At times during the past
few days I had hardly known her as the same girl
whom I had met at the picnic, and whose vigils I
had shared in the sick-room of her father. Then,
even in her moments of greatest sorrow or fright
or anxiety, she was all life and thought and keenness.
Now she was generally *distraite*, and at times in a

sort of negative condition as though her mind—her very being—was not present. At such moments she would have full possession of observation and memory. She would know and remember all that was going on, and had gone on around her; but her coming back to her old self had to me something the sensation of a new person coming into the room. Up to the time of leaving London I had been content whenever she was present. I had over me that delicious sense of security which comes with the consciousness that love is mutual. But now doubt had taken its place. I never knew whether the personality present was my Margaret—the old Margaret whom I had loved at the first glance — or the other new Margaret, whom I hardly understood, and whose intellectual aloofness made an impalpable barrier between us. Sometimes she would become, as it were, awake all at once. At such times, though she would say to me sweet and pleasant things which she had often said before, she would seem most unlike herself. It was almost as if she was speaking parrot-like or at dictation of one who could read words or acts, but not thoughts. After one or two experiences of this kind, my own doubting began to make a barrier; for I could not speak with the ease and freedom which were usual to me. And so hour by hour we drifted further apart. Were it not for the few odd moments when the old Margaret was back with me full of her charm I do not know what would have happened. As it was, each such moment gave me a fresh start and kept my love from changing.

I would have given the world for a confidant; but this was impossible. How could I speak a doubt of Margaret to anyone, even her father! How could I speak a doubt to Margaret, when Margaret herself was the theme! I could only endure—and hope. And of the two the endurance was the lesser pain.

I think that Margaret must have at times felt that there was some cloud between us, for towards the end of the first day she began to shun me a little ; or perhaps it was that she had become more diffident than usual about me. Hitherto she had sought every opportunity of being with me, just as I had tried to be with her ; so that now any avoidance, one of the other, made a new pain to us both.

On this day the household seemed very still. Each one of us was about his own work, or occupied with his own thoughts. We only met at meal times ; and then, though we talked, all seemed more or less preoccupied. There was not in the house even the stir of the routine of service. The precaution of Mr. Trelawny in having three rooms prepared for each of us had rendered servants unnecessary. The dining-room was solidly prepared with cooked provisions for several days. Towards evening I went out by myself for a stroll. I had looked for Margaret to ask her to come with me ; but when I found her, she was in one of her apathetic moods, and the charm of her presence seemed lost to me. Angry with myself, but unable to quell my own spirit of discontent, I went out alone over the rocky headland.

On the cliff, with the wide expanse of wonderful sea before me, and no sound but the dash of waves below and the harsh screams of the seagulls above, my thoughts ran free. Do what I would, they returned continuously to one subject, the solving of the doubt that was upon me. Here in the solitude, amid the wide circle of Nature's force and strife, my mind began to work truly. Unconsciously I found myself asking a question which I would not allow myself to answer. At last the persistence of a mind working truly prevailed ; I found myself face to face with my doubt. The habit of my life began to assert itself, and I analysed the evidence before me.

It was so startling that I had to force myself into obedience to logical effort. My starting-place was this : Margaret was changed—in what way, and by what means. Was it her character, or her mind, or her nature ? for her physical appearance remained the same. I began to group all that I had ever heard of her, beginning at her birth.

It was strange at the very first. She had been, according to Corbeck's statement, born of a dead mother during the time that her father and his friend were in a trance in the tomb at Aswân. That trance was presumably effected by a woman ; a woman mummied, yet preserving as we had every reason to believe from after experience, an astral body subject to a free will and an active intelligence. With that astral body, space ceased to exist. The vast distance between London and Aswân became as naught ; and whatever power of necromancy the Sorceress had might have been exercised over the dead mother, and possibly the dead child.

The dead child ! Was it possible that the child was dead and was made alive again ? Whence then came the animating spirit—the soul ? Logic was pointing the way to me now with a vengeance !

If the Egyptian belief was true for Egyptians, then the "Ka" of the dead Queen and her "Khu" could animate what she might choose. In such case Mar-

garet would not be an individual at all, but simply a
phase of Queen Tera herself; an astral body obedient
to her will!

Here I revolted against logic. Every fibre of my
being resented such a conclusion. How could I
believe that there was no Margaret at all; but just an
animated image, used by the Double of a woman of
forty centuries ago to its own ends . . .! Somehow,
the outlook was brighter to me now, despite the new
doubts.

At least I had Margaret!

Back swung the logical pendulum again. The child
then was not dead. If so, had the Sorceress had anything to do with her birth at all? It was evident—
so I took it again from Corbeck—that there was a
strange likeness between Margaret and the pictures of
Queen Tera. How could this be? It could not be
any birth-mark reproducing what had been in the
mother's mind; for Mrs. Trelawny had never seen
the pictures. Nay, even her father had not seen them
till he had found his way into the tomb only a few
days before her birth. This phase I could not get
rid of so easily as the last; the fibres of my being
remained quiet. There remained to me the horror of
doubt. And even then, so strange is the mind of man,
Doubt itself took a concrete image; a vast and impenetrable gloom, through which flickered irregularly
and spasmodically tiny points of evanescent light,
which seemed to quicken the darkness into a positive
existence.

The remaining possibility of relations between Margaret and the mummied Queen was, that in some
occult way the Sorceress had power to change places
with the other. This view of things could not be so

lightly thrown aside. There were too many suspicious circumstances to warrant this, now that my attention was fixed on it and my intelligence recognised the possibility. Hereupon there began to come into my mind all the strange incomprehensible matters which had whirled through our lives in the last few days. At first they all crowded in upon me in a jumbled mass ; but again the habit of mind of my working life prevailed, and they took order. I found it now easier to control myself ; for there was something to grasp, some work to be done ; though it was of a sorry kind, for it was or might be antagonistic to Margaret. But Margaret was herself at stake ! I was thinking of her and fighting for her ; and yet if I were to work in the dark, I might be even harmful to her. My first weapon in her defence was truth. I must know and understand ; I might then be able to act. Certainly, I could not act beneficently without a just conception and recognition of the facts. Arranged in order these were as follows :

Firstly : the strange likeness of Queen Tera to Margaret who had been born in another country a thousand miles away, where her mother could not possibly have had even a passing knowledge of her appearance.

Secondly : the disappearance of Van Huyn's book when I had read up to the description of the Star Ruby.

Thirdly : the finding of the lamps in the boudoir. Tera with her astral body could have unlocked the door of Corbeck's room in the hotel, and have locked it again after her exit with the lamps. She could in the same way have opened the window, and put the lamps in the boudoir. It need not have been that

Margaret in her own person should have had any hand in this ; but—but it was at least strange.

Fourthly : here the suspicions of the Detective and the Doctor came back to me with renewed force, and with a larger understanding.

Fifthly : there were the occasions on which Margaret foretold with accuracy the coming occasions of quietude, as though she had some conviction or foreknowledge of the intentions of the astral-bodied Queen.

Sixthly : there was her suggestion of the finding of the Ruby which her father had lost. As I thought now afresh over this episode in the light of suspicion in which her own powers were involved, the only conclusion I could come to was—always supposing that the theory of the Queen's astral power was correct—that Queen Tera being anxious that all should go well in the movement from London to Kyllion had in her own way taken the Jewel from Mr. Trelawny's pocket-book, finding it of some use in her supernatural guardianship of the journey. Then in some mysterious way she had, through Margaret, made the suggestion of its loss and finding.

Seventhly, and lastly, was the strange dual existence which Margaret seemed of late to be leading ; and which in some way seemed a consequence or corollary of all that had gone before.

The dual existence ! This was indeed the conclusion which overcame all difficulties and reconciled opposites. If indeed Margaret were not in all ways a free agent, but could be compelled to speak or act as she might be instructed ; or if her whole being could be changed for another without the possibility of any one noticing the doing of it, then all things were pos-

sible. All would depend on the spirit of the individuality by which she could be so compelled. If this
individuality were just and kind and clean, all might
be well. But if not ! . . . The thought was too awful
for words. I ground my teeth with futile rage, as the
ideas of horrible possibilities swept through me.

Up to this morning Margaret's lapses into her new
self had been few and hardly noticeable, save when
once or twice her attitude towards myself had been
marked by a bearing strange to me. But to-day the
contrary was the case ; and the change presaged
badly. It might be that that other individuality was
of the lower, not of the better sort ! Now that I
thought of it I had reason to fear. In the history of
the mummy, from the time of Van Huyn's breaking
into the tomb, the record of deaths that we knew of,
presumably effected by her will and agency, was a
startling one. The Arab who had stolen the hand from
the mummy ; and the one who had taken it from his
body. The Arab chief who had tried to steal the
Jewel from Van Huyn, and whose throat bore the
marks of seven fingers. The two men found dead on
the first night of Trelawny's taking away the sarcophagus ; and the three on the return to the tomb. The
Arab who had opened the secret serdâb. Nine dead
men, one of them slain manifestly by the Queen's own
hand ! And beyond this again the several savage
attacks on Mr. Trelawny in his own room, in which,
aided by her Familiar, she had tried to open the safe
and to extract the Talisman jewel. His device of
fastening the key to his wrist by a steel bangle, though
successful in the end, had wellnigh cost him his life.

If then the Queen, intent on her resurrection under
her own conditions had, so to speak, waded to it

through blood, what might she not do were her purpose thwarted? What terrible step might she not take to effect her wishes? Nay, what were her wishes; what was her ultimate purpose? As yet we had had only Margaret's statement of them, given in all the glorious enthusiasm of her lofty soul. In her record there was no expression of a love to be sought or found. All we knew for certain was that she had set before her the object of resurrection, and that in it the North which she had manifestly loved was to have a special part. But that the resurrection was to be accomplished in the lonely tomb in the Valley of the Sorcerer was apparent. All preparations had been carefully made for accomplishment from within, and for her ultimate exit in her new and living form. The sarcophagus was unlidded. The oil jars, though hermetically sealed, were to be easily opened by hand; and in them provision was made for shrinkage through a vast period of time. Even flint and steel were provided for the production of flame. The Mummy Pit was left open in violation of usage; and beside the stone door on the cliff side was fixed an imperishable chain by which she might in safety descend to earth. But as to what her after intentions were we had no clue. If it was that she meant to begin life again as a humble individual, there was something so noble in the thought that it even warmed my heart to her and turned my wishes to her success.

The very idea seemed to endorse Margaret's magnificent tribute to her purpose, and helped to calm my troubled spirit.

Then and there, with this feeling strong upon me, I determined to warn Margaret and her father of dire possibilities; and to await, as well content as I could in my ignorance, the development of things over which I had no power.

I returned to the house in a different frame of mind to that in which I had left it; and was enchanted to find Margaret—the old Margaret—waiting me.

After dinner, when I was alone for a time with the father and daughter, I opened the subject, though with considerable hesitation :

"Would it not be well to take every possible precaution, in case the Queen may not wish what we are doing, with regard to what may occur before the Experiment; and at or after her waking, if it comes off ?" Margaret's answer came back quickly; so quickly that I was convinced she must have had it ready for some one :

"But she does approve! Surely it cannot be otherwise. Father is doing, with all his brains and all his energy and all his great courage, just exactly what the great Queen had arranged !"

"But," I answered, "that can hardly be. All that she arranged was in a tomb high up in a rock, in a desert solitude, shut away from the world by every conceivable means. She seems to have depended on this isolation to insure against accident. Surely, here in another country and age, with quite different conditions, she may in her anxiety make mistakes and treat any of you—of us—as she did those others in times gone past. Nine men that we know of have been slain by her own hand or by her instigation. She can be remorseless if she will." It did not strike me till afterwards when I was thinking over this conversation, how thoroughly I had accepted the living and conscious condition of Queen Tera as a

fact. Before I spoke, I had feared I might offend
Mr. Trelawny ; but to my pleasant surprise he smiled
quite genially as he answered me :

" My dear fellow, in a way you are quite right. The
Queen did undoubtedly intend isolation ; and, all
told, it would be best that her experiment should
be made as she arranged it. But just think, that
became impossible when once the Dutch explorer
had broken into her tomb. That was not my doing.
I am innocent of it, though it was the cause of my
setting out to rediscover the sepulchre. Mind, I do
not say for a moment that I would not have done
just the same as Van Huyn. I went into the tomb
from curiosity ; and I took away what I did, being
fired with the zeal of acquisitiveness which animates
the collector. But, remember also, that at this time
I did not know of the Queen's intention of resurrection ; I had no idea of the completeness of her
preparations. All that came long afterwards. But
when it did come, I have done all that I could to
carry out her wishes to the full. My only fear is
that I may have misinterpreted some of her cryptic
instructions, or have omitted or overlooked something.
But of this I am certain ; I have left undone nothing
that I can imagine right to be done ; and I have done
nothing that I know of to clash with Queen Tera's
arrangement. I want her Great Experiment to
succeed. To this end I have not spared labour or
time or money—or myself. I have endured hard-
ship, and braved danger. All my brains ; all my
knowledge and learning, such as they are ; all my
endeavours such as they can be, have been, are,
and shall be devoted to this end, till we either
win or lose the great stake that we play for."

"The great stake?" I repeated; "the resurrection of the woman, and the woman's life? The proof that resurrection can be accomplished; by magical powers; by scientific knowledge; or by use of some force which at present the world does not know?"

Then Mr. Trelawny spoke out the hopes of his heart which up to now he had indicated rather than expressed. Once or twice I had heard Corbeck speak of the fiery energy of his youth; but, save for the noble words of Margaret when she had spoken of Queen Tera's hope—which coming from his daughter made possible a belief that her power was in some sense due to heredity—I had seen no marked sign of it. But now his words, sweeping before them like a torrent all antagonistic thought, gave me a new idea of the man.

"'A woman's life!' What is a woman's life in the scale with what we hope for! Why, we are risking already a woman's life; the dearest life to me in all the world, and that grows more dear with every hour that passes. We are risking as well the lives of four men; yours and my own, as well as those two others who have been won to our confidence. 'The proof that resurrection can be accomplished!' That is much. A marvellous thing in this age of science, and the scepticism that knowledge makes. But life and resurrection are themselves but items in what may be won by the accomplishment of this Great Experiment. Imagine what it will be for the world of thought—the true world of human progress—the veritable road to the Stars, the *itur ad astra* of the Ancients—if there can come back to us out of the unknown past one who can yield to us the lore stored in the great

Library of Alexandria, and lost in its consuming
flames. Not only history can be set right, and
the teachings of science made veritable from their
beginnings; but we can be placed on the road to
the knowledge of lost arts, lost learning, lost sciences,
so that our feet may tread on the indicated path to
their ultimate and complete restoration. Why, this
woman can tell us what the world was like before
what is called 'the Flood'; can give us the origin
of that vast astounding myth; can set the mind
back to the consideration of things which to us now
seem primeval, but which were old stories before
the days of the Patriarchs. But this is not the end!
No, not even the beginning! If the story of this
woman be all that we think—which some of us
most firmly believe; if her powers and the restoration of them prove to be what we expect, why,
then we may yet achieve a knowledge beyond
what our age has ever known—beyond what is
believed to-day possible for the children of men.
If indeed this resurrection can be accomplished,
how can we doubt the old knowledge, the old magic,
the old belief! And if this be so, we must take it
that the 'Ka' of this great and learned Queen has
won secrets of more than mortal worth from her
surroundings amongst the stars. This woman in her
life voluntarily went down living to the grave, and
came back again, as we learn from the records in
her tomb; she chose to die her mortal death whilst
young, so that at her resurrection in another age,
beyond a trance of countless magnitude, she might
emerge from her tomb in all the fulness and splendour of her youth and power. Already we have
evidence that though her body slept in patience

K

through those many centuries, her intelligence never passed away, that her resolution never flagged, that her will remained supreme ; and, most important of all, that her memory was unimpaired. Oh, what possibilities are there in the coming of such a being into our midst! One whose history began before the concrete teaching of our Bible ; whose experiences were antecedent to the formulation of the Gods of Greece ; who can link together the Old and the New, Earth and Heaven, and yield to the known worlds of thought and physical existence the mystery of the Unknown—of the Old World in its youth, and of Worlds beyond our ken !"

He paused almost overcome. Margaret had taken his hand when he spoke of her being so dear to him, and held it hard. As he spoke she continued to hold it. But there came over her face that change which I had so often seen of late ; that mysterious veiling of her own personality which gave me the subtle sense of separation from her. In his impassioned vehemence her father did not notice ; but when he stopped she seemed all at once to be herself again. In her glorious eyes came the added brightness of unshed tears ; and with a gesture of passionate love and admiration, she stooped and kissed her father's hand. Then, turning to me, she too spoke :

"Malcolm, you have spoken of the deaths that came from the poor Queen ; or rather that justly came from meddling with her arrangements and thwarting her purpose. Do you not think that, in putting it as you have done, you have been unjust ? Who would not have done just as she did ? Remember she was fighting for her life! Ay, and for more than her life! For life, and love, and all the glorious possibilities of that dim future in the unknown world of the North which had such enchanting hopes for her! Do you not think that she, with all the learning of her time, and with all the great and resistless force of her mighty nature, had hopes of spreading in a wider way the lofty aspirations of her soul! That she hoped to bring to the conquering of unknown worlds, and using to the advantage of her people, all that she had won from sleep and death and time; all of which might and could have been frustrated by the ruthless hand of an assassin or a thief. Were it you, in such case would you not struggle by all means to achieve the object of your life and hope; whose possibilities grew and grew in the passing of those endless years? Can you think that that active brain was at rest during all those weary centuries, whilst her mortal body, swathed in all the protecting environment ordained by the religion and the science of her time, waited the destined hour; whilst her free soul was flitting from world to world amongst the boundless regions of the stars? Had these stars in their myriad and varied life no lessons for her; as they have had for us since we followed the glorious path which she and her people marked for us, when they sent their winged imaginations circling amongst the lamps of the night!"

Here she paused. She too was overcome, and the welling tears ran down her cheeks. I was myself more moved than I can say. This was indeed my Margaret; and in the consciousness of her presence my heart leapt. Out of my happiness came boldness, and I dared to say now what I had feared

would be impossible : something which would call
the attention of Mr. Trelawny to what I imagined
was the dual existence of his daughter. As I took
Margaret's hand in mine and kissed it, I said to
her father :

"Why, sir! she couldn't speak more eloquently if
the very spirit of Queen Tera was with her to animate
her and suggest thoughts ! "

Mr. Trelawny's answer simply overwhelmed me with
surprise. It manifested to me that he too had gone
through just such a process of thought as my own.

"And what if it was ; if it is ! I know well that the
spirit of her mother is within her. If in addition there
be the spirit of that great and wondrous Queen, then
she would be no less dear to me, but doubly dear !
Do not have fear for her, Malcolm Ross ; at least have
no more fear than you may have for the rest of us ! "
Margaret took up the theme, speaking so quickly that
her words seemed a continuation of her father's,
rather than an interruption of them.

"Have no special fear for me, Malcolm. Queen
Tera knows, and will offer us no harm. I know it ! I
know it, as surely as I am lost in the depth of my own
love for you ! "

There was something in her voice so strange to me
that I looked quickly into her eyes. They were bright
as ever, but veiled to my seeing the inward thought
behind them as are the eyes of a caged lion.

Then the two other men came in, and the subject
changed.

CHAPTER XVIII

THE LESSON OF THE "KA"

THAT night we all went to bed early. The next night would be an anxious one, and Mr. Trelawny thought that we should all be fortified with what sleep we could get. The day, too, would be full of work. Everything in connection with the Great Experiment would have to be gone over, so that at the last we might not fail from any unthought-of flaw in our working. We made, of course, arrangements for summoning aid in case such should be needed ; but I do not think that any of us had any real apprehension of danger. Certainly we had no fear of such danger from violence as we had had to guard against in London during Mr. Trelawny's long trance.

For my own part I felt a strange sense of relief in the matter. I had accepted Mr. Trelawny's reasoning that if the Queen were indeed such as we surmised— such as indeed we now took for granted— there would not be any opposition on her part ; for we were carrying out her own wishes to the very last. So far I was at ease—far more at ease than earlier in the day I should have thought possible ; but there were other sources of trouble which I could not blot out from my mind. Chief amongst them was Margaret's strange condition. If it was indeed that she had in her own person a dual existence, what might happen when the two existences became one ? Again, and again, and again I turned this matter over in my mind, till I could have shrieked out in nervous anxiety. It was no consolation to me to remember that Margaret was herself satisfied, and her father acquiescent. Love is, after all, a selfish thing ; and it throws a black shadow on anything between which and the light it stands. I seemed to hear the hands go round the dial of the clock ; I saw darkness turn to gloom, and gloom to grey, and grey to light without pause or hindrance to the succession of my miserable feelings. At last, when it was decently possible without the fear of disturbing others, I got up. I crept along the passage to find if all was well with the others ; for we had arranged that the door of each of our rooms should be left slightly open so that any sound of disturbance would be easily and distinctly heard.

One and all slept ; I could hear the regular breathing of each, and my heart rejoiced that this miserable night of anxiety was safely passed. As I knelt in my own room in a burst of thankful prayer, I knew in the depths of my own heart the measure of my fear. I found my way out of the house, and went down to the water by the long stairway cut in the rock. A swim in the cool bright sea braced my nerves and made me my old self again.

As I came back to the top of the steps I could see the bright sunlight, rising from behind me, turning the rocks across the bay to glittering gold. And yet I felt somehow disturbed. It was all too bright ; as it sometimes is before the coming of a storm. As I paused to watch it, I felt a soft hand on my shoulder ; and, turning, found Margaret close to me ; Margaret as bright and radiant as the morning glory of the sun! It was my own Margaret this time! My old Margaret, without alloy of any other; and I felt that, at least, this last and fatal day was well begun.

But alas! the joy did not last. When we got back to the house from a stroll around the cliffs, the same old routine of yesterday was resumed: gloom and anxiety, hope, high spirits, deep depression, and apathetic aloofness.

But it was to be a day of work; and we all braced ourselves to it with an energy which wrought its own salvation.

After breakfast we all adjourned to the cave, where Mr. Trelawny went over, point by point, the position of each item of our paraphernalia. He explained as he went on why each piece was so placed. He had with him the great rolls of paper with the measured plans and the signs and drawings which he had had made from his own and Corbeck's rough notes. As he had told us, these contained the whole of the hieroglyphics on walls and ceilings and floor of the tomb in the Valley of the Sorcerer. Even had not the measurements, made to scale, recorded the position of each piece of furniture, we could have eventually placed them by a study of the cryptic writings and symbols.

Mr. Trelawny explained to us certain other things, not laid down on the chart. Such as, for instance, that the hollowed part of the table was exactly fitted to the bottom of the Magic Coffer, which was therefore intended to be placed on it. The respective legs of this table were indicated by differently shaped uræi outlined on the floor, the head of each being extended in the direction of the similar uræus twined round the leg. Also that the mummy, when laid on the raised portion in the bottom of the sarcophagus, seemingly made to fit the form, would lie head to the West and feet to the East, thus receiving the natural earth currents. "If this be intended," he said, "as I presume it is, I gather that the force to be used has something to do with magnetism or electricity, or both. It may be, of course, that some other force, such, for instance, as that emanating from radium, is to be employed. I have experimented with the latter, but only in such small quantity as I could obtain ; but so far as I can ascertain the stone of the Coffer is absolutely impervious to its influence. There must be some such unsusceptible substances in nature. Radium does not seemingly manifest itself when distributed through pitchblende ; and there are doubtless other such substances in which it can be imprisoned. Possibly these may belong to that class of 'inert' elements discovered or isolated by Sir William Ramsay. It is therefore possible that in this Coffer, made from an aerolite and therefore perhaps containing some element unknown in our world, may be imprisoned some mighty power which is to be released on its opening."

This appeared to be an end of this branch of the subject ; but as he still kept the fixed look of one who is engaged in a theme we all waited in silence. After a pause he went on :

"There is one thing which has up to now, I confess, puzzled me. It may not be of prime importance ; but in a matter like this, where all is unknown, we must take it that everything is important. I cannot think that in a matter worked out with such extraordinary scrupulosity such a thing should be overlooked. As you may see by the ground-plan of the

tomb the sarcophagus stands near the north wall, with
the Magic Coffer to the south of it. The space covered
by the former is left quite bare of symbol or ornamentation of any kind. At the first glance this would
seem to imply that the drawings had been made *after*
the sarcophagus had been put into its place. But a
more minute examination will show that the symbolisation on the floor is so arranged that a definite effect is
produced. See, here the writings run in correct order
as though they had jumped across the gap. It is only
from certain effects that it becomes clear that there is
a meaning of some kind. What that meaning may
be is what we want to know. Look at the top and
bottom of the vacant space, which lies West and East
corresponding to the head and foot of the sarcophagus.
In both are duplications of the same symbolisation,
but so arranged that the parts of each one of them are
integral portions of some other writing running cross-
wise. It is only when we get a *coup d'œil* from either
the head or the foot that you recognise that there are
symbolisations. See! they are in triplicate at the
corners and the centre of both top and bottom. In
every case there is a sun cut in half by the line of the
sarcophagus, as by the horizon. Close behind each of
these and faced away from it, as though in some way
dependent on it, is the vase which in hieroglyphic
writing symbolises the heart—'Ab' the Egyptians called
it. Beyond each of these again is the figure of a pair
of widespread arms turned upwards from the elbow ;
this is the determinative of the ' Ka ' or ' Double.' But
its relative position is different at top and bottom. At
the head of the sarcophagus the top of the ' Ka ' is
turned towards the mouth of the vase, but at the foot
the extended arms point away from it.

"The symbolisation seems to mean that during the passing of the Sun from West to East—from sunset to sunrise, or through the Under World, otherwise night—the Heart, which is material even in the tomb and cannot leave it, simply revolves, so that it can always rest on 'Ra' the Sun-God, the origin of all good ; but that the Double, which represents the active principle, goes whither it will, the same by night as by day. If this be correct it is a warning—a caution—a reminder that the consciousness of the mummy does not rest but is to be reckoned with.

"Or it may be intended to convey that after the particular night of the resurrection, the 'Ka' would leave the heart altogether, thus typifying that in her resurrection the Queen would be restored to a lower and purely physical existence. In such case what would become of her memory and the experiences of her wide-wandering soul ? The chiefest value of her resurrection would be lost to the world ! This, how-ever, does not alarm me. It is only guess-work after all, and is contradictory to the intellectual belief of the Egyptian theology, that the 'Ka' is an essential portion of humanity." He paused and we all waited. The silence was broken by Doctor Winchester :

"But would not all this imply that the Queen feared intrusion of her tomb ? " Mr. Trelawny smiled as he answered :

"My dear sir, she was prepared for it. The grave robber is no modern application of endeavour ; he was probably known in the Queen's own dynasty. Not only was she prepared for intrusion, but, as shown in several ways, she expected it. The hiding of the lamps in the serdâb, and the institution of the aveng-ing 'treasurer' shows that there was defence, positive

as well as negative. Indeed, from the many indica-
tions afforded in the clues laid out with the most
consummate thought, we may almost gather that she
entertained it as a possibility that others—like ourselves, for instance—might in all seriousness undertake
the work which she had made ready for her own hands
when the time should have come. This very matter
that I have been speaking of is an instance. The clue
is intended for seeing eyes ! "

Again we were silent. It was Margaret who spoke :
"Father, may I have that chart ? I should like to
study it during the day ! "

"Certainly, my dear !" answered Mr. Trelawny
heartily, as he handed it to her. He resumed his
instructions in a different tone, a more matter-of-fact
one suitable to a practical theme which had no
mystery about it :

"I think you had better all understand the working
of the electric light in case any sudden contingency
should arise. I dare say you have noticed that we
have a complete supply in every part of the house,
so that there need not be a dark corner anywhere.
This I had specially arranged. It is worked by a
set of turbines moved by the flowing and ebbing
tide, after the manner of the turbines at Niagara.
I hope by this means to nullify accident and to have
without fail a full supply ready at any time. Come
with me and I will explain the system of circuits, and
point out to you the taps and the fuses." I could not
but notice, as we went with him all over the house,
how absolutely complete the system was, and how he
had guarded himself against any disaster that human
thought could foresee.

But out of the very completeness came a fear !

In such an enterprise as ours the bounds of human thought were but narrow. Beyond it lay the vast of Divine wisdom, and Divine power!

When we came back to the cave, Mr. Trelawny took up another theme:

"We have now to settle definitely the exact hour at which the Great Experiment is to be made. So far as science and mechanism go, if the preparations are complete, all hours are the same. But as we have to deal with preparations made by a woman of extraordinarily subtle mind, and who had full belief in magic and had a cryptic meaning in everything, we should place ourselves in her position before deciding. It is now manifest that the sunset has an important place in the arrangements. As those suns, cut so mathematically by the edge of the sarcophagus, were arranged of full design, we must take our cue from this. Again, we find all along that the number seven has had an important bearing on every phase of the Queen's thought and reasoning and action. The logical result is that the seventh hour after sunset was the time fixed on. This is borne out by the fact that on each of the occasions when action was taken in my house, this was the time chosen. As the sun sets to-night in Cornwall at eight, our hour is to be three in the morning!" He spoke in a matter-of-fact way, though with great gravity; but there was nothing of mystery in his words or manner. Still, we were all impressed to a remarkable degree. I could see this in the other men by the pallor that came on some of their faces, and by the stillness and un-questioning silence with which the decision was received. The only one who remained in any way at ease was Margaret, who had lapsed into one of her moods of abstraction, but who seemed to wake up to a note of gladness. Her father, who was watching her intently, smiled ; her mood was to him a direct confirmation of his theory.

For myself I was almost overcome. The definite fixing of the hour seemed like the voice of Doom. When I think of it now, I can realise how a condemned man feels at his sentence, or at the sounding of the last hour he is to hear.

There could be no going back now! We were in the hands of God!

The hands of God . . .! And yet . . .! What other forces were arrayed ? . . . What would become of us all, poor atoms of earthly dust whirled in the wind which cometh whence and goeth whither no man may know. It was not for myself . . . Margaret . . .!

I was recalled by Mr. Trelawny's firm voice :

" Now we shall see to the lamps and finish our preparations." Accordingly we set to work, and under his supervision made ready the Egyptian lamps, seeing that they were well filled with the cedar oil, and that the wicks were adjusted and in good order. We lighted and tested them one by one, and left them ready so that they would light at once and evenly. When this was done we had a general look ·round ; and fixed all in readiness for our work at night.

All this had taken time, and we were I think all surprised when as we emerged from the cave we heard the great clock in the hall chime four.

We had a late lunch, a thing possible without trouble in the present state of our commissariat arrangements. After it, by Mr. Trelawny's advice, we separated; each to prepare in our own way for the strain of the coming night. Margaret looked pale and somewhat overwrought, so I advised her to lie down and try to sleep. She promised that she would. The abstraction which had been upon her fitfully all day lifted for the time; with all her old sweetness and loving delicacy she kissed me good-bye for the present! With the sense of happiness which this gave me I went out for a walk on the cliffs. I did not want to think; and I had an instinctive feeling that fresh air and God's sunlight, and the myriad beauties of the works of His hand would be the best preparation of fortitude for what was to come.

When I got back, all the party were assembling for a late tea. Coming fresh from the exhilaration of nature, it struck me as almost comic that we, who were nearing the end of so strange—almost monstrous —an undertaking, should be yet bound by the needs and habits of our lives.

All the men of the party were grave; the time of seclusion, even if it had given them rest, had also given opportunity for thought. Margaret was bright, almost buoyant; but I missed about her something of her usual spontaneity. Towards myself there was a shadowy air of reserve, which brought back something of my suspicion. When tea was over, she went out of the room; but returned in a minute with the roll of drawing which she had taken with her earlier in the day. Coming close to Mr. Trelawny, she said:

"Father, I have been carefully considering what you said to-day about the hidden meaning of those suns and hearts and 'Ka's,' and I have been examining the drawings again."

"And with what result, my child?" asked Mr. Trelawny eagerly.

"There is another reading possible!"

"And that?" His voice was now tremulous with anxiety. Margaret spoke with a strange ring in her voice; a ring that cannot be, unless there is the consciousness of truth behind it:

"It means that at the sunset the 'Ka' is to enter the 'Ab'; and it is only at the sunrise that it will leave it!"

"Go on!" said her father hoarsely.

"It means that for this night the Queen's Double, which is otherwise free, will remain in her heart, which is mortal and cannot leave its prison-place in the mummy shrouding. It means that when the sun has dropped into the sea, Queen Tera will cease to exist as a conscious power, till sunrise; unless the Great Experiment can recall her to waking life. It means that there will be nothing whatever for you or others to fear from her in such way as we have all cause to remember. Whatever change may come from the working of the Great Experiment, there can come none from the poor, helpless, dead woman who has waited all those centuries for this night; who has given up to the coming hour all the freedom of eternity, won in the old way, in hope of a new life in a new world such as she longed for . . . !" She stopped suddenly. As she had gone on speaking there had come with her words a strange pathetic, almost pleading, tone which touched me to the quick. As she stopped, I could see, before she turned away her head, that her eyes were full of tears.

For once the heart of her father did not respond to her feeling. He looked exultant, but with a grim masterfulness which reminded me of the set look of his stern face as he had lain in the trance. He did not offer any consolation to his daughter in her sympathetic pain. He only said :

"We may test the accuracy of your surmise, and of her feeling, when the time comes!" Having said so, he went up the stone stairway and into his own room. Margaret's face had a troubled look as she gazed after him.

Strangely enough her trouble did not as usual touch me to the quick.

When Mr. Trelawny had gone, silence reigned. I do not think that any of us wanted to talk. Presently Margaret went to her room, and I went out on the terrace over the sea. The fresh air and the beauty of all before me helped to restore the good spirits which I had known earlier in the day. Presently I felt myself actually rejoicing in the belief that the danger which I had feared from the Queen's violence on the coming night was obviated. I believed in Margaret's belief so thoroughly that it did not occur to me to dispute her reasoning. In a lofty frame of mind, and with less anxiety than I had felt for days, I went to my room and lay down on the sofa.

I was awaked by Corbeck calling to me, hurriedly :

"Come down to the cave as quickly as you can. Mr. Trelawny wants to see us all there at once. Hurry!"

I jumped up and ran down to the cave. All were there except Margaret, who came immediately after me carrying Silvio in her arms. When the cat saw his old enemy he struggled to get down ; but Margaret held him fast and soothed him. I looked at my watch. It was close to eight.

When Margaret was with us her father said directly, with a quiet insistence which was new to me:

"You believe, Margaret, that Queen Tera has voluntarily undertaken to give up her freedom for this night? To become a mummy and nothing more, till the Experiment has been completed? To be content that she shall be powerless under all and any circumstances until after all is over and the act of resurrection has been accomplished, or the effort has failed?" After a pause Margaret answered in a low voice:

"Yes!"

In the pause her whole being, appearance, expression, voice, manner had changed. Even Silvio noticed it, and with a violent effort wriggled away from her arms; she did not seem to notice the act. I expected that the cat, when he had achieved his freedom, would have attacked the mummy; but on this occasion he did not. He seemed too cowed to approach it. He shrunk away, and with a piteous "miaou" came over and rubbed himself against my ankles. I took him up in my arms, and he nestled there content. Mr. Trelawny spoke again:

"You are sure of what you say! You believe it with all your soul?" Margaret's face had lost the abstracted look; it now seemed illuminated with the devotion of one to whom is given to speak of great things. She answered in a voice which, though quiet, vibrated with conviction:

"I know it! My knowledge is beyond belief!"
Mr. Trelawny spoke again:

"Then you are so sure, that were you Queen Tera herself, you would be willing to prove it in any way that I might suggest?"

"Yes, any way!" the answer rang out fearlessly.

He spoke again, in a voice in which was no note of doubt:

"Even in the abandonment of your Familiar to death—to annihilation."

She paused, and I could see that she suffered—suffered horribly. There was in her eyes a hunted look, which no man can, unmoved, see in the eyes of his beloved. I was about to interrupt, when her father's eyes, glancing round with a fierce determination, met mine. I stood silent, almost spellbound; so also the other men. Something was going on before us which we did not understand!

With a few long strides Mr. Trelawny went to the west side of the cave and tore back the shutter which obscured the window. The cool air blew in, and the sunlight streamed over them both, for Margaret was now by his side. He pointed to where the sun was sinking into the sea in a halo of golden fire, and his face was as set as flint. In a voice whose absolute uncompromising hardness I shall hear in my ears at times till my dying day, he said:

"Choose! Speak! When the sun has dipped below the sea, it will be too late!" The glory of the dying sun seemed to light up Margaret's face, till it shone as if lit from within by a noble light, as she answered:

"Even that!"

Then stepping over to where the mummy cat stood on the little table, she placed her hand on it. She had now left the sunlight, and the shadows looked dark and deep over her. In a clear voice she said:

"Were I Tera, I would say 'Take all I have! This night is for the Gods alone!'"

As she spoke the sun dipped, and the cold shadow

suddenly fell on us.   We all stood still for a while.
Silvio jumped from my arms and ran over to his
mistress, rearing himself up against her dress as if
asking to be lifted.   He took no notice whatever of
the mummy now.

Margaret was glorious with all her wonted sweetness
as she said sadly :

"The sun is down, Father !   Shall any of us see it
again ?   The night of nights is come !"

CHAPTER XIX

THE GREAT EXPERIMENT

IF any evidence had been wanted of how absolutely one and all of us had come to believe in the spiritual existence of the Egyptian Queen, it would have been found in the change which in a few minutes had been effected in us by the statement of voluntary negation made, we all believed, through Margaret. Despite the coming of the fearful ordeal, the sense of which it was impossible to forget, we looked and acted as though a great relief had come to us. We had indeed lived in such a state of terrorism during the days when Mr. Trelawny was lying in a trance that the feeling had bitten deeply into us. No one knows till he has experienced it, what it is to be in constant dread of some unknown danger which may come at any time and in any form.

The change was manifested in different ways, according to each nature. Margaret was sad. Doctor Winchester was in high spirits, and keenly observant ; the process of thought which had served as an antidote to fear, being now relieved from this duty, added to his intellectual enthusiasm. Mr. Corbeck seemed to be in a retrospective rather than a speculative mood. I was myself rather inclined to be gay ; the relief from certain anxiety regarding Margaret was sufficient for me for the time.

As to Mr. Trelawny he seemed less changed than any. Perhaps this was only natural, as he had had in his mind the intention for so many years of doing that in which we were to-night engaged, that any event connected with it could only seem to him as an episode, a step to the end. His was that commanding nature which looks so to the end of an undertaking that all else is of secondary importance. Even now, though his terrible sternness relaxed under the relief from the strain, he never flagged nor faltered for a moment in his purpose. He asked us men to come with him; and going to the hall we presently managed to lower into the cave an oak table, fairly long and not too wide, which stood against the wall in the hall. This we placed under the strong cluster of electric lights in the middle of the cave. Margaret looked on for a while; then all at once her face blanched, and in an agitated voice she said:

"What are you going to do, Father?"

"To unroll the mummy of the cat! Queen Tera will not need her Familiar to-night. If she should want him, it might be dangerous to us; so we shall make him safe. You are not alarmed, dear?"

"Oh no!" she answered quickly. "But I was thinking of my Silvio, and how I should feel if he had been the mummy that was to be unswathed!"

Mr. Trelawny got knives and scissors ready, and placed the cat on the table. It was a grim beginning to our work; and it made my heart sink when I thought of what might happen in that lonely house in the mid-gloom of the night. The sense of loneliness and isolation from the world was increased by the moaning of the wind which had now risen ominously, and by the beating of waves on the rocks below. But we had too grave a task before us to be swayed by external manifestations: the unrolling of the mummy began.

There was an incredible number of bandages; and the tearing sound—they being stuck fast to each other by bitumen and gums and spices—and the little cloud of red pungent dust that arose, pressed on the senses of all of us. As the last wrappings came away, we saw the animal seated before us. He was all hunkered up; his hair and teeth and claws were complete. The eyes were closed, but the eyelids had not the fierce look which I expected. The whiskers had been pressed down on the side of the face by the bandaging; but when the pressure was taken away they stood out, just as they would have done in life. He was a magnificent creature, a tiger-cat of great size. But as we looked at him, our first glance of admiration changed to one of fear, and a shudder ran through each one of us; for here was a confirmation of the fears which we had endured.

His mouth and his claws were smeared with the dry, red stains of recent blood!

Doctor Winchester was the first to recover; blood in itself had small disturbing quality for him. He had taken out his magnifying-glass and was examining the stains on the cat's mouth. Mr. Trelawny breathed loudly, as though a strain had been taken from him.

"It is as I expected," he said. "This promises well for what is to follow."

By this time Doctor Winchester was looking at the red stained paws. "As I expected!" he said. "He has seven claws, too! Opening his pocket-book, he took out the piece of blotting-paper marked by Silvio's claws, on which was also marked in pencil a diagram of the cuts made on Mr. Trelawny's wrist. He placed the paper under the mummy cat's paw. The marks fitted exactly.

When we had carefully examined the cat, finding, however, nothing strange about it but its wonderful preservation, Mr. Trelawny lifted it from the table. Margaret started forward, crying out :

"Take care, Father! Take care! He may injure you!"

"Not now, my dear!" he answered as he moved towards the stairway. Her face fell. "Where are you going?" she asked in a faint voice.

"To the kitchen," he answered. "Fire will take away all danger for the future; even an astral body cannot materialise from ashes!" He signed to us to follow him. Margaret turned away with a sob. I went to her; but she motioned me back and whispered :

"No, no! Go with the others. Father may want you. Oh! it seems like murder! The poor Queen's pet. . . . !" The tears were dropping from under the fingers that covered her eyes.

In the kitchen was a fire of wood ready laid. To this Mr. Trelawny applied a match; in a few seconds the kindling had caught and the flames leaped. When the fire was solidly ablaze, he threw the body of the cat into it. For a few seconds it lay a dark mass amidst the flames, and the room was rank with the smell of burning hair. Then the dry body caught fire too. The inflammable substances used in embalming became new fuel, and the flames roared. A few minutes of fierce conflagration; and then we breathed freely. Queen Tera's Familiar was no more!

When we went back to the cave we found Margaret

sitting in the dark. She had switched off the electric light, and only a faint glow of the evening light came through the narrow openings. Her father went quickly over to her and put his arms round her in a loving protective way. She laid her head on his shoulder for a minute, and seemed comforted. Presently she called to me :

"Malcolm, turn up the light!" I carried out her orders, and could see that, though she had been crying, her eyes were now dry. Her father saw it too and looked glad. He said to us in a grave tone :

"Now we had better prepare for our great work. It will not do to leave anything to the last!" Margaret must have had a suspicion of what was coming, for it was with a sinking voice that she asked :

"What are you going to do now ?" Mr. Trelawny too must have had a suspicion of her feelings, for he answered in a low tone :

"To unroll the mummy of Queen Tera!" She came close to him and said pleadingly in a whisper :

"Father, you are not going to unswathe her! All you men . . . ! And in the glare of light!"

"But why not, my dear ?"

"Just think, Father, a woman! All alone! In such a way! In such a place! Oh! it's cruel, cruel!" She was manifestly much overcome. Her cheeks were flaming red, and her eyes were full of indignant tears. Her father saw her distress ; and, sympathising with it, began to comfort her. I was moving off ; but he signed to me to stay. I took it that after the usual manner of men he wanted help on such an occasion, and man-like wished to throw on someone else the task of dealing with a woman in indignant distress. However, he began to appeal first to her reason :

"Not a woman, dear; a mummy! She has been dead nearly five thousand years!"

"What does that matter? Sex is not a matter of years! A woman is a woman, if she had been dead five thousand centuries! And you expect her to arise out of that long sleep! It could not be real death, if she is to rise out of it! You have led me to believe that she will come alive when the Coffer is opened!"

"I did, my dear; and I believe it! But if it isn't death that has been the matter with her all these years, it is something uncommonly like it. Then again, just think; it was men who embalmed her. They didn't have women's rights or lady doctors in ancient Egypt, my dear! And besides," he went on more freely, seeing that she was accepting his argument, if not yielding to it, "we men are accustomed to such things. Corbeck and I have unrolled a hundred mummies; and there were as many women as men amongst them. Doctor Winchester in his work has had to deal with women as well as men, till custom has made him think nothing of sex. Even Ross has in his work as a barrister . . ." He stopped suddenly.

"You were going to help too!" she said to me, with an indignant look.

I said nothing; I thought silence was best. Mr. Trelawny went on hurriedly; I could see that he was glad of interruption, for the part of his argument concerning a barrister's work was becoming decidedly weak:

"My child, you will be with us yourself. Would we do anything which would hurt or offend you? Come now! be reasonable! We are not at a pleasure party. We are all grave men, entering gravely on an experiment which may unfold the wisdom of old times, and enlarge human knowledge indefinitely; which may put the minds of men on new tracks of thought and research. An experiment," as he went on his voice deepened, "which may be fraught with death to any one of us—to us all! We know from what has been, that there are, or may be, vast and unknown dangers ahead of us, of which none in the house to-day may ever see the end. Take it, my child, that we are not acting lightly; but with all the gravity of deeply earnest men! Besides, my dear, whatever feelings you or any of us may have on the subject, it is necessary for the success of the experiment to unswathe her. I think that under any circumstances it would be necessary to remove the wrappings before she became again a live human being instead of a spiritualised corpse with an astral body. Were her original intention carried out, and did she come to new life within her mummy wrappings, it might be to exchange a coffin for a grave! She would die the death of the buried alive! But now, when she has voluntarily abandoned for the time her astral power, there can be no doubt on the subject."

Margaret's face cleared. "All right, Father!" she said as she kissed him. "But oh! it seems a horrible indignity to a Queen, and a woman."

I was moving away to the staircase when she called to me:

"Where are you going?" I came back and took her hand and stroked it as I answered:

"I shall come back when the unrolling is over!" She looked at me long, and a faint suggestion of a smile came over her face as she said:

"Perhaps you had better stay, too! It may be useful to you in your work as a barrister!" She smiled out as she met my eyes : but in an instant she changed. Her face grew grave, and deadly white. In a far away voice she said :

"Father is right! It is a terrible occasion; we need all to be serious over it. But all the same—nay, for that very reason you had better stay, Malcolm! You may be glad, later on, that you were present to-night!"

My heart sank down, down, at her words; but I thought it better to say nothing. Fear was stalking openly enough amongst us already!

By this time Mr. Trelawny, assisted by Mr. Corbeck and Doctor Winchester, had raised the lid of the ironstone sarcophagus which contained the mummy of the Queen. It was a large one; but it was none too big. The mummy was both long and broad and high; and was of such weight that it was no easy task, even for the four of us, to lift it out. Under Mr. Trelawny's direction we laid it out on the table prepared for it.

Then, and then only, did the full horror of the whole thing burst upon me! There, in the full glare of the light, the whole material and sordid side of death seemed staringly real. The outer wrappings, torn and loosened by rude touch, and with the colour either darkened by dust or worn light by friction, seemed creased as by rough treatment; the jagged edges of the wrapping-cloths looked fringed; the painting was patchy, and the varnish chipped. The coverings were evidently many, for the bulk was great. But through all, showed that unhidable human figure, which seems to look more horrible when partially concealed than at any other time. What was before us was Death, and nothing else. All the romance and sentiment of fancy had disappeared. The two elder men, enthusiasts who had often done such work, were not disconcerted ; and Doctor Winchester seemed to hold himself in a business-like attitude, as if before the operating-table. But I felt low-spirited, and miserable, and ashamed ; and besides I was pained and alarmed by Margaret's ghastly pallor.

Then the work began. The unrolling of the mummy cat had prepared me somewhat for it ; but this was so much larger, and so infinitely more elaborate, that it seemed a different thing. Moreover, in addition to the ever present sense of death and humanity, there was a feeling of something finer in all this. The cat had been embalmed with coarser materials ; here, all, when once the outer coverings were removed, was more delicately done. It seemed as if only the finest gums and spices had been used in this embalming. But there were the same surroundings, the same attendant red dust and pungent presence of bitumen ; there was the same sound of rending which marked the tearing away of the bandages. There were an enormous number of these, and their bulk when opened was great. As the men unrolled them, I grew more and more excited. I did not take a part in it myself ; Margaret had looked at me gratefully as I drew back. We clasped hands, and held each other hard. As the unrolling went on, the wrappings became finer, and the smell less laden with bitumen, but more pungent. We all, I think, began to feel it as though it caught or touched us in some special way. This, however, did not interfere with the work ; it went on uninterruptedly. Some of the inner wrappings bore symbols or pictures. These were done sometimes wholly in pale green colour, sometimes in many

colours ; but always with a prevalence of green. Now
and again Mr. Trelawny or Mr. Corbeck would point
out some special drawing béfore laying the bandage
on the pile behind them, which kept growing to a
monstrous height.

At last we knew that the wrappings were coming to
an end. Already the proportions were reduced to
those of a normal figure of the manifest height of the
Queen, who was more than average height. And as
the end drew nearer, so Margaret's pallor grew ; and
her heart beat more and more wildly, till her breast
heaved in a way that frightened me.

Just as her father was taking away the last of the
bandages, he happened to look up and caught the
pained and anxious look of her pale face. He paused,
and taking her concern to be as to the outrage on
modesty, said in a comforting way :

"Do not be uneasy, dear ! See ! there is nothing
to harm you. The Queen has on a robe.—Ay, and a
royal robe, too ! "

The wrapping was a wide piece the whole length of
the body. It being removed, a profusely full robe of
white linen had appeared, covering the body from the
throat to the feet.

And such linen ! We all bent over to look at it.

Margaret lost her concern, in her woman's interest
in fine stuff. Then the rest of us looked with admiration ; for surely such linen was never seen by the
eyes of our age. It was as fine as the finest silk.
But never was spun or woven silk which lay in such
gracious folds, constrict though they were by the close
wrappings of the mummy cloth, and fixed into hardness by the passing of thousands of years.

Round the neck it was delicately embroidered in

pure gold with tiny sprays of sycamore; and round
the feet, similarly worked, was an endless line of lotus
plants of unequal height, and with all the graceful
abandon of natural growth.

Across the body, but manifestly not surrounding it,
was a girdle of jewels. A wondrous girdle, which
shone and glowed with all the forms and phases and
colours of the sky!

The buckle was a great yellow stone, round of outline, deep and curved, as if a yielding globe had been
pressed down. It shone and glowed, as though a
veritable sun lay within; the rays of its light seemed
to strike out and illumine all round. Flanking it were
two great moon-stones of lesser size, whose glowing,
beside the glory of the sun-stone, was like the silvery
sheen of moonlight.

And then on either side, linked by golden clasps of
exquisite shape, was a line of flaming jewels, of which
the colours seemed to glow. Each of these stones
seemed to hold a living star, which twinkled in every
phase of changing light.

Margaret raised her hands in ecstasy. She bent over
to examine more closely; but suddenly drew back
and stood fully erect at her grand height. She seemed
to speak with the conviction of absolute knowledge as
she said :

"That is no cerement! It was not meant for the
clothing of death ! It is a marriage robe!"

Mr. Trelawny leaned over and touched the linen
robe. He lifted a fold at the neck, and I knew from
the quick intake of his breath that something had
surprised him. He lifted yet a little more; and then
he, too, stood back and pointed, saying :

" Margaret is right! That dress is not intended to

be worn by the dead! See! her figure is not robed in it. It is but laid upon her." He lifted the zone of jewels and handed it to Margaret. Then with both hands he raised the ample robe, and laid it across the arms which she extended in a natural impulse. Things of such beauty were too precious to be handled with any but the greatest care.

We all stood awed at the beauty of the figure which, save for the face cloth, now lay completely nude before us. Mr. Trelawny bent over, and with hands that trembled slightly, raised this linen cloth which was of the same fineness as the robe. As he stood back and the whole glorious beauty of the Queen was revealed, I felt a rush of shame sweep over me. It was not right that we should be there, gazing with irreverent eyes on such unclad beauty : it was indecent ; it was almost sacrilegious ! And yet the white wonder of that beautiful form was something to dream of. It was not like death at all ; it was like a statue carven in ivory by the hand of a Praxiteles. There was nothing of that horrible shrinkage which death seems to effect in a moment. There was none of the wrinkled toughness which seems to be a leading characteristic of most mummies. There was not the shrunken attenuation of a body dried in the sand, as I had seen before in museums. All the pores of the body seemed to have been preserved in some wonderful way. The flesh was full and round, as in a living person ; and the skin was as smooth as satin. The colour seemed extraordinary. It was like ivory, new ivory ; except where the right arm, with shattered, bloodstained wrist and missing hand had lain bare to exposure in the sarcophagus for so many tens of centuries.

With a womanly impulse ; with a mouth that

drooped with pity, with eyes that flashed with anger, and cheeks that flamed, Margaret threw over the body the beautiful robe which lay across her arm. Only the face was then to be seen. This was more startling even than the body, for it seemed not dead, but alive. The eyelids were closed; but the long, black, curling lashes lay over on the cheeks. The nostrils, set in grave pride, seemed to have the repose which, when it is seen in life, is greater than the repose of death. The full, red lips, though the mouth was not open, showed the tiniest white line of pearly teeth within. Her hair, glorious in quantity and glossy black as the raven's wing, was piled in great masses over the white forehead, on which a few curling tresses strayed like tendrils. I was amazed at the likeness to Margaret, though I had had my mind prepared for this by Mr. Corbeck's quotation of her father's statement. This woman—I could not think of her as a mummy or a corpse—was the image of Margaret as my eyes had first lit on her. The likeness was increased by the jewelled ornament which she wore in her hair, the "Disk and Plumes," such as Margaret, too, had worn. It, too, was a glorious jewel; one noble pearl of moonlight lustre, flanked by carven pieces of moonstone.

Mr. Trelawny was overcome as he looked. He quite broke down; and when Margaret flew to him and held him close in her arms and comforted him, I heard him murmur brokenly:

" It looks as if you were dead, my child! "

There was a long silence. I could hear without the roar of the wind, which was now risen to a tempest, and the furious dashing of the waves far below. Mr. Trelawny's voice broke the spell:

"Later on we must try and find out the process of embalming. It is not like any that I know. There does not seem to have been any opening cut for the withdrawing of the viscera and organs, which apparently remain intact within the body. Then, again, there is no moisture in the flesh; but its place is supplied with something else, as though wax or stearine had been conveyed into the veins by some subtle process. I wonder could it be possible that at that time they could have used paraffin. It might have been, by some process that we know not, pumped into the veins, where it hardened!"

Margaret, having thrown a white sheet over the Queen's body, asked us to bring it to her own room, where we laid it on her bed. Then she sent us away, saying:

"Leave her alone with me. There are still many hours to pass, and I do not like to leave her lying there, all stark in the glare of light. This may be the Bridal she prepared for—the Bridal of Death; and at least she shall wear her pretty robes."

When presently she brought me back to her room, the dead Queen was dressed in the robe of fine linen with the embroidery of gold; and all her beautiful jewels were in place. Candles were lit around her, and white flowers lay upon her breast.

Hand in hand we stood looking at her for a while. Then with a sigh, Margaret covered her with one of her own snowy sheets. She turned away; and after softly closing the door of the room, went back with me to the others who had now come into the dining-room. Here we all began to talk over the things that had been, and that were to be.

Now and again I could feel that one or other of us

L

was forcing conversation, as if we were not sure of ourselves. The long wait was beginning to tell on our nerves. It was apparent to me that Mr. Trelawny had suffered in that strange trance more than we suspected, or than he cared to show. True, his will and his determination were as strong as ever; but the purely physical side of him had been weakened somewhat. It was indeed only natural that it should be. No man can go through a period of four days of absolute negation of life without being weakened by it somehow.

As the hours crept by, the time passed more and more slowly. The other men seemed to get unconsciously a little drowsy. I wondered if in the case of Mr. Trelawny and Mr. Corbeck, who had already been under the hypnotic influence of the Queen, the same dormance was manifesting itself. Doctor Winchester had periods of distraction which grew longer and more frequent as the time wore on.

As to Margaret, the suspense told on her exceedingly, as might have been expected in the case of a woman. She grew paler and paler still; till at last about midnight, I began to be seriously alarmed about her. I got her to come into the library with me, and tried to make her lie down on a sofa for a little while. As Mr. Trelawny had decided that the experiment was to be made exactly at the seventh hour after sunset, it would be as nearly as possible three o'clock in the morning when the great trial should be made. Even allowing a whole hour for the final preparations, we had still two hours of waiting to go through, and I promised faithfully to watch her and to awake her at any time she might name. She would not hear of it, however. She thanked me sweetly and smiled at me as she did so; but she assured me that she was not

sleepy, and that she was quite able to bear up. That
it was only the suspense and excitement of waiting that
made her pale. I agreed perforce; but I kept her
talking of many things in the library for more than an
hour; so that at last, when she insisted on going back
to her father's room I felt that I had at least done
something to help her pass the time.

We found the three men sitting patiently in silence.
With manlike fortitude they were content to be still
when they felt they had done all in their power. And
so we waited.

The striking of two o'clock seemed to freshen us all
up. Whatever shadows had been settling over us
during the long hours preceding seemed to lift at
once; and we went about our separate duties alert
and with alacrity. We looked first to the windows to
see that they were closed, and we got ready our respirators to put them on when the time should be close
at hand. We had from the first arranged to use them
for we did not know whether some noxious fume
might not come from the magic coffer when it should
be opened. Somehow, it never seemed to occur to
any of us that there was any doubt as to its opening.

Then, under Margaret's guidance we carried the
mummied body of Queen Tera from her room into
her father's, and laid it on a couch. We put the sheet
lightly over it, so that if she should wake she could at
once slip from under it. The severed hand was placed
in its true position on her breast, and under it the
Jewel of Seven Stars which Mr. Trelawny had taken
from the great safe. It seemed to flash and blaze as
he put it in its place.

It was a strange sight, and a strange experience.
The group of grave silent men carried the white still

figure, which looked like an ivory statue when through
our moving the sheet fell back, away from the lighted
candles and the white flowers. We placed it on the
couch in that other room, where the blaze of the
electric lights shone on the great sarcophagus fixed in
the middle of the room ready for the final experiment,
the great experiment consequent on the researches
during a lifetime of these two travelled scholars.
Again, the startling likeness between Margaret and the
mummy, intensified by her own extraordinary pallor,
heightened the strangeness of it all. When all was
finally fixed three-quarters of an hour had gone, for
we were deliberate in all our doings. Margaret
beckoned me, and I went out with her to bring in
Silvio. He came to her purring. She took him up
and handed him to me ; and then did a thing which
moved me strangely and brought home to me keenly
the desperate nature of the enterprise on which we
were embarked. One by one, she blew out the candles
carefully and placed them back in their usual places.
When she had finished she said to me :
    " They are done with now. Whatever comes—life
or death—there will be no purpose in their using
now." Then taking Silvio into her arms, and pressing
him close to her bosom where he purred loudly, we
went back to the room. I closed the door carefully
behind me, feeling as I did so a strange thrill as of
finality. There was to be no going back now. Then
we put on our respirators, and took our places as had
been arranged. I was to stand by the taps of the
electric lights beside the door, ready to turn them off
or on as Mr. Trelawny should direct. Doctor Winchester was to stand behind the couch so that he
should not be between the mummy and the sarco-

phagus; he was to watch carefully what should take place with regard to the Queen. Margaret was to be beside him; she held Silvio ready to place him upon the couch or beside it when she might think right. Mr. Trelawny and Mr. Corbeck were to attend to the lighting of the lamps. When the hands of the clock were close to the hour, they stood ready with their linstocks.

The striking of the silver bell of the clock seemed to smite on our hearts like a knell of doom. One! Two! Three!

Before the third stroke the wicks of the lamps had caught, and I had turned out the electric light. In the dimness of the struggling lamps, and after the bright glow of the electric light, the room and all within it took weird shape, and all seemed in an instant to change. We waited with our hearts beating. I know mine did, and I fancied I could hear the pulsation of the others.

The seconds seemed to pass with leaden wings. It were as though all the world were standing still. The figures of the others stood out dimly, Margaret's white dress alone showing clearly in the gloom. The thick respirators which we all wore added to the strange appearance. The thin light of the lamps showed Mr. Trelawny's square jaw and strong mouth and the brown shaven face of Mr. Corbeck. Their eyes seemed to glare in the light. Across the room Doctor Winchester's eyes twinkled like stars, and Margaret's blazed like black suns. Silvio's eyes were like emeralds.

Would the lamps never burn up!

It was only a few seconds in all till they did blaze up. A slow, steady light, growing more and more bright, and changing in colour from blue to crystal white. So they stayed for a couple of minutes without change in the coffer; till at last there began to appear all over it a delicate glow. This grew and grew, till it became like a blazing jewel, and then like a living thing whose essence of life was light. We waited and waited, our hearts seeming to stand still.

All at once there was a sound like a tiny muffled explosion and the cover lifted right up on a level plane a few inches; there was no mistaking anything now, for the whole room was full of a blaze of light. Then the cover, staying fast at one side rose slowly up on the other, as though yielding to some pressure of balance. The coffer still continued to glow; from it began to steal a faint greenish smoke. I could not smell it fully on account of the respirator; but, even through that, I was conscious of a strange pungent odour. Then this smoke began to grow thicker, and to roll out in volumes of ever increasing density till the whole room began to get obscure. I had a terrible desire to rush over to Margaret, whom I saw through the smoke still standing erect behind the couch. Then, as I looked, I saw Doctor Winchester sink down. He was not unconscious; for he waved his hand back and forward, as though to forbid any one to come to him. At this time the figures of Mr. Trelawny and Mr. Corbeck were becoming indistinct in the smoke which rolled round them in thick billowy clouds. Finally I lost sight of them altogether. The coffer still continued to glow; but the lamps began to grow dim. At first I thought that their light was being overpowered by the thick black smoke; but presently I saw that they were, one by one, burning out. They must have burned quickly to produce such fierce and vivid flames.

I waited and waited expecting every instant to hear
the command to turn up the light; but none came. I
waited still, and looked with harrowing intensity at
the rolling billows of smoke still pouring out of the
glowing casket, whilst the lamps sank down and went
out one by one.

Finally there was but one lamp alight, and that was
dimly blue and flickering. The only effective light in
the room was from the glowing casket. I kept my
eyes fixed toward Margaret; it was for her now that
all my anxiety was claimed. I could just see her
white frock beyond the still white shrouded figure on
the couch. Silvio was troubled; his piteous mewing
was the only sound in the room. Deeper and denser
grew the black mist and its pungency began to assail
my nostrils as well as my eyes. Now the volume of
smoke coming from the coffer seemed to lessen, and
the smoke itself to be less dense. Across the room I
saw something white move where the couch was.
There were several movements. I could just catch
the quick glint of white through the dense smoke in
the fading light; for now the glow of the coffer began
quickly to subside. I could still hear Silvio, but his
mewing came from close under; a moment later I
could feel him piteously crouching on my foot.

Then the last spark of light disappeared, and
through the Egyptian darkness I could see the faint
line of white around the window blinds. I felt that
the time had come to speak; so I pulled off my
respirator and called out:

"Shall I turn up the light?" There was no
answer; so before the thick smoke choked me, I
called again but more loudly:

" Mr. Trelawny, shall I turn up the light?" He

did not answer; but from across the room I heard Margaret's voice, sounding as sweet and clear as a bell:

"Yes, Malcolm!" I turned the tap and the lamps flashed out. But they were only dim points of light in the midst of that murky ball of smoke. In that thick atmosphere there was little possibility of illumination. I ran across to Margaret, guided by her white dress, and caught hold of her and held her hand. She recognised my anxiety and said at once:

"I am all right."

"Thank God!" I said. "How are the others? Quick, let us open all the windows and get rid of this smoke!" To my surprise, she answered in a sleepy way:

"They will be all right. They won't get any harm." I did not stop to inquire how or on what ground she formed such an opinion, but threw up the lower sashes of all the windows, and pulled down the upper. Then I threw open the door.

A few seconds made a perceptible change as the thick, black smoke began to roll out of the windows. Then the lights began to grow into strength and I could see the room. All the men were overcome. Beside the couch Doctor Winchester lay on his back as though he had sunk down and rolled over; and on the farther side of the sarcophagus, where they had stood, lay Mr. Trelawny and Mr. Corbeck. It was a relief to me to see that, though they were unconscious, all three were breathing heavily as though in a stupor. Margaret still stood behind the couch. She seemed at first to be in a partially dazed condition; but every instant appeared to get more command of herself. She stepped forward and helped me to raise her father and drag him close to a window. Together we placed the others similarly, and she flew down to the dining-room and returned with a decanter of brandy. This we proceeded to administer to them all in turn. It was not many minutes after we had opened the windows when all three were struggling back to consciousness. During this time my entire thoughts and efforts had been concentrated on their restoration; but now that this strain was off, I looked round the room to see what had been the effect of the experiment. The thick smoke had nearly cleared away; but the room was still misty and was full of a strange pungent acrid odour.

The great sarcophagus was just as it had been. The coffer was open, and in it, scattered through certain divisions or partitions wrought in its own substance, was a scattering of black ashes. Over all, sarcophagus coffer and, indeed, all in the room, was a sort of black film of greasy soot. I went over to the couch. The white sheet still lay over part of it; but it had been thrown back, as might be when one is stepping out of bed.

But there was no sign of Queen Tera! I took Margaret by the hand and led her over. She reluctantly left her father to whom she was administering, but she came docilely enough. I whispered to her as I held her hand:

"What has become of the Queen? Tell me! You were close at hand, and must have seen if anything happened!" She answered me very softly:

"There was nothing that I could see. Until the smoke grew too dense I kept my eyes on the couch, but there was no change. Then, when all grew so dark that I could not see, I thought I heard a movement close to me. It might have been Doctor Winchester who had sunk down overcome; but I could not be sure. I thought that it might be the Queen waking, so I put down poor Silvio. I did not see what became of him; but I felt as if he had deserted me when I heard him mewing over by the door. I hope he is not offended with me!" As if in answer, Silvio came running into the room and reared himself against her dress, pulling it as though clamouring to be taken up. She stooped down and took him up and began to pet and comfort him.

I went over and examined the couch and all around it most carefully. When Mr. Trelawny and Mr. Corbeck recovered sufficiently, which they did quickly, though Doctor Winchester took longer to come round, we went over it afresh. But all we could find was a sort of ridge of impalpable dust, which gave out a strange dead odour. On the couch lay the jewel of the disk and plumes which the Queen had worn in her hair, and the Star Jewel which had words to command the Gods.

Other than this we never got clue to what had happened. There was just one thing which confirmed our idea of the physical annihilation of the mummy. In the sarcophagus in the hall, where we had placed the mummy of the cat, was a small patch of similar dust.

.   .   .   .

In the autumn Margaret and I were married. On the occasion she wore the mummy robe and zone and the jewel which Queen Tera had worn in her hair. On her breast, set in a ring of gold made like a twisted lotus stalk, she wore the strange Jewel of

Seven Stars which held words to command the Gods
of all the worlds.   At the marriage the sunlight
streaming through the chancel windows fell on it,
and it seemed to glow like a living thing.

The graven words may have been of efficacy; for
Margaret holds to them, and there is no other life
in all the world so happy as my own.

We often think of the great Queen, and we talk
of her freely.   Once, when I said with a sigh that
I was sorry she could not have waked into a new
life in a new world, my wife, putting both her hands
in mine and looking into my eyes with that far-away
eloquent dreamy look which sometimes comes into her
own, said lovingly:

" Do not grieve for her!   Who knows, but she may
have found the joy she sought?   Love and patience
are all that make for happiness in this world; or in
the world of the past or of the future; of the living
or the dead.   She dreamed her dream; and that is
all that any of us can ask!"

THE END